Edwin Arnold

East and West

being papers reprinted

Edwin Arnold

East and West
being papers reprinted

ISBN/EAN: 9783337250898

Printed in Europe, USA, Canada, Australia, Japan

Cover: Foto ©Andreas Hilbeck / pixelio.de

More available books at **www.hansebooks.com**

BUDDHA-GAYA, A.D. 1870.   *Frontispiece.*

State before restoration.

EAST AND WEST

BEING PAPERS
REPRINTED FROM THE "DAILY TELEGRAPH"
AND OTHER SOURCES

BY

SIR EDWIN ARNOLD, M.A., K.C.I.E., C.S.I.

AUTHOR OF

"THE LIGHT OF ASIA," "THE LIGHT OF THE WORLD,"
"SEAS AND LANDS," "WANDERING WORDS,"
ETC. ETC.

WITH FORTY-ONE ILLUSTRATIONS BY
R. T. PRITCHETT

LONGMANS, GREEN, AND CO.

LONDON, NEW YORK, AND BOMBAY

1896

Printed by BALLANTYNE, HANSON & Co.
At the Ballantyne Press

CONTENTS

CHAP.   PAGE

I. THE EGYPTIAN THIEF 1

II. "ASPECTS OF LIFE" . 23

III. A FLIGHT OF LOCUSTS . 55

IV. ASTRONOMY AND RELIGION 67

V. IN THE INDIAN WOODS 91

VI. LOVE THE PRESERVER 107

VII. A REAL THIRST 135

VIII. THE INDIAN UPANISHADS . 149

IX. THE TWO BRIDGES . 169

X. INDIAN VICEROYS 183

XI. UNDER THE SUNSHINE 195

XII. JUNGLE KINGDOMS—

    PART I.—THE WAR BETWEEN MAN AND BEAST . 209

    „ II.—CHARACTERISTICS OF THE CONFLICT . . 218

    „ III.—SNAKES . 230

XIII. A FISHERMAN'S WIFE . 237

XIV. AN ENGINE OF FATE 247

XV. IN THE STONE TRADE 257

XVI. THE TRIUMPH OF JAPAN . 271

CONTENTS

CHAP.		PAGE
XVII.	LOST AND FOUND	291
XVIII.	BUDDHA-GYA .	303
XIX.	THE "GARDEN OF REPOSE"	323
XX.	THE SWORD OF JAPAN	339
XXI.	LIMPETS .	353
XXII.	A DELICATE ENTERTAINMENT	363

LIST OF ILLUSTRATIONS

FULL-PAGE ILLUSTRATIONS

BUDDHA-GAYA, A.D. 1870. (*State before restoration*)

Frontispiece

PAGE

THE WATER CARRIER OF EGYPT . 17

CHINA TEA CLIPPER 32

JERUSALEM AND MOUNT OF OLIVES AND TEMPLE 58

ALGIERS HARBOUR . 198

NORTH SEA TRAWLERS 240

DOWN THE GHÂTS . 252

THE WIND GOD OF JAPAN 285

BUDDHA-GAYA. (*Entrance arches before restoration*) . 305

ASOKA PILLAR AT TIRHOOT 307

THE BUDDHIST CHIEF PRIEST—SRI-MANGALA WELIGAMA
OF PANADÛRE 311

SWORD REST, JAPAN . . 342

ILLUSTRATIONS IN TEXT

HEADPIECE TO CHAPTER I. . . 1

SON OF RAMESES . 1

NILE BOAT . 2

SISTRUM 4

THE GOD "RA." (*Orb of Life*) . . . 7

"HÂTHOR." (*Goddess of Bread and Water*) 10

PAGE

"Papyrus Cyperus" of the Nile .   .   20

Locust and Eggs .   .   .   62

Headpiece to Chapter IV.   69

Sacred Lotus .   97

Banyan Tree .   .   104

Talipot Palm and Bamboo   .   105

Laef Butterflies. (*Protective resemblances*) .   112

Hindoo Funeral   142

Græco-Buddhist Sculpture on Sansiii Tope .   153

Miniature Rock and Tree .   .   260

Tobako-Bon, Pipes, and Saki Bottles . 264

Miniature Garden .   .   268

Headpiece to Chapter XVI. .   273

Rice   .   .   .   276

"Daikon" Radish. (*Raphanus sativus*) .   .   281

Water Gate of Temple, Miya Shima, Island of Itsuku   290

Poona   326

Bangle Shop, Poona   327

A Set of Lotas   .   332

Headpiece to Chapter XXI. .   .   355

Wall Picture or "Kakemono"   366

Japanese Lady   .   .   .   368

Japanese Boy .   .   .   373

I

THE EGYPTIAN THIEF

EAST AND WEST

I

THE EGYPTIAN THIEF

A Tale expanded from the brief Greek text of Herodotus.
(EUTERPE II. *Chap.* 121.)

SON OF RAMESES.

"TAKE chisel and mallet, my son, and cut for me, in the spot I mark upon this porphyry block, a socket three fingers breadth across."

"Wilt thou, oh my Father, thus mar the master-stone of thy building for the treasure-place of Pharaoh? How should a socket be needed on the under-face of this block?"

"Cut even as I bid thee!" gravely replied the elder of the two, the Royal Architect Sanehat; and bending to

A

the lower side of the tilted stone he drew carefully
with red pigment the outline of the orifice which
he desired to have pierced upon the huge mass of
the dressed and polished rock.

.   .   .   .   .

Those who held this conversation—Sanehat the
Royal Builder, and Setnau his eldest son—lived
many thousand years ago. It was in the time of
the very ancient King of Egypt, Rhampsinit, who
ruled in Memphis. The
scene was the Courtyard
of the Palace at the out-
skirts of the great city,
where the massive walls
and gateways of the Royal
House came down to the
banks of a canal leading
to the Nile. Along the edge of the canal lay barges
and river-boats, loaded with ponderous blocks of
hewn and unhewn stone, brought laboriously from
the quarries of Hammâmat beyond the river ; and all
the Courtyard, usually so quiet and well-swept, was
now cumbered with similar dressed and undressed
masses of porphyry, syenite, granite, and the softer
limestone, beyond which soared, amid scaffolding of
palm-sticks, the nearly finished façade of the King's
new treasure-chamber. The day was sultry with the
fierce heat of early summer in the Delta, when the
last hot breath of the Khamsîn withers the fresh
fig-leaves, and Ra the Orb of Life, gleaming in full
majesty from his burning path across the pale sky,

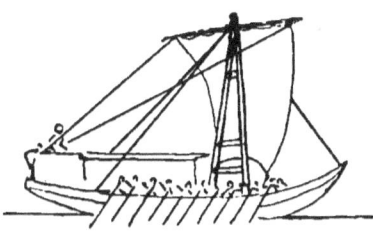

NILE BOAT.

makes all the land look gold in the light, and ebony
in the shadows.　Only native-born children of the
Nile valley could have toiled bareheaded under such
ardent heat; but, temperate as antelopes in their
diet, the Egyptian women and children went and
came with water, slime, and wood on their heads
for the artificers, heedless of the glare, beneath
which a crowd of brown-skinned masons, stone-
workers, sculptors, painters, and common labour-
ing men, stripped stark naked, worked in various
ways, at the direction of Sanehat's sons and fore-
men, to hasten the completion of the mastaba of
King Rhampsinit.　From the canal-banks and from
the neighbouring Nile the creaking noises came of
water-wheels perpetually lifting the precious water
upon the thirsty gardens and fields.　The chatter
and babble of a bazaar close at hand mingled with
fainter cries from the city, and with the far off
beating of temple sistrums and cymbals.　Suddenly
a large drum in the Courtyard gave the signal for
the midday meal of the royal workmen, and, as they
broke off to their rude repast of onions and millet-
cake, the Royal Architect took his staff and slowly
paced, respectfully followed by his son, to his own
abode within a garden of palms and sycamore trees
at the angle where the canal emerged from the Nile ;
for "Sanehat" means the "son of the sycamores."

What caused him to wear so wistful a countenance?　The reason was that, early in the day, the
Master-Builder of Memphis had been summoned to
the presence of the mighty Pharaoh in the inner

hall of the Palace. The King had borne himself
towards his accomplished servant as "a friend of
great sweetness." Sanehat had saluted the Throne
with the palms of his hands and his forehead humbly
placed on the ground. Lying low and long on
his breast before the state chair
of ivory and brown gold, he did
not raise his eyes until the chief
officers lifted him up with gentle
arms, and the girls of the Court
began to beat their triangles, and
sang the song of the "King's
friend," softly chanting—

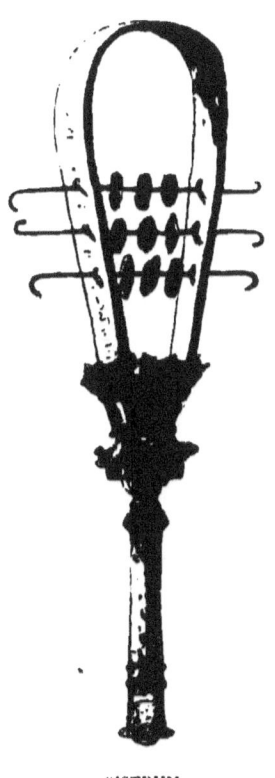

"May thy works prosper, Lord of all
    Lands!
May Phtah give good breath to thy
    nostrils;
May Nub the goddess ornament thy
    years with glory!
The Urœus shines on thy brow like
    the star Sothis;
Grant fair words unto Sanehat thy
    servant,
Who buildeth thee abodes for the
    Gods,
Houses for thy women, and chambers
    for thy treasure."

SISTRUM.

And, hereupon, Rhampsinit the King had bade them
raise him to his feet, and put a collar of gold upon
his neck, and pour fragrant oil upon his head,
saying, "Let him be free of terror. He is a Royal
Friend among my chosen! Bring for him delicate
meats, and drinks of coolness, and place for him

a seat of inlaid wood that he may sit, and that I
may speak with him of my building."

Afterwards the King had held much and earnest
speech with Sanehat, questioning about mighty temples which were in his mind, and structures of
splendour to be devised and erected; and Sanehat
had laid before the eyes of Rhampsinit the plan for
the first pyramid, which was hereafter to be erected
by Cheops. There should be raised from the
sandy tableland of the desert, said he, a tomb-
place for the King, called Khâ—the rising—a place
where the dead Pharaoh should be safe forever until
his soul had need again of the body. The pyramid
completed should have a height of 476 feet on a
base 764 feet square, and should contain in itself
the deepest secrets of mathematics and astronomy.
The King's Sarcophagus should be concealed in the
heart of this stone mountain made by man's hand,
with cunning devices to hide it until after-times.
Under the limestone casing, a movable block, working on a stone pivot, should close the passage to
the death-chamber, so that no intruder could find
the way to violate it. Sanehat showed the King
with what machines the vast blocks might be lifted
to their position, and the great hill of stone built
perfectly from top to bottom. Also what it would
cost in turnips, onions, and garlic for the labourers
employed. But these things were subsequently to
be achieved, and the King, albeit rejoiced at such
vast plans, had ever come back from musing over
the magnificent ideas of his Master-Builder to the

matter of the treasure-chamber attached to his Palace, now nearing completion. Herein he intended to store the accumulated wealth to be devoted to those stupendous future labours. The gold and the amber and the ivory, the agates and carved onyx and bronzes, the priceless gums and perfumes, the gilded lapis lazuli and the lovely blue and green turquoises from the mines of Hammâmat, all were to be deposited in that strong receptacle which Sanehat was constructing in the Palace Court. And one would think, as the Pharaoh loaded his servant with praise for his large conceptions, and promised to make him like to a King's son for worthiness and wealth and fame, that he would surely be in the favour of the Palace till his death, and that the heart of Sanehat would have rejoiced. But at the last, the Chief Interpreter had whispered somewhat to the King, and the King spake a certain sombre word which had sent Sanehat very sad of countenance forth from the Palace, and had caused him to bid his son cut that same socket in the block of porphyry.

Now the word was this. Rhampsinit, hearing the whisper of the Chief Interpreter, gnawed his fingers for a time until he broke his sard signet-ring, and then said gloomily, " Hath thou spoken to no man, O Master-Builder, of the secret entering and quitting of this my new treasure-chamber ? " And the Architect answered, " By the life of my Lord, and by my soul, I have spoken to none." Then Rhampsinit said, " Thou and I alone, therefore, know of the

making of this house and of the keys of its door-
way." And the Architect had answered, " By Ra,
living forever! only thou and I."

Yet, when he had so answered, his heart became
as water within him, for he discerned suddenly the
bitter purpose of the King,
and that he himself should
be in some way or other
slain, in order that only the
Pharaoh might be aware of
the entering of the treasure-
chamber. And therefore was
it that he had gone back sorrowful to the working place,
and therefore had he com-
manded the socket to be cut
in that block of porphyry.

The day arrived when the
treasure-chamber became finished; and all the wealth of
Rhampsinit, brought from
many a storehouse, was laid
out and heaped up in its
recesses. Besides the massive
gateways which led into it,

THE GOD " RA."
Orb of Life.

and the strong walls of stone shutting it close, the
place was guarded by every kind of magic. Statues
animated by the *Ka*, or Double, of the Royal Founder,
protected its angles. An image of black and white
granite at the entrance held in its huge hands a
sceptre and a hooded snake; and that same carved

stone serpent, it was currently reported, would coil round the neck of any robber approaching, and sting him to swift death. Only the King and the Chief Eunuch possessed the curious keys which opened the vast bronze doors of the chamber, or knew how to use them. When all the royal wealth had been deposited there, a great feast was held in the palace, whereat the guests of the King sat crowned with flowers, their heads scented with perfumed oil, the Master-Builder highest among them, throned amid Princes, beside the Pharaoh. At the close of the festival, Rhampsinit poured a measure of wine into his own golden goblet, and gave it to Sanehat, who, bound by loyalty, drank it to the bottom, and took his leave, clad in new robes of favour, and graced with titles of honour: while the people of the Court made way before him, and the dancing girls sang the praise of the "friend of Pharaoh."

Alas! that same night, at the hour when the first cock crows, mortal pains attacked the frame of the Architect. The sweat of death stood cold upon him. His body shook alternately with rigors, and then became as if plunged in the fires of Amenti, so that, perceiving his end to be near, he spake to Rud-didet, his chief wife, saying, "The heart of Pharaoh is harder than the red granite of the desert quarry. The breath of his kindness is deadlier than the kiss of the hungry asp. This night he has put into his wine of amity a poison which no medicine can assuage. Call hither my two sons, and come thou nigh unto me with them, for I shall die to-night, and I have that to say which only thou and these must hear."

Setnau and his younger brother Hemti dutifully attended at the summons, and stood with their mother beside the bed of the dying Architect, while he thus addressed them, in a voice growing more and more feeble: "My sons! and thou, Rud-didet, mother of my sons! the Pharaoh has not willed that any should possess the secrets of his treasure-chamber except himself and our enemy—the Chief Interpreter. To-night he has taken my life with a subtle drug. This, indeed, I had foreseen, and have so devised that when I shall have descended to Amenti, the riches of the King will all be yours. Thou dost remember, Setnau, how I bade thee cut a socket in the block of purple porphyry. Count eleven cubits from the hand of the statue at the corner, and ye shall see a granite slab, rose-coloured, fronting the canal, which moves if ye press its upper third portion. Being disengaged, the porphyry block beside it swings round upon its socket, and ye may enter the chamber from the outside at will. When I am dead, the King's Chief Interpreter will speak fair words, but trust them not. When fitting time arrives, go freely into the King's treasure-house, and make yourselves rich with the royal wealth, for the sake of which he hath betrayed me to death." At this Sanchat the Master-Builder died, and was embalmed after the Egyptian manner, his soul going forth to seek "the Field of Reeds," while in the coffin of his mummy were placed chapters of "The Book of the Dead," to guide him to where Hâthor the Goddess gives that bread and water of death which, once partaken of, enable the departed to enter the Ferry Boat that doth bear spirits to the other world. The dead man had then to answer the questions of that Boat. "Tell me my name," said the Mast; and he must reply, "The Guide of the Great Goddess is thy name." Then the Sailyard asked, "What is my name?" and the dead must reply, "The Backbone of the Heavenly Jackal, Uapû-aîtû, is thy name." And the Masthead inquired, "What is my name?" the right answer being, "The Neck of Amsit, Child of Horus." And the Sail also, demanding its hidden title, must be responded to, "Nûit is thy name, the Starry One!" Knowing all these things, Sanehat went safe to the Shore of Spirits.

" HÂTHOR."
Goddess of Bread and Water.

But when he was gone, the household became neglected by Pharaoh, and poverty pressed upon the Lady Rud-Didet, and Setnau .and Hemti the brothers. Moreover, the King's Interpreter, by and by pretending royal anger against the deceased

Artificer, and that he had laid unlawful hands upon
some of the money and provisions for the workmen
(which was a false accusation), sent officers to exact
restitution, and took away all that could be found
which was valuable in the abode of Sanchat. There
came at last a time in that sorrowful abode when
not more than a jar of oil and a measure of millet
were remaining for the family; but the young men
had been brought up in fear of the Lords of Justice
and Truth, and day by day they sought the favours
of Thoth, who gives wealth, and of Nâpri, who grants
food, working industriously in the yards of the
stone-masons of the city. Soon, however, their
mother fell sick for lack of good nourishment, and
remembering in her heart how cruelly Sanchat had
died, and what he had said in dying, she called her
sons to her side, and gave them command, in these
words: "This will be no sin if we shall hurt those
who have injured us. Ye know well where there
is abundance of wealth and worldly store. What
spake he who was beyond all the builders of Egypt
for knowledge and faithfulness, and who perished
of the shameful wine-cup of Pharaoh, in its show
of friendliness? 'Count eleven cubits along the
wall from the hand of the statue at the corner,
and ye shall perceive a granite slab, rose-grained,
fronting the canal, which will yield if ye press its
upper third portion; and then the dark-coloured
block swings back upon its socket, and ye may enter
the chamber from without, and help yourselves at
will from his goods who hath rewarded good service

with a deadly drink.' Thus did your father speak. Go now therefore by night, and bring for me and for yourselves that which shall fill up our jars and sacks again from the King's Treasury."

Accordingly, the two young men went forth by night, bearing with them a lamp of clay, and a fire-stick to kindle its wick ; and knowing well the place, they measured the eleven cubits from the hand of the statue, found the granite slab, and pressing upon its upper portion, set free the great block of porphyry, which easily revolving upon the socket, opened a passage into the King's treasure-house. First Setnau crept through, while Hemti kept watch outside ; but when the lamp was enkindled, then— lest the guard should spy the shining of its light— Hemti followed his brother, and together they drew the great stone close again, and looked around them. At first little could be discerned of the vast enclosure, but there were bronze lamps filled with perfumed oil swinging from the roof, or placed on pedestals of alabaster ; and these being ready for use, they lighted them all, until the place became bright as day, and every corner of it visible. Then they saw two rows of massive stone columns supporting the vast slabs of the roof, coloured with all sorts of gay painting, and having carved capitals, richly wrought and painted ; and all round the walls were alabaster panels, sculptured with pictures of the products of the King's countries, and of the people bringing these in boats and on asses and oxen, all limned and tinted to the life. And around these

columns, and along the walls of the chamber, were
ranged all kinds of wealth and wonderful possessions
that a Lord of Egypt would store up. There were
the black and the blue wigs of the King, together
with fair diadems of gold, and silk, and stringed
gems belonging to each of them : pots of costly perfume for the anointing of his head and body—cost-
liest of all those gums of the land of Punt which
burn with the smell of Heaven—bottles of agate
and chalcedony holding the black powder for the
eyelids of his ladies, and of red powders for their
cheeks and lips; piles of rich garments in cotton,
and wool, and silk delicately woven and broidered,
and made precious with thread of gold and silver
and with work of pierced pearls and turquoises.
In one corner lay heaped up, like round yellow
flowers from the Sont-tree, little balls of pure gold,
got from the rocks of Ophir, and in another bricks
of silver and of copper; while elsewhere were beads
of many colours and shapes on strings, and curious
enamelled ornaments of burnt earth, and stone and
wood and glass and bronze, with Tabnu, which are
small rings holding a sacred beetle, or a sardonyx, or
a charmed crystal. Lapis lazuli in blocks and rough
lumps lay on one hand, and on the other little
chests of cedar, or boxes of alabaster and bags of
leather stiffened with bitumen, holding all sorts of
jewels,—rubies, sapphires, carnelians, jaspers, turquoises, agates, jacinths, emeralds, and topazes.
There were long strings of polished amber, and
plates of green copper stone, with gods and god-

desses cut out in yellow and red and green marbles,
and *ushabti* for the King's death—little figures of
attendants to wait on him in the Nether World,
having heads of gold and feet of coral or amber.
Also there were pearls from the Sea of Suph—
pearls of all shapes and sizes, in white piles like
the husked rice; some beaded into necklets and
armlets; together with billets of ebony wood and
of sandal wood, sacks of gum arabic, bundles of
ostrich feathers, skins of lions, leopards, and other
animals, not to speak of elephants' tusks, beautiful
weapons of bronze and iron and wood, inlaid and
jewelled, and rows upon rows of painted jars full
of the choicest wines of Egypt.

The two young Egyptians, having feasted their
eyes upon all these treasures of the King, and
marked what should fetch most profit from the
merchants outside, filled the receptacles which they
had brought with bricks of gold and silver, and
precious stones engraved, and amulets of amber and
lazuli, together with enamelled *ushabti* for their
father's mummy place, and departed, carefully re-
placing the great stone behind them. Moreover
Setnau took with him an alabaster flask of the
costly perfume used by the daughters of the King,
marked in gold script with each one's name, and,
further, hid in his girdle a necklet of great pearls for
his wife to wear privately; and they took also an
earthen jar of the King's wine, made of strange
vines from the land of the black men. Afterwards
once and again they did re-enter that treasury,

when the first spoil was expended ; and great cheer made they in their house, and it seemed to Rud-Didet and to her sons that while the cruel Rhampsinit should be rich they also would be well-to-do.

But, on a time, the King coming into his secret place of wealth to overlook his havings, perceived that in this, and that spot, and the other, much was lacking ; here jars of wine, there alabaster flasks and essences, and, beyond, ingots of gold and silver, and precious amulets of carved stone, and some' among the rarest gems and jewels. Yet was there no sign of entrance at the heavy gate, nor mark of violence to wall or roof or lintel or window. Astonished and incensed, he took long counsel with the Chief Interpreter, and by advice of that evil man he caused traps of iron, which would grip and break the haunch of a lion or knee of a river-horse, to be cunningly set in the shadow of the columns, by the side of the principal treasures. Thus was it, that one moonless night, when the two brothers came again, and Hemti had entered, he groping about in the darkness, stumbled into one of these terrible engines, which closing upon his mid-leg, held him fast. Nevertheless he forbade his brother to approach until he had kindled the lamp. Setnau then coming to him, could in no way loosen the jaws of the trap, nor deliver Hemti. Thereupon the fearless young man said : "It may not be that I escape, and the face of me will be known, and death will fall with shame and torment upon my mother and thee. Cut off my head, accordingly, and carry it away with thee, that Rhampsinit may be shent. But fill thy bag also with gold and jewels, for this is the last of our nights of fortune." Thus urged, Setnau cut off the head of his brother Hemti, and placed it in his leathern sack together with much wealth and many precious things, and so went home again to inform Rud-Didet.

Next morning, when the King returned to the treasure-house to see what had occurred, he was beyond measure amazed at finding the dead body of the robber, without a head and stripped of clothing, fixed in the teeth of the trap, and yet no sign around, above, or below, to manifest how the chamber had been plundered. Long and anxious were the counsels of the Palace. At last it was resolved to hang the carcase of the thief upon a cross of wood on the city wall, setting a constant guard of soldiers beside it, who should observe every one passing by, and should straightway arrest and bring to the Palace him or her, whosoever, at sight of the body, displayed any marks of sorrow or compassion. For it went very ill with the ancient Egyptians if the body of a dead person should moulder in the air or earth, or be devoured of worms, or birds, or beasts, or fishes : since in this way, and failing embalmment, the *Ka* or double of the man or woman would possess at last no link by which to return to life, but must wander between the two worlds, the soul fading away as the body

THE WATER CARRIER OF EGYPT. *P.* 17.

crumbled. All which lay heavy upon the heart of his mother, the Lady Rud-Didet, when she heard about the dead man on the wall, so that she spoke bitter things to Setnau, and bade him, by whatsoever means, deliver to her the corpse of her younger son, so that it might have the work of the embalmer done upon him, and the head be stitched fairly upon the neck, and repose in peace in a goodly mummy-chest. Furthermore, when Setnau said this could not be, since no wit of man could outdo the anger and vigilance of the King, Rud-Didet replied that if the body were not brought home before sunrise she would go, in her despair, to the throne of Pharaoh, and inform him how the treasures had been stolen, and where they might be discovered.

Hearing this, the elder son, beside himself with fear and trouble, conceived a subtle plan. Taking a string of asses, just before sundown, he loaded them with skins of sweet heady wine, and disguising himself as an ass-driver, directed the beasts along the wall to the place where the soldiers guarded the corpse. Arriving there, he managed, unnoticed, to cast loose the cords from the necks of two of the skins, so that the wine began to spirt forth, running into the road. At this he wailed aloud, beat his head with his fists, and manifested such loud tokens of distress, that the soldiers heard him; and noticing the waste of the wine, they, instead of helping the man, got vessels, and filled and quaffed them, while the pretended ass-driver cried on all the Gods to curse them, and threatened to invoke

B

against them the justice of Pharaoh. But the
sentinels, having drunk freely of the liquor, and
becoming more amused than angered at the man,
spoke soothing words to him; until at the last the
ass-driver affected to be propitiated, and exchanged
friendly speech with them, finally even offering one
more of his skins wherewith to make merry. Soon,
as the cups went round, the soldiers and the pretended ass-driver became boon companions, they
reclining upon their shields and jollily toping,
while Setnau plied them ever and ever with more
liquor until such time as the whole band grew
utterly fuddled, and overpowered by the strong
drink lay fast asleep in the midst of their spears
and swords, the city also being quite still and empty
because of midnight.

Then Setnau arose, having all this while drank
little, but, indeed, spilled his share of the wine
unseen upon the dust; and taking down the body
of his brother from the cross, he laid it on the
stoutest of his asses, threw over it a mantle from
one of the soldiers, and so carried the corpse home
to his mother the Lady Rud-Didet, who very secretly
performed for Hemti all the due death-rites, and laid
his mended body in a fair box, with beautiful chosen
death-charms, and learned prayers painted upon it,
so that his *Ka* had peace and pleasure, and should
come again to earthly life at the appointed time.

But Rhampsinit the King, having learned how
that the carcase of the robber had been craftily
borne away, grew wroth beyond any patience. And

first he put to cruel death the soldiers and their captain, thrusting some through and through with pointed stakes, and flaying alive the others. Afterwards he devised a strange plan whereby to catch the daring man who had broken into his treasure-house, had plundered his wealth, and had defied his vengeance by delivering the body of an accomplice from shame and decay.

Now Rhampsinit the King had for his eldest daughter a Princess the most beautiful of face and faultless in limbs and maiden symmetry in all Egypt. If a man should gaze upon her countenance, which was as a full moon in the time of millet-reaping, the heart within him became as water, and his strength melted for worship and desire. This great Princess, the High and Sacred Lady Amîtsi, was at that time promised to a mighty and opulent Prince of the Royal Blood; but by reason of bitter anger, and burning rage to discover the offender, Rhampsinit commanded his daughter as follows. He bade her put on the robes of a courtesan, painting her face, and braiding her hair, and suspending outside her house a picture of herself, cunningly limned, so that all men passing by must admire and desire her, sitting at call. And under the picture was written that the favours of Nub-Khesdeb[1] the Harlot were only for him who had wrought in his lifetime the most subtle and most wicked deed ever wrought—and for no man else. Many gallants, accordingly, repaired thither,

---

[1] *Nub-Khesdeb* means: "She whose body is as gold and lazuli."

but it availed not be-
cause their stories did
not satisfy; until Set-
nau, hearing of the
device, and well com-
prehending it, resolved
to outwit the King, and
to embrace the Princess.
To this end he took
with him, under his mantle,
the newly severed arm of
a dead man, and went to
the house of her who was
called Nub-Khesdeb, and
had admittance. For, first
of all, the Princess per-
ceived upon his garments
the smell of that fragrance
stolen from the treasure-
chamber, the like of which
was not in all Egypt except
in the tiring-rooms of the
Queens and the Prin-
cesses. And next the
man spake, saying, "Kiss
me, and I will afterwards
relate to thee the wicked-
est deed ever done, to
wit, when I cut off my
brother's head within the
King's treasury; and also

"PAPYRUS CYPERUS" OF THE NILE.

the most subtle thing, to wit, when I caused the
soldiers on the wall to become drunk with wine,
and took away my brother's body for burial."
Thereupon the Princess in the dark, well-assured
that this was the one she sought, made quickly to
lay fast hold of him, and to call succour; but he
passing the dead man's arm between her hands,
with that deceived her, and so made good his flight
through the door.

When this last doing was reported to Rhampsinit, he was astonished at the shrewdness and
boldness of the thief. He therefore swore an oath
by the life of Osiris, that there should be a free
pardon for him and his, and great rewards, and
that the Princess Amîtsi herself should be given
to him in marriage, along with a dower of lands
and cattle and slaves, if he would reveal himself,
and be true man of the State and faithful. Which
oath the heralds proclaimed in all the cities and
towns and villages, and the news coming quickly
to the ears of Setnau, he resolved to cast himself
upon the clemency of Pharaoh, and therefore went
to the Palace and told all which he had wrought,
whereon the King forgave the thief, as the most
knowing of such living men as he had seen, and
wiser than all the other Egyptians.

London, *May* 17, 1895.

II

"ASPECTS OF LIFE"

II

"ASPECTS OF LIFE"

An Address delivered in the Town Hall, Birmingham, on the 10th of October 1893, as President of the Midland Institute.

IT is thirty-five years from the day when I last stood in Birmingham. More than a generation has, in fact, elapsed since, as a very young man, newly graduated at Oxford, I had the good fortune to be selected as a Master in your King Edward's School. And now a much greater honour, one far beyond my merits, has fallen upon me—to be chosen to address this important and enlightened Institute, in your famous, patriotic, and prosperous city. I should hold it an impertinence to dwell at any length on that which must be too obvious— my inability to discharge with becoming credit the responsibilities of such a succession. For you have established upon the records of your Institute, in its list of Presidents, a dynasty of such intellectual and social splendour as hardly any other association could rival. Finding myself in the place which they have rendered august, it is with true respect that I recall some among the names of my brilliant predecessors. That master of all English hearts has spoken here

—Charles Dickens ; as well as those illustrious phy-
sicists Professors Huxley, and Tyndall, and Lord
Kelvin. The wide and gentle genius of my friend
Sir John Lubbock has graced this seat, and the
kindly learning of my old tutor, Arthur Stanley ;
together with the research and the philosophy of renowned historians like Mr. Lecky, Professor Seeley,
and Mr. Froude.   You have been addressed by
a Primate of All England in his Grace of Can-
terbury ; by an Indian Viceroy in Lord Northbrook ;
by a chief of critics in Mr. James Russell Lowell ;
and by an accomplished astronomer in Sir Robert
Ball. The glory of these and other names which
glow upon your catalogue during the past quarter
of a century forbids to him who follows them here
to-day any hope of being worthy of so grand an
inheritance. He must regard himself as but a
link of metal in the chain of gold, contented if
the current of your high traditions passes safely
by him, and relying for your indulgence on two
qualities only — an appreciation of the eminence
of his antecessors, and a desire to show his regard
for this important Institute, and his gratitude for
its choice of him, by saying the best he may.

That galaxy of great minds to which I have
alluded has illuminated well-nigh all possible topics
of speech in your Hall. I have indeed asked myself with no small anxiety what was left which
might be handled with freshness and profit, since
it would not seem decorous to talk of science, of
history, of education, and many other tempting

subjects, after such commanding authorities. Still, the experience of any one, honestly stated, has a value; and, seeing that I am here again after so many years, it is natural to question myself, and it may not be useless to answer briefly before you, what I have learned—to what chief conclusions study, observation, travel, public toils, and private meditations have led me — upon life in general. Will it be worth while frankly to compare the aspirations of the youth of twenty-one with the realisations of the grown-up man of the world? Shall I venture once more, and for an hour or two, to become a teacher in Birmingham? If you can have the patience to listen, I think I will have the courage to speak; and my address to-day shall, therefore, be upon some aspects of human life, free, of course, from all theology and politics.

I fear I must alienate certain friendly minds, and appear to commence by presumption, when I say that I return to Birmingham just as convinced of what can never be proved as when I left it. I have found life in the highest degree charming and interesting, and this notwithstanding an ample share of what are styled—sometimes I think a little too querulously—its "pains and sorrows." I quitted Birmingham in the pleasant beginning of my days, glad to live; I come back to it, after much experience and many labours, glad to have lived, well satisfied with my share in the world, and a resolute philosophical opponent of those who love dismal dialectics and drape the Universe in the black

hangings of pessimism. If there have been ages
in which, because it did not know much, our race
had good reason not to hope much, the time seems
to me to be now arrived when the despair which has
been so fashionable grows foolish as well as needless.
It is true we have inherited so much fear and supersti-
tion from the past; dogmatic religions and artificial
moralities have wrought so much to degrade natural
virtue and check instinctive joy; our inner vision
is still so rudimentary and our sense-knowledge so
limited, that I dare not say worse of the pessimists
than that they seem to me very stupid. As for that
noble love of fact and truth which is at the bottom
of sincere agnosticism, there is nothing, I think, to
be more respected. We must not deceive each
other with soft sayings. Ajax demanding light
from Zeus, even though he must die in that light,
is the immortal example of a faithful and valiant
human spirit. Speaking from this place in 1877,
Professor Tyndall well remarked : " When facts
present themselves, let us venture to face them, and
let us be equally bold to confess ignorance where it
prevails." But the day seems to be arrived when
there is really so much to make us think well of the
destiny of mankind ; such fair reason to rejoice in the
mere fact of existence ; so large a promise of ever-ex-
tending human knowledge and insight ; such general
softening of manners, spreading of intelligence, and
enlarging of average happiness, that it appears more
becoming for man, the chief at least of animals, to
be singing with the lark in the sky than croaking

with the frog in the swamp. Mahommedans follow a habit of reciting their morning formula of praise— the *Fatihah*—as soon as the light enables them to distinguish a black garment from a white one. I think we also have by this time passed far enough through the night of ignorance and fear to discern in our beliefs what is the black of wilful blindness from the white of rightful hopefulness, and to realise the truth of that fine line of Mr. Frederick Myers, " God will forgive us all but our despair."

From the lowest points of view, hope is very cheap and gladness acts as a sovereign medicine. Consider the social, moral, and individual advantages of a cheerful view of life contrasted with the cheerless view. Sunshine has not a stronger effect in developing the beauty of flowers and the form of leaves than radiance of mind and lightness of heart in bringing forth all which is best in men and women. We have partly found this out as regards children, and Society conspires pretty generally nowadays to render their early years happy. The Japanese recognised that same high duty two thousand years ago, and possess in consequence the best mannered and most joyous little ones in the world. But why stop at childhood? I should like to see the pastimes and recreations of the people made henceforth a department of administrative solicitude. I should like to have a Minister of Public Amusement sitting in every Cabinet, and Municipal Councils spending rates royally upon new popular pleasures of the right kind. There is nothing better than to be happy ;

joy is the real root of morality ; no virtue is worth
praising which does not spring from minds contented and convinced, and free of dread and gloom.
No religion was ever divine which relied on terror instead of love ; and no philosophy will bear any good
fruit which propounds despair and deduces annihilation. This is where, by their own true instincts, the
greater poets have done so much more for mankind
than most of its benefactors, delighting as they do in
life, and preserving amid its deepest mysteries and
hardest puzzles a divine serenity about its origin and
purpose. Observe our English Shakespeare ! How
calm, how complacent! how assured his glorious
genius always abides ! A page of him taken almost
anywhere—set beside a page of modern pessimism
—is like the speech of a prince in his pleasure-house
compared with the moanings of a sick wretch in a
spital. All genuine poets, from Homer to Browning,
are radically joyous. Keats writes :—

> "They shall be accounted poet-kings
> Who simply tell the most heart-easing things."

And Hafiz says : "It was whispered of me in
Shiraz that I was sad, but what had I to do with
sadness?" Art, in all its highest forms, bears no
message so imperative as to emphasise the beauty
and maintain the dignity and delight of life ; and
you may judge first-class writers and painters as
we shall some day judge philosophers, by their
fidelity to this wholesome errand of joy.

Poets, however, are not much accepted as autho-

rities in certain quarters; and beyond doubt we
must have better reasons than their melodious
verses furnish if we are to be securely glad of life
and serenely unperturbed by death.   Yet, upon
the face of facts, is life—even were it transient—
so bad a thing as some people make out?   Look
at common modern existence as we see it, and
note to what rich elaboration and large degrees
of comfort it has come.   I leave aside for the
moment uncivilised nations, and the bygone struggles
of our race; its wars and woes, its tyrannies and
superstitions; all of which history has greatly exaggerated, not telling us of the contemporaneous
contentments.   I invite you briefly to contemplate
the material side of an artisan's existence in your
own Birmingham.   Let alone the greatness of
being an Englishman, and the supreme safety and
liberty of his daily life, what king of old records
ever fared so royally?   What magician of fairy
tales ever owned so many slaves to bring him
treasures and pleasures at a wish?   Observe his
dinner board!   Without being luxurious, the whole
globe has played him serving-man to spread it.
Russia gave.the hemp, or India or South Carolina
the cotton, for that cloth which his wife lays upon
it.   The Eastern Islands placed there those con-
diments and spices which were once the secret
relishes of the wealthy.   Australian Downs send
him frozen mutton or canned beef; the prairies of
America meal for his biscuit and pudding; and
if he will eat fruit, the orchards of Tasmania and

the palm woods of the West Indies proffer delicious
gifts; while the orange groves of Florida and of
the Hesperides cheapen for his use those "golden
apples" which dragons used to guard. His coffee
comes from where jewelled humming-birds hang
in the bowers of Brazil, or purple butterflies flutter
amid the Javan mangroves. Great clipper ships,
racing by night and day under clouds of canvas,
convey to him his tea from China or Assam, or
from the green Singhalese Hills. The sugar which
sweetens it was crushed from canes that waved
by the Nile or the Orinoco; and the plating of
the spoon with which he stirs it was dug for
him from Mexican or Nevadan mines. The cur-
rants in his dumpling are a tribute from classic
Greece, and his tinned salmon or kippered herring
a token from the seas and rivers of Canada or
Norway. He may partake, if he will, of rice that
ripened under the hot skies of Patna or Rangoon;
of cocoa, that "food of the gods," plucked under
the burning blue of the Equator. For his rasher
of bacon the hog-express runs daily with 10,000
grunting victims into Chicago; Dutch or Brittany
hens have laid him his eggs, and Danish cows
grazed the daisies of Elsinore to produce his cheese
and butter. If he drinks beer, it is odds that
Belgium and Bavaria have contributed to it the
barley and the hops; and, when he has finished
eating, it will be the Mississippi flats or the gardens
of the Antilles that fill for him his pipe with the
comforting tobacco. He has fared, I say, at home

P. 32.

CHINA TEA CLIPPER.

as no Heliogabálus or Lucullus ever fared; and
then, for a trifle, his daily newspaper puts at his
command information from the whole globe, the
freshness and fulness of which make the news-
bearers of Augustus Cæsar, thronging hourly into
Rome, ridiculous. At work, machinery of wonderful invention redeems his toil from servitude and
elevates it to an art. Is he fond of reading?
There are free libraries open to him, full of intellectual and imaginative wealth. Is he artistic?
Galleries rich with beautiful paintings and statues
are prepared for him. Has he children? They
can be excellently educated for next to nothing.
Would he communicate with absent friends? His
messengers pass in the Queen's livery, faithfully
bearing his letters everywhere by sea and land;
or in hour of urgency the Ariel of electricity will
flash for him a message to the ends of the kingdom at the price of a quart of small beer. Steam
shall carry him wherever he would go for a half-
penny a mile; and when he is ill, the charitable
institutions he has too often forgotten in health
render him such succour as sick goddesses never
got from Æsculapius, nor Ulysses at the white
hands of Queen Helen. Does he encounter accident? For him as for all others the benignant
science of our time, with the hypodermic syringe
or a waft of chloroform, has abolished agony;
while for dignity of citizenship he may help, when
election time comes, by his vote, to sustain or to
shake down the noblest empire ever built by genius

C

and valour. Let fancy fill up the imperfect picture
with those thousand helps and adornments that
civilisation has brought even to lowly lives; and
does it not seem stupid and ungrateful to say, as
some go about saying, that such an existence,
even if it were transitory, is not for itself distinctly
worth possessing?

But, will it last? That ordinary human life is
fairly agreeable, stands sufficiently confessed by the
fact that people want it to go on in the same way
for ever. Very few even among our gloomiest pessimists appear to be in any particular hurry to die.
And they, too, are obliged to allow that human life
exhibits everywhere an almost universal advance in
social elevation and range of perception. Two fatal
blows, among others, have fallen upon the old
narrow-minded theologies and philosophies. One
was the Copernican discovery, that, instead of being
the centre of things, furnished with sun, moon, and
stars for mere lamps, and created as the sole care of
Heaven, our globe is but a small obscure islet of the
celestial archipelago, an almost insignificant speck in
the galaxies of glory filling space. The chief religions of the world have not even yet adjusted their
doctrines to the great verities of Galileo and Newton,
although they will have to adjust them. A second
revolutionary announcement which has altered bygone ideas is that of the revealed vastness of geological time followed by Darwin's "Origin of Species."
Modern astronomy and evolution have silently swept
away "dark-tangled schemes of sad salvation" and

the belief in special creations. It seemed at first to some conservative minds that all was hereby lost for human hope and pride, if we were, indeed, so closely akin to lower life and so humbly placed in the stellar systems. But those prodigious truths have really enhanced unspeakably the dignity and value of human existence. If Earth knows now that she is only, as it were, a bit of drift-wood in the "blue Pacific of Infinity," she has also learned that she influences by attraction every orb in the sky, and is influenced by every orb. The descent of man from an ascidian mollusc immediately implies his ascent towards unimagined perfections. If we started so low down, we have already climbed up most promisingly. The amphioxus has no cerebrum at all; the halibut, as big as a man, possesses that organ in size smaller than a melon-seed; while the cranial capacity of the Australian savage exceeds that of the gorilla by ten cubic inches, and our Birmingham artisan's skull is better than the "black fellow's" by forty cubic inches; to say nothing of those convolutions of the brain in the civilised man which are its most important feature. There, by the way, is planted the physical throne of that consciousness which puzzles the boldest materialist, and obliges him—if really scientific—to confess his ignorance. An illustrious interpreter of the ways of Nature, Professor Tyndall, asked from this very place, "What is the causal connection, if any, between the objective and the subjective—between molecular motion in the brain and states of consciousness? Does water think and

feel when it runs into frost-ferns upon a window
pane? If not, why should the molecular motion of
the brain be yoked to this mysterious companion,
consciousness   His answer was, " I do not know,
and nobody knows." In the same honest spirit Dr.
Burdon Sanderson said in his address this year
before the British Association at Nottingham :
" Between sensation and the beginning of action
there is an intervening region which the physiologist
willingly resigns to psychology, feeling his incompetence to use the only instrument by which it can be
explored, that of introspection." I quote these sen-
tences not to lead you into the wilderness of physio-
logy, but merely to show that science has no fatal or
final word to say about the prospects of continuous
Life. She capitulates here, by the lips of two of her
truest and most fearless spokesmen, to the Unseen
and the Unknown. Do not, therefore, think that you
are warned off from endless hope and utmost pro-
babilities of immortal and ever-increasing individual
life and gladness by the scalpel of the brain-doctor
or the dyspeptic logic of the agnostic. A boundless
aspiration is not only cheap, but strictly reasonable ;
and what has come from Evolution in the visible
region is nothing to what may come from it in the
invisible. The dove of right Reason can bring you
back a branch of olive from the waste of physiologi-
cal waters where the raven of Unfaith never finds so
much as a single leaf.

The " Cosmic process," as Professor Huxley calls
it, has led us thus far; yet that justly famous

expositor of science, in his Romanes Lecture at
Oxford, delivered on 18th May last, arraigned the
Cosmos for immorality, and declared that "the
ethical progress of society depends not on imitating the cosmic process, but on combating it." I
could not speak of my illustrious predecessor here
without gratitude and admiration, and should ordi-
narily distrust myself in differing from him. But
so luminous a mind certainly overlooked the fact
that the ethical faculty and the ethical ideal
which he contrasted with the course of nature
have likewise come, by Evolution, forth from the
cosmic process, just as much as those things that
shock him in the natural world. As I have
written in my "Light of Asia"—

> "Out of the dark it wrought the heart of man,
>   Out of dull shells the pheasant's pencilled neck ;
> Ever at toil it leads to loveliness
> All seeming wrath and wreck.
>
> It is not marred nor stayed in any use,
> All liketh it : the sweet white milk it brings
> To mothers' breasts : it brings the white drops, too,
> Wherewith the young snake stings."

"Reckless of good or evil," writes another highly
enlightened metaphysician — Mr. John Fisk, of
America—"natural selection develops at once the
mother's tender love for her infant and the horrible
teeth of the ravening shark." But the cosmic
process is not immoral on that account; not even
cruel ! On the contrary, it is supremely equitable
and ultimately tender. It is as sedulous to pro-

vide the shark with the means of living as the
new-born heir of a queen with his natural food.
Professor Huxley accordingly erred, I think, in
saying at Oxford, "The practice of that which is
ethically best—what we call Goodness or Virtue—
involves a course of conduct in all respects opposed
to that which leads to success in the cosmic struggle
for existence. In place of ruthless self-assertion it
demands self-restraint. In the place of thrusting
aside or treading down all competitors, it requires
that the individual shall not merely respect but
shall help his fellows. Its influence is directed
not so much to the survival of the fittest as the
fitting of as many as possible to survive." Yes ;
but the nobler specialised justice referred to in this
passage is exactly what has been developed out of
the initial impartialities of the natural course. The
"morality" has come forth from the "immorality."
Out of the simple instinct of gregariousness we
see Nature making something like citizens even of
bees and ants, penguins and seals—teaching rudimentary ethics by lessons of the savage struggle
itself; and in the brain and heart of man she
attains to that noblest goal of all morality embodied in Christ's Golden Rule. Is there not a
clear demonstration here of the fundamental and
far-off beneficence of the cosmic process if we
will only get two foolish notions out of our heads
—one that the universe was made for us alone,
and the other that death is an ending and an evil?
I do not know how Mr. Huxley could more amply

justify the ultimate objects of the cosmic process than, being as he is its brilliant product, thus to reproach it with precisely what he has derived from it. It is Coriolanus at the head of his army splendidly rebuking his mother, Volumnia, by warrant of those very qualities which he drew in at her breasts. Well might she say—

> "Thy valiantness was mine, thou suck'dst it from me;
> But owe thy pride thyself."

The gifted lecturer put the problem back, I readily confess, into a very different region when he asked at Oxford, " Why among the endless possibilities open to omnipotence—that of sinless, happy existence among the rest — should this present actuality be selected in which sin and misery abound?" That eternal dilemma puzzled the Buddha himself; as in the "Light of Asia," where Prince Gautama says—

> "Since, if all-powerful, He made us so,
> He is not good; if not all-powerful,
> He is not God."

There is no present answer to it. Mr. John Stuart Mill, in a valuable letter, which I possess, upon the question, wrote me: " I can believe in a God or Gods, but not, as matters appear to stand, in an Omnipotent Deity." As to the "sin and misery" business, however, is it not nowadays absurdly exaggerated? I have alluded to the almost universal willingness to live, which of itself shows that pleasure and satisfaction largely preponderate

over pain and discontent. The average number of
days of sickness in every ten years for each man
is said to be only sixteen.   Under rules of scientific
hygiene and principles of health better practised,
our span of life—be this desirable or the reverse—
has, by the evidence of insurance societies, considerably increased.   The power of unalleviated
physical pain to terrify or trouble is practically
at an end with the general use of those benign
anæsthetics which have brought a new era of
confidence to the hospital and sick - room, and
taken away all its horror from the surgeon's knife.
Doubtless, to judge from your average daily journal,
murders and suicides, crimes and catastrophes, wars
and feuds and frauds, would seem to remain the
staple of the human record.   But be it remembered
that, for obvious reasons, all our worst and darkest
is collected there.   One might as well judge of
public health by the painful cases described in a
medical publication as of the vast mass of solid
human happiness and innocent living joy by the
daily catalogue of these really trivial exceptions to
it.   As for " sins " (the most serious of which are
only such as are malicious), though the population
increases, they seem steadily to diminish.   We had
87,668 " habituals " in 1868 ; now the evil roll is
only 52,153.   When the population was 19,257,000
in 1889 there were 2589 persons undergoing penal
servitude ; now, with a population of 27,830,179.
the number is only 947.   In 1878, the entire
number of prisoners in our gaols was 20,833 ;

the entire number at the same date last year was
12,663, though the population had increased by six
millions. Pauperism is also declining. In 1870,
1,079.391 persons were in receipt of relief; in 1891,
with an addition of more than seven million inhabitants, there were only 774,905. The upshot of these
figures—without pressing them too much—seems
surely to be that the "cosmic process," in our own
little corner of the universe, is not doing so badly.

If, in truth, that process contained and developed
no other wonder of love and wide-reaching purpose
than the far-sighted instinct of motherly affection,
Professor Huxley's indictment against it would have
to be abandoned. I say nothing here of the beauty
which its action has produced on land and water,
in wood, and field, and garden; of the glories of
form and colour, and the delights of sound and
taste and touch; nor of the faculty to rejoice in
these which it has also bred out of the salutary
struggle. I would be content to trust a defence
of the cosmic scheme to that one profound and
ever-present passion for futurity which burns at its
centre—the love, namely, of the mother for her
offspring. Why, except for glorious ultimate ends
and personal rewards, should this exist in all its
strange gradations, from the fish which feels the
diluted rudiments of its mandate, to the fierce and
fearless maternal devotion of the tigress and she-
bear, and the unwearying and unselfish tenderness
of the Christian mother? Why should the eider
duck pluck the down from her breast to make

her delicate nest at one end of the scale, and
the Princess Alice, at the other, die so divinely
from the kisses of her sick child, if the universe
were not bound together in some sweet secret of
a common life to come, and in some far-off profits
of a vast hidden partnership, as to which female
parents are the semi-conscious trustees? I have
always greatly admired an answer made to me by
an American woman, when I was wondering at the
patience of a nursing wife with her complaining
child, and at the general marvels of maternal care
throughout nature. "Well!" she said, "stranger,
God Almighty can't be everywhere at once, and
so I guess He invented mothers."

Nevertheless, in spite of parental protection and
individual effort to live, the cosmic process no
doubt has plenty of innocent victims, and to some
minds seems to be likely to end by cutting short
all which it has developed, including progress,
pleasures, arts, learning, races, realms, and eventually the planet itself; nay, even the solar system
amid which these were produced. But that is
only in the visible sphere! The cosmic process
perhaps secretly mocks at those whom it thus
succeeds in deceiving for their own good, like a
mother administering hidden medicine. Its strenu-
ous purpose, in the midst of its slaughters and by
means of its very terrors and cruelties, may be to
make everything strive to live. If its tribes and
races knew too much, they would not be sufficiently anxious to exist. Two conditions have been

necessary to the full exploitation of our earthly passage — dread of death and ignorance of the future. Nature hoodwinks her children everywhere. When she has trained a bird to feed on butterflies, she teaches the butterfly to look like the dead leaf of a tree; when she has given the fish-hawk his keen vision, she makes his food —the fish—take on the colours of the weeds and river-stones to escape him. She has put man to school here with Death and Pain and Want for his stern teachers; but possibly it is only because we are children that we think our instructors merciless. Deeper down we evidently know better than to be afraid of them. Note, in those moments when they leave a man to the best and greatest that is in him, how we let go all grip of those lower instructions. Pliny says in vigorous Latin that the cessation of the breath is probably the most delightful moment in life, and I myself have had the honour of conducting to the dinner-table a charming actress, twice drowned (and twice restored to consciousness), who protested that dying was the nicest sensation she knew. As is written in my "Death and—Afterwards": "What a blow to the philosophy of negation appears the sailor leaping from the taffrail of his ship into an angry sea to save his comrade or to perish with him! He has never read either Leopardi or Schopenhauer, perhaps not that heavenly verse, 'Whoso loseth his life for My sake, the same shall save it.' But arguments, which are as far beyond dismal philo-

sophies as the unconscious life is deeper than the
conscious, sufficiently persuade him to plunge.
'Love that stronger is than death' bids him
dare, for Love's imperious sake, the weltering
abyss; and any such deed of sacrifice and heroic
contempt of peril in itself almost proves that man
knows more than he believes himself to know
about his own immortality. Every miner working
for wife and children in a 'fiery' pit, every soldier
standing cool and firm for his country and flag
in the face of instant death, offers a similar en-
dorsement of Walt Whitman's indignant sentence,
'If rats and maggots end us, then alarum! for
we are betrayed.' It is quite possible that in
respect to the mysteries of life and death we
precisely resemble the good knight Don Quixote,
when he hung by his wrist from the stable window,
and imagined that a tremendous abyss yawned beneath his feet. Fate, in the character of Maritornes,
cuts the thong, with lightsome laughter; and the
gallant gentleman falls—four inches!"

As to this aspect of the question, Asia—from
which you have derived all your past religious ideas,
and from which you have many more to learn—
is far in advance of our West. St. Paul's great
declaration, "The things seen are temporal; the
things not seen are eternal"—accepted timidly here
by the pious, but regarded as a mere phrase by
materialists—is in India a commonplace of daily
certainty. Nobody there doubts the continuity of
life, any more than he doubts that the setting sun

will rise again, the same orb, to-morrow. I have
heard a Mahratta woman, while chiding a child
for spilling milk, exclaim, "You must have been
a very bad girl in your last life!" The popular
reason why Hindoo widows do not re-marry is
because the loss of a betrothed or wedded husband
is looked upon as the fatal expiation for some
extreme offence in a previous existence, to be
borne with patient continence in this one; on
which condition the family of the deceased husband
will faithfully maintain the widow, as still belonging to the dead man, and to be surely reunited
with him. This was the basis of the heroic though
tragical custom of "Sati," or widow-burning, one of
the grandest defiances ever flung by human faith
and love at the face of the doctrine of annihilation.
The respect for the animal world, general in Hindoo
and Buddhist societies, is founded, with the tenet
of transmigration, on the same fixed belief in the
endurance and evolving advance of every individual
being. No spot is empty of life to the Indian mind.
A Deccani or Bengali labourer, at his meal in the
jungle, throws behind him fragments of his chupatty
for the invisible Bhuts and Prets to eat. In India,
as in Japan, festivals (*shraddha, shojin*) are made for
the dead with scrupulous regularity, at which their
seats are duly set. The East is saturated with the
mental and social results of this universal acceptance
of the notion that individual life is inextinguishable.
A dignified calm spreads throughout the Oriental
populations, a permanent uninquiring placidity,

noticeable by the most careless or prejudiced eye.
India would never indeed have invented the locomotive, or the Gatling gun ; but her poorest peasants,
by inheritance from profound philosophies, and by the
religious atmosphere of their land, stand at a point
of view far beyond the laboured subtleties of a
Priestley or a Hegel. And if they could be familiar,
as you are, with the splendid achievements and vast
researches of modern science they would not, any
the more, abandon their fixed faith in the Unseen
and the Unknown. Rather would they think it odd
that Western savants should teach the law of the
conservation of force only to abandon it when the
highest and most elaborated of all forces come into
question ; that they should study cell-life under
their microscopes and not perceive that the same
Protamœba they examine—that shapeless jelly—has
been living forty thousand years, as certainly as
forty minutes ; that an illustrious chemist like
Professor Dewar should compress the air we breathe
into a sky-blue liquor, and, when he lets it loose
again, fail to suggest to his audience that what their
eyes see of the real life and furniture of the universe
is next to nothing. The wisest Indian philosophy
has never boggled, like ours, over that silly word
"supernatural." The Upanishad says : "What is
in the Visible, exists also in the Invisible ; and
what is in Brahm's world, that is also here." The
Ultimate, albeit unreachable, is as real to the Asiatic
mind as rice ; and in the Bhagavad-Gita Arjuna is
actually permitted to behold the embodied Infinite.

Indeed, it is rather this present existence which
India regards as the illusion, the Maya. To see the
stars we must wait for night, and to live we must die.
Nor is it uninteresting to note in Hindoo classics
how these large and happy serenities of Oriental
view have softened personifications of Death. I have
translated from the Sanskrit of the Mahabharata,[1]
among other episodes, two remarkable examples of
this. In one the Princess Savitri follows Yama, the
god of death, who has taken away her husband's
soul, and sings to him such beautiful words of love
and faith that, after bestowing many boons to show
his delight in her virtue, the vanquished deity at
last gives back to her the spirit of her lord. In the
other, "The Birth of Death," it is represented how
Death was created by the Supreme Being, in the
form of a most lovely and compassionate girl, to
lighten the earth of that growing burden of living
things of which it had complained. But Death,
"Mrityu," is pictured as too full of love and tenderness for all living creatures to kill them, until
"Bhagavan" turns the tears which she has shed
upon his hand into diseases, and ordains that she
shall bring lives to an end indirectly by these :

> "So passed she from the Almighty Presence, mute,
> The tender angel made to slay mankind,
> And works the will of Heaven, and slays what lives ;
> Not with her own kind hand—she doth not kill !
> By ills and pests which foolish passions breed,
> As many as those pitying tears that rolled
> Forth from her eyes, they perish." [2]

---

[1] *Vide* Indian Idylls.　　　　[2] Indian Idylls.

I do not presume to say that Asia is wiser than Europe or than our illustrious agnostic Professors, but certainly her children live more happily and die more easily. Since it is not the eye which sees, or the ear that hears, but the Self behind those instruments, they believe in that Self, and discount by peace its assured perpetuity. Masters of metaphysics, they sweep the puzzle of Being aside with one decisive maxim: "Never can the Thought know the Thinker." Of that which daunts and troubles us, the boundless mystery of the Universe, their quiet genius has made a daily delight, congenial to the limited powers but illimitable desires of the ever-ascending soul. They have perceived, without seeking to explain, the two supreme celestial laws that govern the Cosmos— Dharma which is Love, and Karma which is Justice. By light of these they have partially discerned how, under an immutable and sometimes seemingly pitiless Equity, all things will advance from good to better, and from better to better still, until it be time for a new and higher order. "*Ahinsa*," therefore, "the doing no injury." is their central commandment, as it was that of Christ in the "Golden Rule," and as it is the last word of Hafiz in his Persian verse.

> "Do no one wrong, and then do what thou wilt,
> My statutes recognise no other guilt."

They await death, not as some of us do, like complaining prisoners under a tyrannical sentence without appeal, attending with gloomy courage the last day in this condemned cell, the flesh ; but rather like glad children of a Great Mother, whose will is sweet and good, whose ways are wise, and who must lull them to the kind, brief sleep of death by-and-by, in order that they may wake ready for happier life in the new sunshine of another and a larger daylight.

If you would banish the evil taste of pessimism from your lips, read sometimes a page or two of the "Leaves of Grass." There died recently in Philadelphia that great and gifted, if somewhat outspoken, Poet of the West, my dear and venerated friend Walt Whitman, who had somehow learned this vast Asiatic complacency which comes from acceptance of the cosmic process and from goodwill to all its living things. Walt Whitman will tell you that :

" Whatever happens to anybody it will be turned to beautiful
       results,
  And nothing can happen more beautiful than death."

He will say :

" All goes outward and onward, nothing collapses !
  And to die is different from what anybody supposed—and luckier !"

He sings right cheerily :

" I know I am deathless ;
  I know this orbit of mine cannot be swept by a carpenter's
       compass :
  I know I shall not pass like a child's carlacue cut out with a
       burnt stick in the dark."

D

Yes! Read a little sometimes in that large-minded and clear-sighted Master—alive with the huge new life of America—who has seen with eyes divinely opened and inspired heart how persistently kind is the unkindness of the Cosmos, and how the beginnings of its work point to far-off consummations, alike in the visible and invisible. The Cosmos is not immoral for him. He writes:

"I believe a leaf of grass is no less than the journey-work of the star;
And the pismire perfect; and a grain of sand; and the egg of the wren;
And the tree toad a *chef d'œuvre* for the highest;
And the running blackberry an adornment for the parlours of heaven;
And a mouse miracle enough to stagger sextillions of infidels."

In his wide affection for humanity, his sense of comradeship with all life, high or low, you may perceive what Buddhism taught to Asia, and what Christ tried to teach to Christendom; that the secrets of content, the spells which bring us into harmony with the cosmic process, are, faith in its purpose, work for its furtherance, and fixed good-will towards all creatures (*Ahinsa*, the desire to help, the readiness to love), which qualities the Cosmos has cheaply evolved by rivalries, and destruction, and the temporary wretchedness of hating. Nor is it only inspired teachers and authentic poets who have seen this. The shrewdest minds all know it. Talleyrand was sharing once in a round game of "questions and answers" at a French château, where one of the queries was, "What is the proper object of life?" which received an almost unanimous reply in the word "Happiness." The next question ran, "What is the secret of securing it?" but this caused deliberation, and greatly perplexed a young and gay Countess, who accordingly consulted in private the Prince of Benevento. That cynical old diplomat, who had seen and done everything, and had no illusions left, exclaimed with impetuous simplicity: "Le secret du bonheur, chère Madame! il n'y en a qu'un — la bienveillance!"

To what point, then, have I to-day ventured to lead you? To this. I say aloud to my age, "Sursum corda!" Lift up your hearts! I say that it seems time for enlightened minds to lay aside misdoubt regarding the continuity of individual life, as wholly contrary to the balance of evidence; to taste the easy pleasure of trust in the cosmic process, as gradually justifying itself; to become partners in the objects of that process by active help, earnest rejoicing, goodwill to all that live; and so to pass at last out of the rudimentary stage where fear and incertitude have been necessary and natural. We must put aside that deeper question which Mr. Huxley asks, as to why it all is so; and must take things as they are. Nay; there is a charm and an advantage in this, similar to the delight which a healthy man feels in breathing the air in which he was born, the delicate medium which so softly and fittingly surrounds him. Mr.

Ruskin has admirably written : "Our happiness as
thinking beings must hang on our being content
to accept only partial knowledge, even in those
matters which chiefly concern us. . . . Our whole
pleasure and power of energetic action depend
upon our being able to breathe and live in a
cloud ; content to see it opening here and closing
there, delighting to catch, through the thinnest
films of it, glimpses of stable and substantial
things ; but yet perceiving a nobleness even in
concealment, and rejoicing that the kindly veil is
spread where the untempered light might have
scorched us, or the infinite clearness wearied." If,
as seems certain, the social virtues have been
evolved out of the social alliance forced upon man
by the fierce and universal struggle of life, then
we will not call the Cosmos immoral. And if,
out of the uncertainty that hangs over death and
the future have sprung, like flowers in a shadowed
place, fortitude and self-sacrifice, faith and pity,
poetry, art, and religion, we will not call the
Cosmos blundering. If it be keen necessity that
has sharpened wits, deadly dangers that have bred
courage, anxious fears that have produced resolve
and aspiration, and death that has intensified and
glorified love, we will not think the Cosmos cruel.
Among Sir Walter Besant's charming works is
one remarkable book entitled "The Holy Rose,"
in which that ingenious author draws a thoughtful
and instructive picture of society relieved from the
law of change and dissolution. A German savant

has discovered the elixir which prolongs human life indefinitely, and nobody any more in his new City of hard facts grows old or in any way alters. A vast and featureless equality is established, a ghastly democratic sameness; everybody is like everybody else, and takes an idle share in the common commodities which an all-powerful science commands, instead of more happily joining under the shield of a natural justice, in the old-fashioned common struggle. The end is a superb but miserable monotony, which is broken up at last by a glad return on the part of the leaders in the improved order to the pleasant anxieties and agreeable mysteries of life as we all to-day know it. I neither ask you, nor am I competent to ask you, to live any other life. It has been good enough, and sweet enough, and wonderful enough for me; and I rejoice to believe there is no end to it, and nowhere any limit to what we have to learn. It would be death, indeed, if there were any such boundary fixed! Never can "the thought compass the thinker," and never shall we get nearer, nor need we wish to get nearer, to a final definition of the infinite existence than that mystical verse from the Sanscrit—

> "He is unknown to those who think they know,
> And known to those who know they know Him not."

But my humble contention is that, having now such ever-augmented glimpses of the wisdom and benignity of the cosmic process, we ought all to begin henceforth to import into life a quite new

delight, an entirely fresh solace, a very much
happier comradeship and confidence. If Epic-
tetus, the lame Phrygian slave, could cry, "Lead
me, Zeus and Necessity! whithersoever ye ordain :
I will follow," an enlightened Englishman to-day
might, I think, repeat—at once with the fullest
freedom of the philosopher and with the lowliest
simplicity of the child ; neither attaching himself
to any special dogmas nor detaching himself from
the Eternal Love, which is the last and largest
and truest name for God ; those words that fold
the wings of the soul, and stay the beatings of
the heart—" Thy will be done ! "

III

A FLIGHT OF LOCUSTS

A FLIGHT OF LOCUSTS

A SENSATION was caused, not long ago, in the House
of Commons, when an honourable member rose and
exhibited specimens of locusts and of locust-eggs,
which had been discovered in some compressed
hay or straw imported into Essex from the East.
Legislators who had never seen locusts "at home"
laughed; but it would be no laughing matter if the
omnivorous insect could indeed be acclimatised in
this country. I say this who have seen locusts
nibble a green country into grey within the course
of one afternoon. We were sitting on a hill upon
the southern side of the great plain of Esdraelon, in
the Holy Land. We had been riding down through
Palestine, from Damascus to Jerusalem—beyond all
doubt the most interesting stretch of country that
can anywhere be traversed. We had passed with our
little caravan under Mount Hermon and the back
of Carmel, past the Sea of Galilee to Nazareth, and,
after tarrying there a few days in the Latin Convent,
were pushing on again for Nablous. So many sick
children and women had been encountered on the
road that a warm desire arose to afford them the
benefit to their fevers and agues and other maladies

of Western medicine. Except for a few indigenous
drugs, the only treatment followed by these poor
Syrian Mohammedans was to get a "mollah" to
write a verse from the Koran upon a strip of parchment, and then wash the sacred characters off with a
little water or milk, and drink the liquid. That was
not much of a febrifuge ; and since there chanced to
be a clever Armenian physician resident at Nazareth,
who only wanted some place as a dispensary to help
the people medically, I bought, through a Mussulman
of the country, those very seven acres of ground on
which the synagogue stood where Christ stood up
to read the law. The land extended on the brow
of an eminence overlooking the little city, generally
identified by Biblical scholars as the "Hill of Pre-
cipitation," and no doubt this is, indeed, the very
place whence the angry Jew's tried to cast down our
Lord headlong. The idea was to convert a little,
domed building, standing upon the ground, into a
small hospital; and having obtained a "firmân"
from the Sultan, and secured the site, I did afterwards send beds and hospital appurtenances to the
place, with a stone for the gateway, inscribed in
Arabic characters, "The Catharine Arnold Hospital." But quarrels broke out between the Greeks
and Latins ; blood was shed ; and the small enterprise succumbed for the time, though I believe it
is now being renewed, and under the same firmân
which I obtained. The business had kept us longer
than was proposed in Nazareth, and it was raining
hard when we started once more down the rocky

JERUSALEM AND MOUNT OF OLIVES AND TEMPLE.

P. 58.

path leading from the city into the plain. In consequence, the road was bad, and the brook Kishon, which flows across it, was greatly swollen. My dragoman, stupid and pig-headed, like most of his class, had for his own purposes opposed our departure; and when we came to the ford, and the first two of the laden mules had sunk into the slime and water up to their belly-bands, he exclaimed, rather insolently, " I told you so, Effendi. *Tarik mafeesh!* there is no road." But I was resolute to go forward, and instead of trying for a passage on this and that side of the regular way, which, indeed, seemed to be a quagmire, I spurred my horse along the middle of it and ordered them to follow. As I had supposed, there was a hard bottom there, and we got across with comparative ease and safety, the face of Nedjm becoming black in consequence all the rest of the day.

So we crossed Kishon and came close up to Mount Gilboa, on a green hill overlooking the site of the ancient Jezreel. The rain had blown away; the sun had dried up the plain; and the rolling hillsides where we stopped for our mid-day meal on the sunny slope glistened under the departing clouds. It would be difficult to find in all the world a more interesting spot for those who knew fairly well the associations of the surrounding country. Within sight were Carmel and Megiddo; the emerald downs overlooking the village of Nain; the cliffs that held the cave where the Witch of Endor lived; Shunem, and, in advance, Engaddi and Dothan, with the

mountains of Samaria ; while we actually overlooked
the vineyard of Naboth, full of the memories of the
prophet Elijah, King Ahab, and the proud and
queenly Jezebel, whose character is so much per-
verted by some who have chronicled the life and
death of the great and terrible Sidonian Princess.

But it is not for its wonderful associations that
I chiefly remember that green Syrian hill glittering
in the sunshine. It is rather on account of having
seen there one of the great sights of the natural world
which may be described a thousand times without
much impressing the mind, but, once witnessed,
leaves an indelible recollection and a feeling almost
of awe at those united infinitesimal forces of the
lower animal world which would overcome evolution
itself and banish man from his own planet, if it were
not for the wise equilibrium that the cosmic process has established by slaying as well as creating.
Should all the spawn of herrings, shed into the
North Sea, come to mature fish, its waters would in
fifty years be so crowded with shoals that the keel
of a ship could not pass. The ants alone, if they
had a free antenna, would soon occupy the whole
earth. The earth-worms, as Darwin showed us,
have by manufacturing arable soil, done more for
the cultivation of the globe than all the farmers and
agriculturists that ever lived and have come to own
it. Such facts as the mischief caused by the intro-
duction of sparrows into America and of rabbits into
Australia show that it is perilous to interfere with the
arrangements of Nature. I remember being justly

rebuked by Sir John Lubbock for having offered to
bring him back some white ants from India. "No,
no!" my wise friend said; "I would not be the man
to introduce the white ant into Great Britain for all
in the cellars of the Bank of England!"

I saw for the first time that afternoon a flight of
locusts! We were sitting on the hill with our backs
turned to the west wind, which was softly blowing
from the Mediterranean. The horses were picketed
close by, grazing the sweet mountain grass. The
Arabs of our caravans were cooking a "pillaw" at
a little distance off. Around us were laid out the
wherewithals of a light lunch, amongst which was an
open marmalade jar. I was thinking of Ahab, and
wondering how he could put up so long with Elijah,
especially when on this very spot the prophet said to
the king, "As the Lord liveth, in this place where
dogs licked the blood of Naboth shall dogs lick thy
blood—even thine"—when suddenly right into the
marmalade there dropped what I took for a large
grasshopper. It was yellow and green, with long
jumping legs and a big head, and while I was taking
it out of the jar two others fell into a plate of soup,
and half a dozen more of the same kind upon a dish
of salad. At the same moment my horse stamped
violently, and I saw more of these grasshoppers
pelting his hocks and haunches. Turning round to
find whence this insect-shower came, I witnessed
what was to me an extraordinary spectacle, though
common enough, of course, in the East. A large
cloud, denser in its lower than its upper part, filled

an eighth part of the western hemicycle. The remoter portion of it was as thick, as brown, and as brumous, as a London fog. The nearer side opened

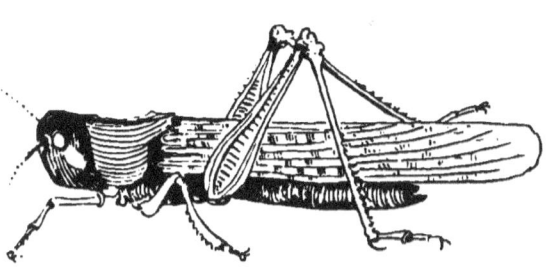

suddenly up into millions, and billions, and trillions, and sextillions of the same green and yellow insect, pelting in a close-winged crowd quite as thickly as flakes of snow could fall upon all the hillsides near and far. You could not stand a moment against the aggressive and offensive rain of these buzzing creatures. The horses even swung themselves round and stood with lowered crests, taking the storm upon their backs and flanks. You had to turn up the collar of your coat to keep them out of your neck, and to button the front not to have your pockets filled with the repulsive swarm, which in two minutes had so peppered the whole scene round about that its colour and character became entirely altered. Every little creature of the interminable flight, on alighting, veered himself round head to

Eggs in Capsule

Eggs full size.

LOCUST AND EGGS.

wind on the earth just as if he had dropped anchor
and swung to the breeze; and it was curious to
notice that the general tint on the ground of their
countless bodies was brown if you looked to windward, and green if you gazed to leeward. But
very quickly the only green to be seen round
about was the hue afforded by this sudden invasion.
Even while we prepared to yield up the spot to
them and pack our lunch baskets for departure,
they had cleared off grass and leaves and every
verdant thing around; and where they rose again
from the soil, or from any clump of trees, in a hungry
throng, the place they quitted had already assumed
a barren and wintry aspect. The Syrian peasants
passing along the roads were beating their breasts
and cursing the ill-fortune of this plague. Some of
them, none the less, gathered up a clothful of the
noxious things; for the locust is distinctly edible.
Half in wrath and revenge, and half for a novelty in
diet, the Arabs to this day eat a few of them, roasting
them in wire nets or in earthen vessels over a slow
fire till the wings and legs drop off, and the locust
becomes crisp, in which state it tastes, as I am able
to say from personal experiment, something like an
unsalted prawn. But it seemed as if, had all Syria
and the globe itself taken to living on locusts, they
would hardly have made a sensible mark upon the
extraordinary number that drifted that day over our
heads. St. John the Baptist is said to have supported existence upon that sort of "locust" which
grows on the carob-tree, a kind of sweet bean; but

this is very probably a mistake of the commentators, who did not wish Sacred History to feed so distinguished a character upon a diet supposed so disgusting. Probably he, however, ate dried grasshoppers, for there is no doubt at all that Easterns have always retaliated upon these devourers of their crops by in turn devouring them. No better proof is wanted of this than the constant practice of the Arabs to-day, and that verse in Leviticus which runs, " Thou mayest eat the locust after his kind, the bald locust after his kind, the beetle after his kind, and the grasshopper after his kind."

The flying plague passed away almost as quickly as it had come, disappearing over Jezreel and the Jordan in the same long, low, brown cloud. But the earth remained for a long time strewn with them, almost as closely as if none had taken wing. Every depression in the ground, every horse-hoof mark, was filled with dozens or scores of them, spitting a green juice, and always head to wind ; and what we observed was nothing—be it remembered—compared to the flights witnessed in Southern Africa and elsewhere. Borrow, in his Travels, speaks of the ground being covered by them over an area of 2000 square miles. Travellers tell of wide rivers the water of which becomes invisible on account of the dead bodies of these insects floating on the surface. The Albert Nyanza is called by the natives the " Muta Nzigi," or " lake of the white locusts," from the enormous masses of these creatures which drown in its waves and are washed up on its shores in

pestiferous heaps. That is the worst of the locust.
In inhabited countries it is almost more dreadful
dead than alive—poisoning the cattle and spreading
disease. It must be, however, an excellent manure
in desolate regions, and no doubt, in some wonderful way of nature, manages to expiate its ravages by
its agricultural usefulness. In Cyprus the English
Government has waged a long and costly war with
this *Gryllus migratorius*, but if anybody had sat
with us at lunch that day upon the hill in Esdraelon,
it seems to me he would have backed the locusts
against the strongest and richest Government that
ever went to war with its winged hosts.

E

IV

ASTRONOMY AND RELIGION

ASTRONOMY & RELIGION.

GREAT results often spring from very small causes. In the ancient town of Middleburgh, in Holland, on a clear autumn day in the year of grace 1606, an old optician named Jan Lippershey had a little job in hand, which was to repair the spectacles of a worthy Mynheer, member of the City Council. He had laid the thick circular glasses, to be re-set, on his work-table, in front of a large old-fashioned mullioned window that looked over the roofs to a flat country in the midst of which rose a church-spire with a clock. The church was about half a league distant, and the figures of the clock were small and in the crabbed Gothic character. By the old craftsman's side played his grandchild,

who had taken up the lenses and was applying
them in an idle mood this way and that to his
eye. Suddenly the child uttered a Dutch exclamation of delight and cried, " Oh, grandfather, I can
see the hour ! " And in effect he had by accident so adjusted the two glasses that a telescopic
result was produced ; and Jan Lippershey, repeating the experiment, read with facility the time from
that casement, holding the glasses in the same
manner.

From such a chance moment dated the invention
of the telescope ; and from that same moment also,
a new era of scientific knowledge dawned, which
must result, though it has not yet resulted, in a
new era of religious thought.

Galileo heard of what the optician's little grand-
son had found out, and in the year 1609 he constructed the earliest telescope. It was not much
more powerful than the opera-glass which the pilot
or the racing man now employs ; but by its aid the
illustrious astronomer was the first to view the
spots on the sun ; to see four moons revolving
round Jupiter ; to descry mountains and plains in
the moon ; to watch the phases of Venus, and to
distinguish many stars which had been invisible
before. Those earliest observations revolutionised
all astral science. Ptolemy and the ancients silently
and suddenly abdicated in favour of Copernicus,
Galileo himself, and Tycho Brahe. There was
come to an end for ever that old conceited ignorance which pictured our planet as the centre of

the Universe, with the moon and the stars for night-lights, and the sun the brilliant but humble attendant of the earth. Little as this immense advance in knowledge has been yet realised by the common imagination, the Church of Rome had an instinct of the revolution; but neither her then mighty power, nor any other influence, could prevent a sudden and swift transformation in human ideas. The least informed mind cannot well take itself back now to the time when a Hebrew writer really believed and recorded that, at the command of Joshua, the moon stood still in the valley of Ajalon, while another inspired scribe could chronicle it as a serious fact that the sun had gone back on its course to prolong the life of King Hezekiah. Galileo, upon whom the prodigious new veracities instantly and imperatively flashed, was compelled by the priests verbally to recant his splendid declarations. But rising from his knees he muttered the famous reservation, "*E pur se muove;*" and for all ages to come there was thus created out of that accidental deed of the little Dutch boy at play, a new heaven and a new earth for mankind.

Galileo, in his "Sidereal Messenger," made a map of eighty new stars which he had discovered in the constellations of Orion's Belt and the "Sword;" and since then astronomer after astronomer, as is well known, has added various groups and galaxies to the two or three thousand conspicuous stars of the first six magnitudes which can be always seen with the naked eye. It is curious and not complimentary to the good sense of mankind that those stars should have been looked upon as merely intended to spangle the sky and give light at night. As lamps they were always a failure. Sixty times the total starlight on the clearest night would not equal the illumination given by the moon ; and thirty-three million times their radiance would be required to equal sunlight. Yet the stars which are seen even by a powerful telescope are now known to be only an insignificant proportion of those actually existing inside " Visible Space." Telescopic photography, as practised to-day by all the observatories, reveals in almost every apparently blank region of the celestial sphere, countless new and distant worlds, lying far beyond all methods of mortal computation and measurement. The only foot-rule with which we can at all estimate the scale of distances in the " Visible Universe" is light. This travels along the ether at the rate of 186,000 miles in a second, so that the ray which we receive from the sun left his surface eight minutes before it has reached our eyes. By ingenious processes based on complex arithmetic, astronomers have determined the distance of about eighty stars, and the nearest of all of them to our system is *Alpha Centauri*. The radiance of this star takes, however, about four years to reach human vision ; while that which we perceive from *Alpha Tauri* or *Aldebaran* was projected from its glittering source twenty-seven years ago ; and most of those seen deeper in the

night sky are so far off that their present light
left them three or four hundred years back. Many
are to-day visible whose beams have travelled to
our gaze only after a lapse of thousands of years,
and there must be radiant streams now on their
way from heavenly bodies in the empyrean which
will only reach the eyes of our very far off posterity.

To what comparative insignificance do these well-
known and well-assured facts reduce the little
corner of space in which our own trivial family
of planets has its being and its motion. It seems
much to say that the earth is distant from the
sun ninety-three millions of miles, so that to
travel thither at the average rate of a tourist by
steam and rail would ask an interval of six hundred
years. And the outside planet of our family,
Neptune, is two thousand eight hundred and twenty-
five millions of miles from the sun, so that we
may roughly call the diameter of our flying system
in space five thousand six hundred and fifty millions
of miles. But vast as this sounds, our solar
system sinks into a speck when one reflects that
if we should represent the interval between the
sun and the earth by one inch, then to put
Aldebaran into his proper place and proportion
our chart would have to be nine leagues wide.
At this moment the great work is everywhere
advancing of making a photographic picture of
the entire visible heavens; all stars down to the
14th magnitude are being reproduced. Twenty-
two thousand separate plates will complete the

planisphere, and it is estimated already that as
many as twenty million distinct stars will appear
upon the unparalleled and astonishing map.

It is vain to endeavour to reduce into intelligible
or adequate language the vastness of material
creation revealed in such a chart; a vastness aug-
mented by the measureless variety of the bodies
and systems included in the immense conspectus.
Gazing near at hand there are indeed all sorts of
absorbing wonders on and around the sun himself;
a world of marvels exists in those "rice-grains"
upon his surface which look like specks and are
all larger than Great Britain, in the "willow
leaves," the "granules," the "faculæ," the "spots;"
in those scarlet flags of flame called "prominences;"
and in the "corona," which at the time of a solar
eclipse is seen stretching for millions of miles
outside the orb.   Those early theologians who
taught that the sun was made to warm and
illuminate this our poor little planetary island did
not know that only one part in two thousand two
hundred millions of his heat and light are received
by the earth.   The rest, in the boundless prodi-
gality of Nature, goes away into space to do, no
doubt, much subtle work.   And then, besides the
sun, there are tantalising mysteries in

> "That orbèd maiden
> With white fire laden
> Whom mortals call the moon."

One side of her we have never beheld, but that
which is always turned towards her elder sister is

painted in silvers and greys, with a landscape of
acclivities and levels which nobody really understands. Astronomers say too rashly that there can
be no life on the moon, because there is no atmosphere there and no moisture. Dead silence must
reign over moonland, they aver, since there is no
air to vibrate; barrenness must prevail since there
falls no rain; and the heat of the sun must
alternately scorch it, and then be withdrawn, producing a cold greater than any which Professor
Dewar can create. Then there are the planets of
which we know just a little, as people often do of
their own particular families. Mercury and Venus
inside our own orbit, Mars outside it; and, beyond
him, stately Jupiter, Saturn with his Ring, Uranus,
and Neptune. Comparatively near as these are,
and presenting well-marked features to the glass,
they are yet so far divided and so minute compared
to the space they swim in, that if the earth were
represented by a football at Hyde Park Corner,
Neptune would be such a four-foot globe as an
acrobat walks upon, placed at Oxford. Between
Mars and Jupiter swarm in the ether those silver
bees of the system called asteroids, perhaps the
fragments of an exploded planet, the baby children
of our system, already 370 in number, and increasing
with yearly observations. The largest of them,
Vesta, is but 300 miles in diameter. Beyond
Jupiter, again, circle those large mysterious planets
about which astronomers too arrogantly say that
they must be lifeless, failing to perceive that life

equates itself everywhere to its conditions, and that
just as lungs are the correlation and the consequence
of an atmosphere of oxygen and nitrogen, and gills
the adaptation to water as a medium to existence,
so there may be creatures on the sun which thrive
upon incandescent hydrogen, moon - people who
flourish without air or water ; Jovians and Saturnians
well contented with an abode in a state of vapour ;
and Uranians with a scheme of body and being
unimagined, but suitable to their environments, and
real as the stomach of a railway director. Then
beyond these our close neighbours are the comets,
the stars, the nebulæ, the " Milky Way," that " river
of light and life " which, searched by the glass,
presents itself as a fathomless channel of sweeping
stars. Inconceivably distant from him, man has yet
means to-day which bring those within the range of
his knowledge. The spectroscope aided by photography tells us the substance and the chemistry of
those remote worlds. Dr. Huggins has found hydrogen in the " nebulæ," and Secchi in certain stars
also ; while the rate at which they approach or
recede can be accurately measured. Thus *Aldebaran*
is going away from us at thirty miles a second, and
Gamma Leonis approaching us at a slightly lower
speed. The great telescope of the Lick Observa-
tory, which I myself had the privilege one night
of using, has settled the fact that the nebula of
Orion is flying from us at ten miles a second.
We know in fact enough of this marvellous " Visible
Universe " to be proud and glad of our increasing

knowledge, but never to presume upon it as final or sufficient.

Indeed, our best acquaintance with its wonders must always be held provisional. The organ wherewith we are aware of it is an imperfect one, insensible to many colours beyond the red and the violet which certain insects appear to perceive. Light itself is nothing but a vibration of what we call, without understanding it, the ether; and sight is a sense easily deceived and of very feeble range. It is probable that only a slight exaltation of the power of our optic nerve would present the picture of the starry sky to us in a very different aspect. To our vision the waste of space appears astounding, much as the Pacific Ocean seems far too large for its archipelagoes. The boundless vault looks as though wasted in containing at such enormous intervals the tiny specks that are its worlds and suns. Would it wear anything like so open an aspect if we had better or different eyes? To see the stars at all it is necessary to wait for the darkness of night: to be aware of those crimson fountains of glory streaming into space from the sun, we have to borrow the help of the moon's interposed disc. Since all heavenly bodies exercise an influence, gravitatory and other-wise, upon all other bodies, it is conceivable that a kind of vision may hereafter exist to which their mutual contact and interaction would be perceptible. We see nothing now which is not of the nature to reflect upon our retinas or to project upon them those light-waves of which alone our light-sense can take any cognisance. The fish that dimly perceives a star through his water-world composed of oxygen and hydrogen, is not in a much worse position for reliable astronomical observations than man, with his limited visual spectrum, at the bottom of his own ocean of oxygen, nitrogen, and the new gas.

Astronomy has taken, however, an immense start forward in estimating the Cosmos, since that discovery by the little Dutch boy, which put her solemn sisters, Philosophy and Religion, quite out of step. The spell of habit binds, nevertheless, even astronomers themselves. Not only do they use contentedly the phrases consecrated by ancient ignorance, such as "Sunrise" and "Sunset," spoken incorrectly of an orb which, as far as we are concerned, neither rises nor sets; but most of them cannot shake themselves free from absolutely primitive ideas about life. You shall read them gravely declaring the uninhabitability of the sun, the moon, and the planets, as before remarked, because of physical differences forsooth between those bodies and our earth. They go on contentedly with the old stellar chartography which Ptolemy introduced when he divided the stars into forty-eight constellations, giving to each of them the name of a character in classic mythology. Modern astronomers, unwilling or unable to improve upon this, have added about twenty more pagan names to those of Ptolemy; and even when fantastic figures are not delineated round the groups of stars, the

ancient appellations are still retained. No doubt
there is a convenience in this, as it helps the " star-
gazer" to map out his sky; and a good observer
will know the " Lyre," the " Swan," the " Plough,"
and "Cassiopeia" as well as any teacher of
geography the outlines of various states and
countries. But no attempt has been made to
break away into a new and more adequate astro-
graphy, based as it might be on the marvellous
symmetries and geometrical collocations of the
sky. This subject of astral perspective has indeed
engaged singularly little scientific attention. The
pursuit which should excite and delight most of all
the scientific imagination, is content to view its
universe as an indefinitely or infinitely expanding
hollow sphere, the boundaries of which perpetually
recede before the increasing power of the lens or
the resolute exercise of inductive reason. But if
our experimentalists suspended in a vast glass
globe endless numbers of electric lamps of different
sizes, and surveyed the illumination from a point
inside or outside, how long would it be before
chance furnished us with such a shapely arrangement as those of the three jewels in the belt of
Orion; the rhomboid in Charles' Wain; or the
measured localisation of the stars in the Southern
Cross ? The best thing that could happen for
mankind would be if a great astronomer had been
born a poet, or if a great poet should become an
astronomer; for we sadly need newer and nobler
ideas about the chief of sciences.

But if, in view of the good and useful work
which astronomers are undoubtedly doing in col-
lecting facts and adding to the range of actual
knowledge, we excuse them for not rising to the
rich sublimity of the Cosmic side of their business,
it is not so easy to forgive modern Philosophy and
modern Theology. Physical and metaphysical
writers are equally to blame for the very slight
influence which they have permitted latter-day
astronomy to exercise upon their disquisitions. Yet
the meaning of the word " metaphysics " would almost appear to suggest that every great enlargement
of view in Natural Science ought to be followed by
an expansion of thought in Speculative Philosophy.
" Metaphysics " is a fine sonorous word, like " Meso-
potamia," but it merely means that when Aristotle
had finished writing about the objects in creation,
τά φυσικά, he commenced quite naturally to discourse
about " μέτα τά φυσικά," or " the things that come
next after objects of creation." Surely that is an
obvious sequence ; and if our metaphysicians,
especially those of the pessimistic school, would
saturate themselves with the new truths of astronomy, extending their mental focus to even the
present range of the Visible Universe, we should
not read dreary and dismal jeremiads about the
origin and end of life, nor in the social field
witness such a folly as Anarchism raising its selfish
and ridiculous banner under the stately march of
the stars. Of all the fools' paradises ever built by
man, the idlest and the meanest is that one of mere

material comfort and easy subsistence without work, which seems to satisfy certain base democratic ideals. If life be what some among our demagogues teach to their stupid but passionate listeners, a three score and ten years span, spent best if spent in meat and drink and voting, then Carlyle was justified when, gazing on the stars he cried, "Ah, sir! 'tis a sorry sight!" As I myself have written in "Lotus and Jewel":

> " Either the Universe in Chaos, Chance,
>   Or else the Universe is Order, Law:
>   If that, die and let go the drunken dance ;
>   If this, live and rejoice in love and awe ! "

In vain has the star-bespangled Night, giver of sleep and rest, comforter of men, revealed under her dark mantle the splendid secret of worlds upon worlds and boundless Being, if not even this has sufficed to silence upon the lips of bitter and dis-believing man doubt as to the ultimate rightfulness of Nature, whose law of order, evolution, and harmonious issues is written in such large silver letters upon the skies.

Nothing, in truth, so much exalts our sense-perception, and, at the same time, admonishes and humiliates it, as the manifestations of Astronomy. With the tube of the Lick telescope directed into the thickest milky effulgence of the thronged galaxy, the eye seems to plunge into the actual glory of infinitude, and literally to see the illimitable. If there be immutable reasons why we should tem-

F

porarily live in what we call the "present," amid
illusions of time and space—which must be false
in the sense of the Hindoo Maya, but need not be
non-existent—how could there be devised a nobler
consolation, a loftier promise, than in such glimpses,
which convince the mind of the infinity and immortality that it cannot in this life understand?
On such a head there are two notable passages
in the New Testament. One is where the great
Teacher of Nazareth, perhaps with His divine
eyes fixed at the time upon the shining firmament, said pityingly, "In My Father's house are
many mansions: if it were not so I would have
told you." And the other passage is a saying
from the same tender and holy lips: "The kingdom
of heaven is nigh unto you, yea, even at your
very gates." Probably these last words, at once so
simple and so mysterious, condense a prodigious
physical fact. It may well be that the next great
secret of existence is hidden from us by a veil
so thin, that its very thinness makes it impene-
trable. A touch, a turn, a change, as slight as
when the light pebble lying on the thin ice
feels it melt and falls to the bottom, may be all
that is necessary to lift the curtain of another
and utterly transformed Universe which is yet
not really another, but only this same one that
we see imperfectly with present eyes, and think
of timidly with present thoughts. As Browning
sings of his fair dream which came so near to
realisation :

"Only to break a door of glass,
Only a bridge of cloud to pass,
Only one wicked Mage to stab,
And, look you, we had kissed Queen Mab!"

So it may be with many, possibly with most,
at that natural promotion and permutation called
Death. Mathematicians talk, as about something
more solid than a dream, in regard of what they
call a higher space, that of Four Dimensions; and
advanced photographers are hoping it may some
day be feasible to take pictures with the ultra-
red rays, which pass through opaque matter, and
to which flesh is lately proved to be transparent.

Returning, however, to what is visible and
known, the infinite vitality of the Universe must
be borne in mind, as well as its boundless extent
and variety. The late Mr. Richard A. Proctor
has well written in his "Other Worlds than Ours"
these eloquent words :

"Instead of millions of inert masses, we see
the whole heavens instinct with energy—astir with
busy life. The great masses of luminous vapour,
though occupying countless millions of cubic miles
of space, are moved by unknown forces like clouds
before the summer breeze; star-mist is condensing
into clusters; star-clusters are forming into suns;
streams and clusters of minor orbs are swayed by
unknown attractive energies; and primary suns,
singly or in systems, are pursuing their stately
path through space, rejoicing as giants to run
their course, extending on all sides the mighty

arm of their attraction, gathering from ever new
regions of space supplies of motive energy, to be
transformed into the various forms of force—light
and heat, and electricity—and distributed in lavish
abundance to the worlds which circle round them."

Perhaps the most deplorable survival of primitive
human ignorance about the heavens is the doubt
which orthodox astronomers still maintain upon
the question, whether life exists amid all these
fair and wonderful mansions of life. And here,
indeed, is where there seems to come in the truest
and most urgent necessity that religion should ex-
tend the boundaries of her doctrines in order to
render them a little more adequate to the range
of scientific acquisitions. Take, for instance, what
is called the "Scheme of Salvation" as it is
preached by ordinary interpreters. How lament-
ably it continues to be narrowed down into the
limits of the old-fashioned notions of the " world ! "
Let me hasten to concede that no discovery, no
generalisation, no new revelation of the vastness,
variety, and vital fulness of the Cosmos could ever
rob of its divine value the inner meanings of what
is eternally true. The idea of redemption by love,
for example, which has a thousand illustrations
even in the little sphere of human experience,
would probably only derive greater and greater
magnificence of demonstration if we could see
and know its operation in systems developed beyond our own, and amid that immense, and to-
day inconceivable, march of evolution, of which

we get only shadows here. But is it not evident that we must think more largely than to imagine for ourselves, or to let those whom we teach imagine, that the Son of God was once absent from such an universe as we now perceive—from the splendid spaciousness of His dominions of light and life—wholly abstracted in the care and charge of "this little O, the earth?" The love of God, manifested in Him, was doubtless then and always present with us, as with all the Cosmos; but, to think becomingly and proportionately to facts, we must recognise that it was also, and simultaneously, present in every abode of planetary and stellar—perhaps of galactic and nebular—society. We meditate too meanly upon heavenly love, and divine government, and the life of man, and his lives which are to be, when our minds still thus wear the garments of old theologies, while our hands hold the telescope and the spectroscope. We have enlarged enormously our conceptions of the · Universe, but apparently forgotten to magnify our beliefs. A school-girl of to-day knows that the specks of silver in the ocean of the night are sun-worlds; but her rector or teacher reads her still the legends of Joshua and Hezekiah, and permits her to think that for thirty years long, some eighteen hundred and ninety-four years ago, a million million orbs and systems—full of living beings—were without the second Person of the Trinity, absent on urgent duty upon an atom of a world invisible to the very nearest of them.

It is charming to observe with what simplicity the delicate and gentle genius of Mr. Ruskin, in his "Frondes Agrestes," has grappled with this incompatibility between old tenets and modern discoveries. He begins by deploring how little men care to know or think about the sky "in which Nature has done more for the sake of pleasing man—more for the sole and evident purpose of talking with him and teaching him—than in any other of her works." "And yet," writes Mr. Ruskin (Section 3, p. 35), "we never attend to it, we never make it a subject of thought, except as it has to do with our animal sensations; we look upon all by which it speaks to us more clearly than to brutes, upon all which bears witness to the intentions of the Supreme that we are to receive more from the covering vault than the light and the dew which we share with the weed and the worm, only as a succession of meaningless and monotonous accidents, too common and too vain to be worthy of a moment of watchfulness, or a glance of admiration."

Again, speaking of the infinitude of things to know, and of the much that never can be known, revealed in the starry firmament, he says :

"None but proud or weak men would mourn over this, for we may always know more, if we choose, by working on; but the pleasure is, I think, to humble people, in knowing that the journey is endless, the treasure inexhaustible—watching the cloud still march before them with its summitless pillar

and being sure that, to the end of time, and to the
length of eternity, the mysteries of its infinity will
still open farther and farther, their dimness being
the sign and necessary adjunct of their inexhaust-
ibleness."

But, brought face to face with the largeness of
the Cosmos and the littleness—at least as relates
to verbal definition—of the pre-Galileo religions,
Mr. Ruskin takes refuge in the provisional and, so
to speak, personal character of the orthodox doctrines, and the "Scheme." "We must not," he
argues, "define and explain ourselves into dim and
distant suspicion of an inactive God inhabiting
inconceivable places, and fading into the multi-
tudinous formalisms of the laws of Nature. All
errors of this kind arise from the originally mistaken idea that man can, 'by searching, find out
God—find out the Almighty to perfection'—whereas
it is clearly necessary, from the beginning to the
end of time, that God's way of revealing Himself
to His creatures should be a *simple* way, which *all*
those creatures may understand. Whether taught
or untaught, whether of mean capacity or enlarged,
it is necessary that communion with their Creator
should be possible to all; and the admission to
such communion must be rested, not on their
having a knowledge of astronomy, but on their
having a human soul. In order to render this
communion possible, the Deity has stooped from
His throne, and has, not only in the person of
the Son, taken upon Him the veil of our human

flesh, but, in the person of the Father, taken upon
Him the veil of our human *thoughts*, and permitted
us, by His own spoken authority, to conceive Him
simply and clearly as a loving father and friend :
a being to be walked with and reasoned with, to
be moved by our entreaties, angered by our rebellion, alienated by our coldness, pleased by our
love, and glorified by our labour; and finally, to
be beheld in immediate and active presence in all
the powers and changes of creation. This conception of God, which is the child's, is evidently
the only one which can be universal, and, therefore, the only one which *for us* can be true."

This is all true, beautiful, and to the purpose of
the eminent author's thought; but it is an explanation of the survival of old religious ideas, rather
than a justification of them. The astronomer and
the house-cat enjoy, of course, the sunshine equally,
but the former understands, as the latter does
not, some at least of the wonders of that golden
warmth. My representation is, that the divine
significations of those of the old doctrines which
have eternal truth in them ought by their ex-
pounders to be henceforward immeasurably expanded
and advanced, in the light of astronomical announce-
ments. My object in these purely suggestive pages
(for to exhaust the point would demand many such
another paper) is to indicate how new, superb, and
noble are the meanings which the ancient formulas
might receive from current facts, if their professional
interpreters could and would rise to the heights

whither " star-eyed science " to-day beckons them. " Life," " Love," " Redemption," "Creation," " Evil," " Good," and that most vast and vague name of " God " are words of ever unfolding might and majesty, which need to-day bolder and more hopeful re-translation into that glorious, albeit ever mystical, language of which the starry heavens display at least the silver cypher.

V

IN THE INDIAN WOODS

IN THE INDIAN WOODS

COUNTRIES have faces, as individuals have. The countenance of one land differs from the countenance of another, by features and complexions strongly contrasted, to eyes which know how to discriminate and observe. This is not merely true of such marked distinctions as exist between arctic and temperate, or tropical and sub-tropical, zones. Anybody can, of course, perceive at a moment's glance whether he is in the treeless latitude of the Orkneys or wandering amid the lavish vegetation of Ceylon and Java. I imply much subtler peculiarities and far finer *differentiæ* by which the watchful traveller shall know, almost to a single degree of latitude, where he stands at the moment of observation. It depends upon three things—firstly, the general geological character of the country ; secondly, its fauna and flora ; thirdly, its peoples, towns, and villages ; but the last may be altogether absent from view without diminishing the faculty to recognise what is quite justly styled the "face" of a country. For myself I retain the very clearest and plainest conception in my mind's eye of the face of any coast or land I ever visited, and if I were a painter of sufficient skill I feel that

it would be possible to set accurately and swiftly
upon canvas the typical landscapes or seascapes of
Provence, of North Africa, of Italy, of Greece, of
Bulgaria, of Asia Minor, of Egypt, of India, of Ceylon,
of China, of Japan, of Western and Eastern America,
and, in fact, of any special region. Occasionally,
just as you meet with visages in a crowd which
exactly resemble others well known, so you will
encounter striking and precise resemblances between
distant and unconnected spots. Boston Common
with Beacon Street, for example, are so exactly like
Piccadilly and the Green Park, that even a Londoner,
suddenly transported to New England, might be
deceived ; and I know a little green recess upon the
banks of the Nile which reproduces to a tree, to a
bush, to a crag, to the spread of shining sand and
climbing flowers, another nook familiar to me on the
shore of the river Moota-Moola, near Poona. But,
generally speaking, countries differ even more notably than individuals, and the main reason is, not
their geology, which gives outline and surface, but
their zoology, and especially their botany. It does
not need a scientific eye to notice and remember the
specialisation which these two confer. The good
observer, even if unable to name many of the living
creatures and most of the plants and trees which he
passes by, remarks them, remembers them, and will
no more afterwards fail to recall the particular district by their means than he will forget the colour
of the eyes of the woman that he has loved, or the
way in which she wore her hair or her robe.

These thoughts arise in glancing at a volume which has just been published under the title of "The Flowering Plants of Western India," by the Rev. Alexander Kyd Nairne, late of the Bombay Civil Service. It is a small octavo, aiming at little more than to catalogue, with running semi-scientific notes, the various plants and trees met with on what was my side of India. But the modest work is, as far as it goes, performed so well, that by its previous study India might become another and a happier world to the intelligent "griffin," who should have this book always with him. I can truly say that in turning the pages of Mr. Nairne's laborious and faith-, ful little compilation, I have revisited India in a way not possible under any ordinary literary guidance. It is pleasant to find how, in glancing through these pages, forest and jungle friends come back, under the old Mahratta and Hindu names, as vividly as if one turned the leaves of a vast album of the portraits of vanished companions. Without criticising Mr. Nairne's useful work from a scientific point of view, I am here proposing to hold on to his erudite botanical skirt, and as he himself wanders amidst those warm and beautiful wildernesses of Asia, to say briefly what I also remember of them, and how the loveliness of a blossom or the glory of a tree is linked in my own memory with this or that adventure, legend, or impression.

Quite irregularly, then, and with no regard to orders and classifications, let us plunge into these plant-catalogues as one used to pluck bridle and

turn away from the *dâk* road to take the forest
paths.   And, first, we are in a garden-ground.
Remark this garden plant, one of the magnolias,
michelia champaca.   It is good to begin with,
for it smells of India.   Shelley, however, had only
heard of it when he wrote :

> "The Champâk odours fail
> Like sweet thoughts in a dream,"

and he would not, perhaps, have greatly admired
the little tree itself, which bears blooms at the
end of naked and swollen stalks.   But the pale
white flowers with the yellow hearts possess truly
the very fragrance of the East.   The Hindoo women
weave them into their hair and offer them in
temples, and in Ceylon images of Buddha are
carved from the thick trunk.   Pluck one waxen
star and pass on, holding it to the delighted
nostril, for this is the odour of the *Veds* and of
the *Upanishads,* the very perfume of classical
India.   That bush close by is the custard apple,
Sita s fruit, *sitaphal,* and yonder twists and clings
gulovel, the climber, *tinospora cordifolia.*   The
fruit of it is good for fever, and the plant is so
full of vitality, that a yard or two of the small
yellow - blossomed   stem,   twisted   round   a   tree
branch, will send down roots to the earth, and,
in the soft, warm air, soon becomes a shrub for
itself.   Now we come to a pool, and could well
stop at it all day for the wonderful things to be
seen in any bit of Indian water.   Those fair

floating blooms—red, white, or blue—are the *Kamal*, the starry water-lily, and the large red

SACRED LOTUS.

lilies are *Padmà*, the sacred lotus of India, from which, according to Sanskrit scriptures, Brahma

G

sprang, and of which the old Hindu literature is
full. There are a hundred and thirty-five different names in the *Devanagari* for this sacred
blossom. Notice how it springs, pure and perfect,
from the black slime, and understand why it is
the type of the human soul disengaging itself,
under the light of Heaven, from the contamina-
tions and illusions of the world. Over the pool
is growing a mesua-tree, *nâg champa*, native to
the Konkan, but cultivated elsewhere, of which
Sir William Jones truly said, "It is one of the
most beautiful on earth, with blooms like white
roses and buds and shoots of the deepest crimson."
They plant this in Ceylon near to every Buddhist
temple. The little herb near it, also displaying
rosy stems, is the *lal âmbâri*, the roselle, "red
sorrel" of the West Indies, of which all Anglo-
Indian housewives make jelly. And yonder, tower-
ing to the sky, its flowers blood-red, its trunk and
branches covered with prickles, is the silk-cotton
tree, *bombax malabaricum* (called in these parts
shewa). Do not stop to do more than admire the
flowers shooting like flames upon the bare branches,
for any Anglo-Indian would weary you with a
hundred stories about it. Near at hand is seen
climbing a rudraksh, the *mâdhavi*, the flower *par
excellence* of Sanskrit lyrical poetry, with large
pointed shining leaves and perfumed blooms, pure
white, except for the fifth petal being dusted with
pale gold. This is also the *atimukhta*, and you must
add a blossom of it to our imaginary bouquet.

Any English eye will know that next flower! It is the common balsam, *tirda;* but we never had it in England till the Portuguese brought it hence in the sixteenth century. That tall, thorny tree, with round grey fruit like a golf-ball, is the wood-apple, and near it, closely akin, the Bil, *Ægle marmelos,* the fruit of which is good for dysentery, and belongs to the citrons and the oranges. But who would think that yonder small white flowers and glossy leaves, which smell so unpleasantly, on the little tree beside the Bil, belong to the satin-wood, which cuts into such lovely slabs—like watered ribbon—and furnishes panels for palaces?

Along the road are planted "Neems," which look like acacias by their leaves, and lilacs by their lovely scented panicles of purple blossom. The little thorny tree there, with yellow cherry-shaped fruit, is more important than it appears, being *Zizyphus Jujuba,* the Bher, which some Mohammedans deem to be the *Sidra* of the Koran, the tree that the Prophet found growing at the boundary of the Seventh Heaven on the night when he went to visit Paradise. And another *Zizyphus,* rather like this, but with white fruit, to be found in the ghâts, is the accepted Lotos of the "Odyssey," the food of the Lotophagi, of which the "Odyssey" says, to cite my translation :

"Whoso hath tasted the honey-sweet fruit from the stem of the lotus
Never once wishes to leave it, and never once thinks to go homewards ;

There would he stay, if he could, content with the eaters of
Lotos,
Plucking and eating its magic, forgetting the thought of re-
turning."

We have seen many a mango-tree, *amba*, since
starting, with dark, massive foliage, and, in the
season, most delicious fruit which, but for a slight
flavour of turpentine, would be so perfect. Nothing
is more grateful than the scent of the white mango
blossoms at night in the Indian spring. On the higher
ground the wild indigo was growing, the jungly-nîl,
which is so important on the other side as a cultivated plant; and we forgot to remark in the garden
hedge the climbing Gunj, *Abrus precatorius*, the
pretty bright seeds of which, scarlet tipped with
black, are used by goldsmiths as weights for gold
and diamonds, and by Portuguese Catholics for
rosaries. The "gram" in the fields, upon which
Indian horses live—*channa*—is akin to this, and
so is the Indian "Coral Tree," with its large scarlet
flowers. We must not fail to notice the "gold-
mohur," which makes the Bombay gardens splendid
in the cold season, with its gilded blooms, which
the French West Indians call "Flowers of Paradise."
And here is the *Bawa*, with blooms like falling rain
of gold and pods like swords, holding seeds that
furnish the physic senna; and, ah! there is the
Asoka, most famous of all trees in Sanskrit poetry,
the name meaning "sorrowless"—or heart's-ease, as
in that line of Damayanti's appeal, *Satyandma
Bhawa Asoka! Asoka Sokanashanam:*

" Truly, Heart's-ease, if, good Heart's-ease !
Thou could'st ease my heart of pain."

This other common tree, seen everywhere on
the dry maidans, is an acacia—the *babul*—very
prickly, with yellow, fragrant flowers and flat
woolly pods, among which the weaverbirds love
to hang their nests, safe from the snakes. Akin
to it are the Mimosas, one of which, like its lowly
sister the sensitive plant *lájálu lájari*, is never
cut down by the Mohammedans, because of its
pretty way of bending down its branches towards
the stranger who comes under its shadow. The
sensitive plant is not much seen in Western India,
but in Ceylon there are whole banks and meadows
of it, through which, as you walk, it is as though
the earth was alive with the delicate, shrinking
leaflets of the grass, which shudder and close up
in a pale and quick confusion. Note in the village
tank the " water-chestnut " growing, " Shingari,"
of which ancient Hindus thought so highly that
they put it among the lunar constellations. You
ask what is the spreading plant, everywhere lying
along the hot plain, with bright, hairy leaves and
round globes of green and yellow. That is the
jangli kakri, sister to bitter colocynth, and wild
cousin of the melon and cucumber. All this while,
too, we have failed to notice the still more common
nágphanna, the " prickly pear," sprawling with
broad, fleshy, savagely-armed leaves upon every
rocky eminence and around every garden and
village. You cannot touch leaf or blood-red fruit

without filling your hand with miscroscopic darts.
We used to cure our Deccan ponies of kicking by
backing them into a clump of this "Barbary fig,"
and it is wonderful how the cobras manage to
live among its pins and needles. Closely akin to it
is the "night-blowing Cereus," the glorious white
and gold blossom of which comes forth suddenly
by night and only lasts for a few splendid hours.

It is interesting that we come now upon a
Kadamba tree, for this too, with its large heart-
shaped leaves, perfumed flowers of white and
yellow, and fruit like a mandarin orange, was re-
verenced by ancient India. Its blossoms smell
like new wine, and had irresistible power to recall
an absent and forgetful lover. From its branches
Krishna watched the *Gopis*, or milkmaids of Brin-
dâban, and under its shade the god danced with
them. Here on the Ghauts is also growing the
ixora — *Kurât* — called the torch-tree because its
green branches are used for flambeaux ; and Indian
people style this other little smooth shrub *pâpat*,
and its berries "Matheran coffee." But, indeed, the
real coffee belongs to the *Ixoras*.

The pimpernel grows about Western India —
our "shepherd's clock," but it is a tiny herb
with blue flowers. A large, handsome tree is the
"mowra" — *Bassia latifolia* — with a hard and
lasting timber and flowers which smell like rats
and mice, but produce, when dried, a spirit only
too attractive to hard drinkers. Of the fruit they
make bangles, and from the seeds oil and stearic

acid. On some of these trunks climb wild the
various forms of Indian jasmine, "mogri," also
largely cultivated for their delicate odour and
to weave those garlands which Hindu hospitality
loves to hang upon the neck and wrists of a
guest. And there—nay, indeed, everywhere upon
the sandy uplands—is the "Karanda" bush, with
tinted white flowers guarded by long thorns, and
purple, sticky fruit, under the tufted roots of
which often lies the grey Mahratta hare. In the
nullahs are Oleander plants, oftentimes with white
and yellow, instead of the well-known red blossoms,
which are so beautiful and so poisonous. And
hardly a patch of forest-ground or fringe of jungle-
shade but will show the greenish-white flowers and
shining ovate leaves of the strychnine-tree, *Kájra*,
which has death in its button-shaped seeds. By
the large ovate leaves, rough underneath, you know
the teak-tree—never so tall in Western India as
in Burmah—and under it a straggling plant of
the wild basil, whose cultivated variety is the
Kala tulsi, the holy shrub of the wife of Mahadeo,
planted near every temple and at the doors of
Hindu houses.

This milk-bush, which is an Euphorbia, has come
from Africa, but is now quite Indian. It is a
cousin of the prickly-pear, though so different in
aspect. Every broken twig bleeds a white and
sticky juice. In our imaginary passage through
jungle, garden, plain, and hill we shall have
frequently passed two famous trees of India—the

Banyan and the Pipal. The first is unmistakable,
by its habit of dropping down boughs from the air,
which take root and become trunks, making, as is
written in the "Light of Asia,"

> "An ample shade,
> Cloistered with columned, dropping stems; and roofed
> With vaults of glittering green."

Some of these noble and wonderful trees spread

BANYAN TREE.

over space enough to encamp a regiment. The
other is the *Ficus Religiosa*, the sacred tree of
Buddha, whose long smooth leaves, for ever
vibrating in the air, are said to whisper to the
gods all that men do, or say, or think on earth
below. Also the plantains encountered were too
common to notice, though, indeed, nothing can be
more beautiful than their fresh broad flags, before

the wind has broken the glossy green silk of them into ribbons.

TALIPOT PALM & BAMBOO.

For palms one must be near the sea-coast, albeit certain species of these lovely and stately

trees will be encountered almost anywhere. Many
and many a notable plant and bush and flower has,
meantime, escaped attention. The "Keori," for
instance, or screw pine—which botanists call Pan-
danus, and the Sanskrit poets *Ketaka*—possesses in
its tender white flowers the very sweetest fragrance
of the whole range of perfumes—an odour such as
might breathe from an angel's lips giving the kiss
of welcome to a soul entering into heaven. Moreover, we did not speak of what was seen a
hundred times, the *erandi*, or castor-oil bush; nor
of the sandal-wood tree, *Chandan*, which has the
fragrant wood, and furnishes the "oil of the
thirteen virtues;" nor of the *Sampsàn* shrub, of
which the mongoose is said to eat after being
bitten by a cobra; and those two botanical
miracles, the *chàr baje*, or "four o'clock," so styled
because its flowers open every afternoon at
that time, and the *Desmodium gyrans*, which
twists and untwists twice in every twenty-four
hours. Nor was mention made of the papaw
tree, which will turn tough meat into tender
if suspended among its branches; nor of a
thousand other things of interest, curiosity, and
beauty in those fields and groves of India, touched
upon briefly, but with a loving and scientific
patience and observation, in the pages of this
book of Mr. Nairne, which has been the companion of our fanciful stroll in the Indian groves
and gardens.

VI

LOVE THE PRESERVER

VI

LOVE THE PRESERVER

On the 10th of October 1893 I delivered an address in the Town Hall of Birmingham, as President of the Birmingham and Midland Institute. Its subject was "Aspects of Life," and in the course of it I spoke the following words :—

"I would be content to trust a defence of the cosmic scheme to that one profound and ever-present passion for futurity which is at its centre—the love, namely, of the mother for her offspring. Why, except for ultimate ends and personal rewards, should this exist, in all its strange gradations, from the fish, which feels the diluted rudiments of its mandate, to the fierce maternal devotion of the tigress and she-bear, and the unwearying and unselfish tenderness of the Christian mother? Why should the eider duck pluck the down from her breast to make her delicate nest, at one end of the scale, and the Princess Alice, at the other, die so divinely from the kisses of her sick child, if the Universe were not bound together in some sweet secret of a common life to come ; in some far-off profits of a vast hidden partnership, as to which female parents are the semi-conscious trustees? I

have always greatly admired an answer made to
me by an American woman, when I was wondering
at the patience of a nursing wife with her complaining child, and at the general marvels of
maternal care throughout nature. 'Well!' she
said, 'God Almighty can't be everywhere at once,
and so, I guess, He invented mothers.'"

The more one thinks upon this universal parental
instinct, the more wonderful and significant it must
seem. Throughout the animated world of creation
we see species preying upon species; each tribe
reluctantly supplying the food of another; until
the spectacle of widespread warfare culminates in
man himself, his huge standing armies and sanguinary battles. The peace, beauty, and purpose
of the Universe appear to be miserably gainsayed by
such mutual hostilities. It seems as if nothing
could live except at the price of life: "Each slays
a slayer, and in turn is slain." Yet side by side
with these mournful and mysterious facts there
exists another set of facts not half sufficiently considered and admired—I mean the omnipresent instinct of parent-creatures to protect, preserve, and
further the lives and development of their own
kind, and specially of their own offspring. Although
books of Natural History are full of instances of
this ubiquitous phenomenon, it has never received
adequate philosophic regard. We see it shining
everywhere, like the sun among clouds, like starlight in darkness; a visible spirit of beneficence
comprehending all, redeeming all, and revealing all.

It is the ever-active, vigilant, and practical verification of the divine declaration, "God is Love,"— and, as I said in my Presidential Address, I believe that nothing more is needed than a close study of the beautiful varieties of this parental passion to justify our highest hopes for the future of all living things, and to console us for a hundred unexplained mysteries of the Universe.

Let me, therefore, recall a few examples from various grades of animated creation of this strange and subtle altruism, which keeps the currents of life flowing in all their channels. It begins very low down; so low, that it would not be difficult to find glimpses and forecasts of it in the most humble orders of animalculæ. Nay, one may discover, even in the vegetable world, innumerable analogies to the parental propensity, shown principally by structure, or by elaborate provision for fertilisation and dissemination of seed, albeit of course destitute of intention and consciousness. But let us be content to begin with insects. Walking one day in the mountains of Japan near Atami, I observed, and touched with my stick, a small conical lump of clay on a rock. It fell to the ground, and then I saw with regret that I had broken into a nest of the ichneumon fly. Inside the tiny earthen hut built by the mother was its larva, a greyish grub; and by the side of this three or four fat spiders and another insect were stored up. The parent had stung each of these in the cephalo-thorax with a stupefying juice from

her own body, suspending life without extinguishing it, and they were laid up there to provide
the larva with food at the time of its
emergence. What forethought! what
devotion! what
sagacity! How
intense must be
the spirit of
providential af-
fection in that
wasp-like fly to
build a house
for its child, to
fill it with pro-
vender scientifi-
cally conserved,
and then to de-
part, never to
be thanked or
rewarded, never
again so much
as to see the
object of all this
solicitude!

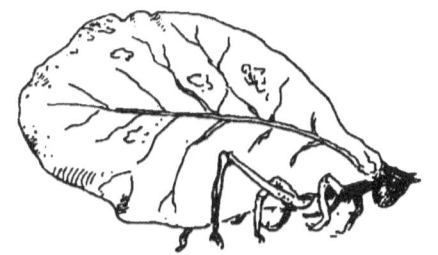

The spider is ex-
tremely attached
to the white silk
bundle contain-

LEAF BUTTERFLIES.

Protective resemblances.

ing its eggs, and will endeavour to save this when
the attempt must prove almost certainly destructive
to herself. But a chief store-house for treasure-

facts on the subject is the book upon ants, bees,
and wasps, written by my honoured and illustrious
friend Sir John Lubbock. Every English and
American boy and girl should peruse that volume,
since it shows, better perhaps than anything ever
written, how strong and imperative is the passion
to nurture and preserve, even in these insignificant
creatures. There are many things truly about ants
which astonish and instruct. It is clear that they
possess powers unknown to man. In a community
of 500,000 every ant can, and does, recognise his
fellow-citizen. They see ultra-violet colours invisible to our eyes; they have a sense of direction
beyond what we can do even with compass and
map; they keep herds of insect-cattle; capture and
train slaves; form cities with tunnels, chambers,
roads, and bridges; are aware beforehand of seasons,
and store food; carry on wars, and maintain in
perfect loyalty the monarchical system. But it is
about their signal care of the young ants that I
am here speaking; and a curious point presents
itself that this "mothering" is done by workers
who are neither male nor female. There is only
one mother to a nest of ants, however large, and
she is the queen, who marries once, and has an
indefinite number of offspring. Many ants are of
a very fierce and fearless disposition. In times of
anger they fight and bite with such ferocity, that
the Brazilian Indians take advantage of this to
suture any flesh wounds. If they have a deep
cut they take two or three black ants and make

H

them bite the lips of the gash, thus bringing them
together, after which they snip off the ant heads,
which so hold the wound united as though by stitches.
But the tenderness of these little things towards the
young of each community is amazing. The eggs
of the queen hatch within about a fortnight into
the *larva* or grub, which soon becomes the *pupa*
or chrysalis, and finally the perfect insect or "*imago.*"
It is the special duty of the young workers to look
after these in all stages; to carry them each day
where they will get warmth and moisture; to arrange
them before the queen in groups like the classes
of a school; and when they emerge, to assist them
into perfect life. But the eggs themselves need to
be nursed into *larvæ* by having the surface licked,
and the workers, old and young alike, stand for
hours round them performing this service. The
larvæ sometimes spin cocoons and so become *pupæ*,
which must also be kept carefully warmed, moist,
and clean. When they are to emerge, the workers
help them out by biting the larval cases. The
new-born ant wears, on appearance, a thin membrane over its body like a shirt, which is tenderly
pulled off, and the tiny being is then washed,
brushed, and fed. A good observer studying the
genus *Atta* writes: "The attitude of the cleansed
all this while was one of intense satisfaction, quite
resembling that of a family dog when you are
scratching the back of his neck. The insect
stretches out her limbs and, as her friend takes
them successively in hand, yields them limp and

supple to manipulation. She rolls gently over on
her side, even quite over on her back, and, with
all her limbs relaxed, presents a perfect picture of
muscular surrender and ease. The pleasure which
the tiny creatures take in being thus 'combed' and
'sponged' is really enjoyable to the observer. I
have seen an ant kneel down before another and
thrust forward its head droopingly, quite under the
other's face, and lie there motionless, thus express-
ing as plainly as sign-language could her desire to
be cleansed. I at once understood the gesture, and
so did the supplicated ant, for she immediately went
to work." The young ants are carefully educated,
led about the city, taught civil and domestic duties,
until their skins harden and they can go outside to
fight and forage. They not only recognise every
member of their own crowded communities, but
they know at sight the "*pupæ*," the children of the
city, although to our eyes these are just like those
of another. And when there is danger to the little
state, it is the children, in the form of those white
grubs, whom they all hasten to save, and for whose
sake they store up honey-dew and other food, feeding them like pigeons from mouth to mouth. This
tenderness is, as I have said, the more remarkable
because of the natural savageness of ants to strangers.
If such an ant, even belonging to the same species,
be placed among 100,000, she will be attacked and
killed, or driven out of the nest. But they remember
their friends and the city-children even after a year's
separation. Along with an intense desire to pre-

serve and nurture their young, the ants have other
striking social qualities which it is difficult to call
by any name except that of " virtue." They are
singularly kind to the blind wood-lice—*platyarthrus*
—and the small white *beckia*, which habitually live
as domestic pets in the nests. They succour each
other in distress with great assiduity, and on finding
food communicate the discovery to their fellows.
Day after day they bring their ant-babies into the
presence of the queen, as if for a royal nursery-
parade. I myself once witnessed such a display
when Sir John Lubbock drew off the glass lid from
one of his ant-cities. I noticed also on that occasion
that all the worker-ants and nurses stood facing Her
Majesty ; and Sir John told me they never if they
could help it turn their backs upon her. The very
sight of their sovereign, who is the Mother of their
city, affords an evident delight to the minute citizens.

Sir John writes: " On one occasion, while moving some ants from one nest into another for
exhibition at the Royal Institution, I unfortunately
crushed the queen and killed her. The others,
however, did not desert her, or draw her out as they
do dead workers, but, on the contrary, carried her
into the new nest, and subsequently into a larger
one with which I supplied them, congregating round
her for weeks just as if she had been alive. One
could hardly help fancying that they were mourning
her loss, or hoping anxiously for her recovery."

Day by day, as has been observed, the worker-
ants bring the *larvæ* and *pupæ* to the queen for

inspection. More than stores of honey or dried food, these represent the treasure of the community. They are the first and last care of all the citizens, under whatever circumstances. Sir John mentions an ant which he kept in a bottle for observation, and left imprisoned by inadvertence during a whole week's absence. "On my return," he says, "I took her out of the bottle, placing her on a little heap of *larvæ*, about three feet from the nest. Under these circumstances I did not expect her to attend to duty ; but though she had been six days in confinement, the brave little creature immediately picked up a larva, carried it off to the nest, and, after half-an-hour's rest, returned for another."

And yet they are so industrious after food, that Ford counted in one large nest twenty-eight dead insects brought in per minute, which gives about 100,000 accumulated in a day ; and in the Hebrew *Mischna*, rules are even laid down about the proper ownership and distribution of grain taken from ant-hills. Still, all is subordinated to that ruling passion of the care of their young. I have often noticed in India a large level disk round an ant-entrance strewn very smoothly with fine débris. This is where the little harvesters bite off the radicles of their gathered grass-seeds to keep them from sprouting inside. When the hunting-ants—the Drivers—of West Africa act in concert, nothing can resist them. Natives say the great python, before he dares to swallow his prey, searches around to see if any Driver-ants be near, lest they should kill and consume him whilst he is gorged with food. We arrogantly call many creatures "little" whose world-work is nevertheless large. Beavers created many of the lakes and marshes of Canada by their dykes and lodges. The arable land of the globe is almost wholly due to earth-worms. The city of Paris is built mainly of infusoria, and all the peninsula of Florida consists of small shells and coral crust, the remnants of sea-lice.

But these fascinating creatures, the ants and their wisdom, must not divert us from our point, which is the universally pervading parental or nursing instinct. Among the bees, also, there exists that third sex—the workers or neuters—in which the egg-laying organ is often modified into a sting, though none the less they cherish the eggs of the hive. Who taught them when the bee-egg passes from *larva* to *pupa*, and infant-bee, to feed it on brood-paste or chyle, and after three days to give the workers the special food of honey? For a week the young bee sits at home secreting wax, which the others take from its pockets as fast as produced; then it turns nurse itself, afterwards for three weeks it gathers honey, and then helps build the comb; the central energy being here, as always, to keep up the succession of life by nourishing and guarding the young.

I might cite a thousand other examples from the insect world of parental love and guardianship manifested by wasps, bees, beetles, saw-flies, &c., but I must pass upwards on the great ladder of life:

The same divine, mysterious, commanding power dominates the reptile world. In obedience to it, the turtle climbs the sea-beach by moonlight and hides her eggs in the warm sand. The snake deposits her egg-string in the heap of dead fermenting leaves or the warm dunghill. There is a toad in Surinam (Pipa) which carries, and even hatches, its eggs in hollows formed upon the soft skin of its back. Poisonous serpents are never more dangerous than when basking near a brood of their young ones ; though the Sanskrit proverb runs :

"*Hunger hears not, cares not, spares not. No boon from the starving beg,*

"*When the snake is pinched with famine, verily ! she eats her egg.*"

These, like the fishes, produce many offspring, so that the sentiment of maternity, or of personal guardianship, cannot be strong. The number of ova in the herring is 250,000 ; in the lump-fish, 155,000 ; in the halibut, 3,500,000 ; and in the female cod-fish, 9,344,000 ! Yet although the mother and father fishes will never recognise their countless hatched spawn, what vast solicitude they show to give them a good start in life ! The *Aspredo Batrachus*, somewhat after the fashion of the Surinam toad, presses her newly-deposited eggs into the soft integument of her belly, and so carries them about until mature. The *Solenostoma* has a ventral pouch, where the fish guards her young, like a marine kangaroo. The *Arius* nurses them in a hollow part of his pharynx. There is a group of

Siluroid fishes, haunting those rivers of tropical
America which flow into the Atlantic, that are
called by naturalists *Doradinæ*. These have the
curious faculty and habit of travelling during the
hot season from any piece of water about to dry
up to some other and larger pool. Those overland
journeys are sometimes of such a length that the
fish spend whole nights and days upon them, and
the Indians who chance to meet a marching column
can fill many baskets with the easy prey thus placed
in their hands. Now, these *Doradinæ* make regular and well-contrived nests for their eggs, which
they place inside the nests, and watch with much
care, male and female taking turns to guard, until
the eggs are all hatched into small fry. The nest is
constructed of leaves at the beginning of the rainy
season, and is sometimes placed in a hole scooped out
from the bank of the pool. Fish-nests are, indeed,
common enough! The bull-heads and stickle-backs
of English ponds are very clever architects in this line,
and build subaqueous bowers out of grass, water-
plants, and leaves, which they glue together with
slime from their own bodies. Within these they
play, the currents and ripples not being strong
enough to destroy their pretty work. Some nest-
bowers are shaped like tents, some like ladies' muffs,
open at each end. The male fish is alone the builder ;
and when he has finished his labour to his liking,
he finds a tiny mate, captivates her with finny
caresses, and leads her into his nest, where she
deposits her eggs. Then the male fish will fetch

another, and yet another small wife, with the same
blandishments, until enough ova have been laid to
stock his nursery; whereupon he sternly mounts
guard over the precious treasures, not allowing any
other fishes, even females, to approach the sacred
spot until the young are hatched and sufficiently
developed to take care of themselves.

The *Arius*, a species of Siluroid, already mentioned as carrying ova about in a pharyngeal pouch,
is imitated in this by the *Chromidæ*, fishes of the
Sea of Galilee. The sea-horses—hippocampi—carefully nurse their young in a sub-caudal bag, while
the parent sits upright in the brine, its tail grasping
a sea-weed. In this attitude they, and the pipe-fish
which follow the same habit, so much resemble filmy
stems and floating leaves of sea-grass, that the fishes
that feed on their offspring are deceived, and take
them for marine plants.

Next as to birds. There exists in America a cuckoo
which builds its own nest, and lays eggs quite in
proportion to its size. Our English cuckoo, on the
contrary, as everybody knows, and as Shakespeare
has mentioned, lays one small egg, and deposits it
in a nest of some other bird. When hatched out,
this interloper turns the legitimate nestlings forth,
and enjoys the undivided attention of the poor little
deceived foster-mother. The astuteness displayed
by the female cuckoo in getting her egg into places
too small to admit her is remarkable. In the island
of Colonsay, young cuckoos have been found in
holes of rock and wall, with such narrow openings

that none but very tiny birds could enter them. The eggs are first laid on the ground, and then carried by the cuckoo herself in her capacious bill and put through the narrow opening of the nest. The cuckoo, too, occasionally takes away one of the eggs from the nest in which she leaves her unusual present. Mr. Hoy, a Norfolk naturalist, writes: " I once observed a cuckoo enter a wagtail's nest, which I had noticed before to contain one egg. In a few minutes the cuckoo crept from the hole, and was flying away with something in its beak, which proved to be the egg of the wagtail, which it dropped on my firing my gun. On examining the nest I found that the cuckoo had only made an exchange, leaving its own egg for the one taken." Mr. Gray, of the British Museum, found that the old cuckoo by no means deserted their young, but stayed in the neighbourhood, and took up full care of the fledgeling when it could fly.

Why should the cuckoo alone among birds thus delegate the duties of motherhood to a bird of another species ? Various theories have been advanced to explain the phenomenon. Richard Jefferies was of opinion that the cuckoo did not rear its own young because the task of feeding three or four young cuckoos was more than any single pair of birds could accomplish. The incredible voracity of the cuckoo, he says, cannot be computed. The two robins, or pair of hedge-sparrows, in whose nest the young cuckoo is bred, work all the day through and cannot satisfy him.

The cuckoo's difficulty, or one of its difficulties, seems to be in the providing sufficient food for its ravenous young. Three of them would wear out their mother completely, especially if—as may possibly be the case—the male cuckoo will not help in feeding.

How strange, again, is the grotesque devotion of the ostrich. Several hen birds unite and lay first a few eggs in one nest and then in another, and these are hatched by the males. This instinct may probably be accounted for by the fact of the hens laying a large number of eggs, but, like the cuckoo, at intervals of two or three days.

What, again, can exceed the self-abnegation and patience of a sitting hen? Where did she learn the art of warming her eggs into chicks from her own bodily heat, except from the universal and protean spirit of parental love, which is the secret of the continuity of life. ."It is quite impossible," says the *Encyclopædia Britannica*, "that any animal can ever have kept its eggs warm with the intelligent purpose of hatching out their contents, so we can only suppose that the incubating instinct began by warm-blooded animals showing that kind of attention to their eggs which we find to be frequently manifested by lower and cold-blooded animals. Thus crabs and spiders carry their eggs about for the purpose of protecting them." But how inexhaustible the sense of duty grows with the fond bird! A hen hatched a pea-fowl's egg. Now, a pea-chicken needs eighteen months of

mother's care, and it was found that this hen
devoted herself for all that period to her task,
and never flagged in watchfulness till the peacock left her. Such is the ardour of this passion
that it will spend itself upon any objects rather
than be wasted. A hen sitting on "dummies"
was given at the end of several weeks three
newly born ferrets. She took to these almost
immediately, and remained with them for a fortnight, after which they were removed from her.
During the whole of this time she had to sit on
the nest; for, of course, the young ferrets were
not able to follow her about as young chickens
could. Two or three times a day she would fly
off her nest, calling upon her brood to follow;
but on hearing their cries of distress because of
cold, she always returned immediately and sat
with patience for six or seven hours more. She
only needed one day to learn the meaning of
these cries, and after that she would always run
in an agitated manner to any place where the
crying ferrets were concealed. Yet it could not
be possible to conceive a greater contrast than
that between the shrill piping notes of a young
chicken and the hoarse, ugly noise of a young ferret.
It is of importance to add that the hen very soon
learnt to accommodate herself to the entirely novel
mode of feeding which her young ones required;
for, although at first she showed much uneasiness
when the ferrets were taken from her to be fed,
before long she used to cluck when she saw the milk

brought, and, finally, surveyed the feeding with high satisfaction. But she never became accustomed to the ferrets' attempts at sucking, and to the last used to fly off the nest with a cackle when nipped by the young mammals in their search for the teats.

Who has not noticed with wonder and interest the pretty cunning with which the hen partridge and other birds will counterfeit injury and help-lessness to lure the invader of any sacred nursing ground from the vicinity of the nest. Albeit well aware of this habit I myself have been over and over again led away from a partridge's " clutch " by the absolutely perfect acting of the mother, who seemed to have a broken wing, until she had drawn me far enough to fly off safely, with pinions as strong as was her tender love. The Scoutie ailen, as the Richardson's skua is called in Shetland, carries the ordinary arts of deception to as great perfection as any bird. It can limp like a partridge, and drop as if shot from the sky, to lie on its side feebly flapping one wing. A writer says: " The bird is not content with such tame devices as these, but, as in Flaubert's 'Salammbo,' when Hamilcar learns that a sacrifice of first-born to Moloch has been decreed, and hides the little Hannibal in the slaves' quarters, afterwards struggling with the priests, who tear from his arms a jewelled and scented slave boy ; so, too, the Scoutie, when hard pressed, deliberately leads on to the nest of the gulls—whom it despises, and whose eggs it will suck—and at the side of

another mother's brood goes through the signs of
maternal distress in order to save her own."

The woodcock constantly carries its young from
place to place in its claws. Moor-hens will remove
not only their young, but their eggs and nest if a
sudden rise in the river or lake by which they build
threatens either. Many ground building birds (as
little allied as are sandpipers and meadow pipits)
feign lameness to draw an enemy away from the
brood ; and — most signal proof of all that this
parental pity knows no fear—birds will feed the
young that have been taken from them through
the bars of a cage—a horrible thing they will never
knowingly approach at other times.

Passing onward to mammals, the whole world
knows the fervent force of maternity and paternity
in what are too lightly called the "brutes." A
rabbit, which at other times never uses its teeth
in defence, will bite the hand extended to seize
her young. I have seen in India the mountain bear
turn in mid flight, and, bleeding from more than
one wound, fearlessly face the sportsmen to save
or avenge her cubs. I have watched the hyæna
dam playing at the mouth of a cave with her
hideous young, as proudly and fondly as any human
mother with her twins ; and bringing to them, before
she would eat anything herself, the tid-bits of the
carrion. Sometimes this maternal tenderness among
the forest creatures wears a grotesque air, as when
you observe the elephant-mothers squirting water
over their little ones, and keeping them to the

right path in the jungle with frequent banging of
the trunk. Sometimes it is overwhelmingly comic,
as when you see the baby monkey in the fields of
Guzerat clinging to its mother's furry sides, while
she goes off bounding over rocks and up the stems
of trees, nowise apparently regarding her pendant
burden. Sometimes it makes you think ferocity
lovely, if ever you have watched a tigress licking
her tigrettes bright and smooth in the cradle of
the lemon-grass ; and sometimes it has rendered
weakness majestic, as when the cows stand round
their calves in the Indian wilderness to keep the
tigress at bay.   But always, in carnivora and herbi-
vora alike, you find it ; and you find it an imperative,
dominant, moral control, extinguishing selfishness,
neutralising hunger and thirst—a sovereign passion
in every breed and genus—the passion to nourish
its young and preserve them alive.   In this familiar
and varied area of the mammalia everybody can
observe for himself the strength of the parental
principle :—can see how, over and over again, the
feeblest as well as the fiercest creatures lay down
their lives to save those of which they are the
natural guardians.

So are we brought step by step up the golden
stairway of Existence—finding this divine, commanding impulse so close an adjunct of animal
being, at all its stages, lowest and highest alike,
that, possibly to make its mystery less incompre-
hensible, people have called it "instinct."   In
humanity, of course, it is crowned with reason,

and hallowed by religion—attaining utmost perfection as a propensity refined into a virtue and a
Christian grace. All grades, however, of the
maternal passion are visible in the history of man,
from that of the savage mother who dies, like a
she-wolf, of thirst, suckling her dusky babe, to the
Princess Alice ; from the Madonna's love, celestially
rendered by the pencil of Raphael, to the child's
motherly little cry, who will not go to sleep
without her doll. The forethought and provision
of the insect ; the family habits of the fish and
reptiles ; the domestic solicitudes of the birds ;
the household pride and passions of the beasts—all
these find representations in the parental feelings
of the human species, where especially is seen that
proud humility of the mother towards her child
which makes maternity a religion. I have nowhere
met with it more exquisitely or lovingly expressed
that in these lines of an old English poem : [1]

> " Upon my lap my sovereign sits,
>   And sucks upon my breast ;
> Meantime his love maintains my life,
>   And gives my sense its rest.
>   Sing lullaby, my little boy ;
>   Sing lullaby, my only joy !
>
> When thou hast taken thy repast
>   Repose, my Babe, on me ;
> So may thy mother and thy nurse
>   Thy cradle also be.
>   Sing lullaby, etc. etc.

---

[1] From Martin Peerson's " Private Music," A.D. 1620.

I grieve that duty doth not work
 All which my wishing would,
Because I would not do to thee
 But in the best I should.
  Sing lullaby, etc. etc.

Yet, as I am, and as I may,
 I must and will be thine,
Though all too little for thyself
 Vouchsafing to be mine.
  Sing lullaby, my little boy ;
  Sing lullaby, my only joy !

In reading such verses one touches the highest
eminence of that spirit into which the simply
initiatory phenomena of reproduction have developed, and one understands the full meaning of
that ancient Hebrew fancy, which made every bride
of Israel secretly cherish the hope that she might
possibly become mother of the Messiah. That
illustrious American, my late most honoured friend,
Emerson, wrote—with just such self-consecrated and
Madonna-like mother-love in his mind, "We are all
born princes!" born provided, he meant, with all this
gentleness and devotion ready to receive our natal
weakness.

What, then, is the origin, and what the purpose
of this parental impulse—which the Greeks called
storgë—running as it does through the whole animate
world? This is the problem which I desire to set
on foot, and about which I have myself certain new
and daring ideas which cannot be developed without
much greater space, and far deeper investigations

I

than the present opportunity permits to my pen.
The question is not in any sense answered by styling
such an altruistic passion "instinct," which, rising
by development to a virtue, is providentially intended
to provide for the preservation of all the forms of
life that would otherwise be extinguished by mutual
destruction and natural decay. Such is really a
Vedic view; it is the Hindu conception of Shiva the
Destroyer, and Vishnu the Conserver as two forms
of one Deity. Instincts oftentimes go wrong. Flies
frequently lay eggs in the flowers of the *stapelia
hirsuta*, and other ill-smelling blossoms, taking them
to be meat in a state of putrefaction; but though
their young perish, the parental intention and knowledge are there. Instinct acts automatically, yet the
calculated thought of ants in peril is first to save the
children of the colony. Some, indeed, in the long
list of creation appear indifferent: the English
" meadowbrown " butterfly drops its eggs at absolute
random in the grass, and knows no more about
them. But in many the passion is strong, though
they will never behold its fruit. My son—Mr. Lester
Arnold, an accomplished naturalist, and author of the
well-known work " Phra, the Phœnician "—tells me
that certain summer wasps never see their offspring;
indeed, none of a certain kind can have done so for
ages, since the young are hatched long after the
previous generation has passed away. And, nevertheless, the females of these wasps, to whom the
form and fashion of their children must be absolutely
unknown, spend their lives in making admirable

arrangements for the future broods! This is, to my
own mind, no more to be put down scornfully as
"mere instinct," than the conduct of the human
mother who, in her last mortal illness, teaches her
little girl to read and sew, or of the human father
who insures his life for his family, sacrificing his own
present advantage for their future profit. We find
the feeling purest and most self-denying in the most
enlightened men and women; but if we could know
the lives of those deep-sea fishes which swim in the
dark abysses of ocean lighted only by the electric
lanterns of their own bodies, we should witness
germs at least of the same spirit of self-sacrifice,
initiatory signs of interest in a generation which
will not be theirs to see. Mr. T. E. Fuller in the
Westminster Review lately published the following admirable words:—

"If the old doctrine of a moral sense as a
distinct propension should prove untenable, where
shall we find "good" in the "Kosmos" as we
find sunlight on the hills or colour in the rain-
bow? Surely, if anywhere, in the love of offspring
—of mother and child—which is a vital force in
the whole animal kingdom, and as real a fact of
Nature as birth or death.

"It has its vagaries, as all natural emotions
have. Like the polar force, it has its local and
deflecting attractions disturbing, if not destroying,
the main current; but it is as strong as the richest
æsthetic emotion, and has far-reaching issues wherever life is. It broadens into love of family and

race, and is at the root of the disciplined patriotism
by which nations are made great; and why not of
all the altruistic instincts?

"It involves protection to weakness, service to the
feeble and the suffering, and a passionate unselfish-
ness which no self-interested action can utterly
destroy. In fact, each new life born into the world
in the entire animal kingdom is nurtured by a sacri-
ficial love.

"From the history of that love we might frame
a moral code as orderly and beautiful as the laws
which interpret the motion of sun and stars!

"It is not a mere product of civilisation, but, like
all other natural instincts, it has developed and
become more complex as it has built itself into the
generations."

I agree with these eloquent paragraphs, but am
inclined to launch my thought far beyond them
upon this great and neglected subject; and I invite
the thinkers upon Natural History to meditate its
marvellous and profound physical and metaphysical
ranges. All other "instincts" have the benefit of the
agent for one of their issues. Why not this also?
Who knows but that, from the devoted female spider
to the American woman now nursing at her breast
the future President of the United States, every
mother insect, fish, bird, or mammal has indeed some
far-off real personal interest in lives beyond her life?
How notable that as the standard of existence
rises offspring grow fewer, but the sentiment more
intense and prolonged! How strange that the law

of mutual slaughter in creation should be balanced
by so universal and compassionate a law of parental
conservation out of which grows the family, the
tribe, patriotism, and, lastly, philanthropy! Behind
this commanding and preserving passion—in itself
the essence of faith, and by its nature the enemy
of selfishness—shines, to my eyes, visibly and
brilliantly, that which has been called "The Love
of God." The more I muse on it, the more I
myself am convinced that doctrines deeper than
Darwinism, and possibly the grandest assurances
of immortality, and the strongest demonstrations
of the identity and continuity of all Life, hide
behind this Mystery of Maternity and this Majesty
of Paternity.

VII

A REAL THIRST

VII

A REAL THIRST

It is remarkable how few of us have ever been really thirsty throughout life. I am not speaking of the very ordinary feeling which arises after hearty exercise, or a long walk, or a vigorous game of cricket or football, which people call being thirsty, and which makes a draught of whatever proper beverage is taken so agreeable as well as so necessary. Everybody at such times has realised the justice of that sententious phrase of Sir Andrew Aguecheek, "'Twere as good a deed as to drink when one's dry;" and, indeed, under favourable circumstances, the appetite for refreshment on such occasions may rise to the sublime heights of what the Chicago men call a "ten-dollar thirst." But all this lies within the ordinary experience of existence, and gives little or no idea of what are the pangs of a true drought when the body has gone without liquid of any sort or kind for an extended period under hot skies or along with strong exertion. The sensation on these occasions passes completely beyond the pleasurable connection between the need and the satisfaction. The want of something to moisten the parched throat and fill the dried and burning veins tran-

scends all limit of wish or desire, and becomes an
agony probably far keener than any arising from
hunger. It happened once, and once only, to myself to experience the beginning of this real anguish
of thirst, and the mere fact of it has stamped for
ever on my memory a long night ride in India, a
lost road, and the ineffable relief of the hospitable
cup which put an end to my distress.

India is nowadays so intersected with railways,
that you may go almost anywhere by what the
natives call the "fire-carriage." But in 1860 this
was not at all the case. Railway-lines then were
few and far between, and when one had a considerable distance to traverse, it was usually accomplished by what we called "laying a dâk." This
might be either a carriage dâk or horse dâk, the
carriage being usually a rattle-trap vehicle known
sarcastically as a "shigram," because that word
means "swift." If you intended to do the journey
in the saddle, you sent word a week before to the
Parsee mail contractor in the Bazaar, with orders to
place horses all along the road by which you were to
pass, at intervals of six koss, that is to say, twelve
miles. These animals would be nothing much in the
way of breed or good looks, and full of every kind
of vice ; but they could do their twelve miles, with a
break or two, at an easy canter, and it was astonishing how quickly one might get along, wasting no
more time at the stages than was necessary to shift
the saddle and bridle. I had to ride from Poona up
to the hill-sanitarium of Mahabuleshwar—a distance,

if I rightly remember, considerably over 100 miles by the Sattara route; and very pleasant the beginning of my ride was. Lightly equipped, and carrying nothing in the way of provisions except a bottle of soda-water, I rode upon my own little Arab horse through the Potters' quarter of the Deccan capital, where the incessant beating of hammers upon brass and copper filled all the air; and so out into the fair country under the famous hill of Parvati. My Indian horse-boy was to meet me at the first stage to take "Mr. Brown" back to his stable. After hard work at the College it was good to be out upon the open plain in the soft afternoon air. The Indian rural districts are always picturesque and interesting, interspersed as they are with villages, and full of animal life. In almost every bush the jungle dove, with its jewelled neck, cooed; the white egrets stalked about in every pool; the bee-eater, bright green and bronze, chased the butter-flies; the "seven brown sisters," little birds that always keep together in bands of seven or nine, chattered in the thicket; green paroquets flashed past in screaming coveys, and the kites and vultures circled in the air. There was a spot I knew, near a temple, where, under a great stone, a cobra had his residence; he was lying out basking in the sun as we passed. Nobody thereabouts would have dreamed of injuring the old grey snake, which I had often seen before, and passed by that afternoon as usual, not interfering with his harmless solitude.

At the end of the first stage a wall-eyed, flat-sided

Deccan pony was waiting, and, the saddle and bridle
being shifted, we started for stage number two at
a gallop. No whip or spur would elicit from such
cattle any satisfactory pace, but that they know their
fodder and shelter would be at the end of the twelve
miles, and they go vivaciously to get them over.
Night was settling down upon the plain as the foot-
hills of the Ghauts came into sight—that lovely
Indian night which is so soothing after the burning
Eastern day; and near the villages you heard the
yell of the jackals, and saw some of them stealing
like shadows across the fields. All through the
night I rode in the same manner, always finding at
each station the Mahratta postboy standing in the
road with the new "mount," which kicked and bit
during the process of saddling, and sometimes tried
hard to get a piece out of the leg of his rider while
mounting. Once off, however, we went along
mechanically, but at midnight the road became
steeper, winding among the hills, and, there being
no moon, nothing better than a foot-pace could be
achieved. I had not sufficiently calculated for this,
and was not nearly so far advanced on my journey
at the break of day as I had hoped to be. The slow
pace and the long ride had made me sleepy, and
twice or thrice in the brief interval of changing
horses I fell into slumber on the ground, and had to
be awakened by the *ghorawallahs* to get into the
saddle. But the coming of dawn over the Indian
landscape woke me up thoroughly again. I have
always thought sunrise the most beautiful spectacle

in Nature; and in India particularly, the daybreak effects are miracles of loveliness. First there comes into the sky what the Easterns call the "wolf-tail" —a long grey brush of something which is neither light nor darkness, sweeping across the east, well above the horizon. Then there passes over the sleeping world the *Dam-i-subh*, the "breath of the morning," which arises quite suddenly and sweeps over the grass and among the leaves, for all the world like the sigh of the great earth turning and waking. And then the sky-horizon, which has changed from grey to pale blue, catches sudden fire; the lower rims of the light clouds are touched with rose-colour and gold, and the sun leaps up, flooding the face of Nature with life and glory. There never was any answer more apposite than a Parsee lady once made to the Bishop of London, when the right reverend prelate was asking her in a tone of horror whether it could possibly be true that her people in India worshipped the sun. "Yes, indeed, my lord," she said, "and so would your lordship, too, if you had ever seen him."

By this time, fairly hungry and thirsty, I could see in the distance the gleam of the river Krishna, and the pinnacles of the temples in the town of Waee. Here, no doubt, I should get milk, eggs, at the worst, water to drink, for the night's riding had made me thirsty. It was perhaps nine o'clock when I rode down to the river and into the main street of this very sacred place. But alas! it was a season when cholera had been very prevalent, and the disease was positively raging in this holy but extremely dirty town. The Hindoos as a race live happily and die placidly, but the spectacle presented by that plague-stricken centre was none the less very painful. All along the river banks, hastily erected funeral pyres were flaming and smoking. At many a door bamboos were being lashed together

HINDOO FUNERAL.

to bear the newly dead to the burning. In the temples priests were praying, and citizens and peasants bringing their small pathetic offerings of propitiation. I was asked by a dozen voices if I was a *hakim*, a *vaidya*, a doctor; but I had neither skill nor medicines, and rode sorrowfully through this scene of death and suffering across the river-ford to the travellers' bungalow on the slope of the opposite hill. Here, in dismounting, my Deccan pony jibbed and drove me against a post, which, unluckily, broke the bottle of soda-water which I had thus far carried. The attendant at the bungalow had died of cholera. Nobody was in his place. There was nothing to be got, and nobody to get it. I did not dare to touch water from the river, every ripple of which must have been full of cholera-germ, and there was nothing, therefore, for it but to lie down on the cane charpoy and try to sleep away the hot hours of the day, with the hope in the early afternoon of riding quickly up the hills and into the station, where friends and comforts were awaiting me. It is a curious fact that, as I lay half asleep that day in Waee, hearing at intervals the funeral cry of the poor townsfolk, "Ram bholo, bhao, Ram!" (Call upon Rama, oh, my brothers!), what with the great heat of the day and the dampness of my clothing from a light rain, the figures of my watch-dial as I lay upon my face were melted off and nearly obliterated. It may be judged by this that the season was warm as well as sickly. I remember how the sight of the river, sparkling under the steps and porticoes of the marble temples, made me long to go down among the dead and dying, and plunge into it. But I was not yet quite thirsty enough for this rashness, and, at starting again, set my fresh steed at the quickest pace he could command along the slope of the hills leading to the station. I quite expected, in the uplands and glens in front of me, to come across some stream or pool, the water of which would be

safe to drink ; for it was now getting on for twenty-
four hours since I had taken any liquid whatever,
and I was beginning to feel that second phase of
thirst, when to drink is no longer a desire but a
passion and a pain.   The horse I was riding was the
last of the *dâk*, and the best, his duty being to carry
me the eighteen or twenty miles remaining.   Although already suffering, I thought little of this
distance, since, being in good health, nothing was
yet the matter with me except a parched throat ;
but in the confidence that I should soon be safe at
the station, I asked a Mahratta peasant whom I met
if he knew where there was any water or milk, and
when he answered in the negative, I inquired which
of the two turnings before me in the forest-road led
to Mahabuleshwar.   That question, too carelessly
put, cost me dear.   Mahabuleshwar, which means
" the place of the great Lord of Strength," is really
the name merely of a temple and of a sacred peak deep
in the hills.   The station, although known generally
by that appellation, is locally called Malcolm-Peth,
and it was this for which I ought to have inquired.
The peasant, ignorant of my plight, and thinking I
wanted to visit the shrine, pointed me along the
steep way to the right, which I rashly followed for
more than two hours and a half, until the sun was
near setting, and then the utter absence of any signs
of a large station told me too plainly that I had lost
my way, and was deep in the wilds of the Ghauts,
thirty hours by this time without any liquid, and perhaps eighteen or twenty miles away from my home.

Twilight is brief in India, and before long the road became invisible. My horse was tired, and proceeding now at only a foot pace. The night-cries began to rise from the jungle, and I heard much too plainly for my comfort upon the left the sharp quick cough that a tiger gives when he is calling to his mate. I had, of course, no weapon with me, but my chief thought was for water, and I listened intently amid the forest noises for any sound of a running or falling rivulet, towards which I would have gone at any hazard. But until the rains come in earnest these Western Ghauts are very dry, and there was no such welcome sign. On the side of the path, however, I could just make out a native hut, to the entrance of which I guided my horse. I pushed open the door, which was unfastened, and, the interior being quite dark, I struck a light. In the gleam of the lucifer-match I saw something very unpleasant—the naked body of a man lying upon a charpoy, evidently dead. I am not very nervous about such things; but with cholera in the district, and every token that this poor fellow had been suddenly overtaken by it, it was better to be in the open air, though I was by this time so bitterly thirsty that I looked into the chatties by the wall of his hut to see if there was anything to drink. Luckily, perhaps, for me they were empty. The water-pot, its contents spilt, lay upon its side by the bed; and I was glad to get into the forest again. But by this time, though the night fell cool, I was really beginning to feel the true pangs of a mortal

K

drought. Had there been a moon, I might, perhaps, have searched for some jungle fruit; but all was gloom. You could just descry the opening in the trees where the road passed, but it seemed out of the question to retrace my steps. When thirst reaches this point you begin to get fever and sharp headache. The lips are dry and crack, and the back of your throat becomes like blistered parchment. I really at that juncture had a wild idea of opening a vein in my horse's neck and sucking it. But he had been a good little beast, and a better inspiration took me. I caressed him, pulled a handful of grass and gave it him to eat, and then, mounting again, laid the bridle on his neck and let him take his own way. He turned round and went down the path by which we had come, now and then quickening his pace. In this way we perhaps traversed five or six miles, till I was beginning to feel too sick to keep the saddle. Just at that moment, in an open place where a little light entered, my horse stopped and pricked up his ears. For a time I could not guess the reason, but presently I heard, in a hollow below our road, the noise of something rustling through the thicket, and suddenly there emerged into the path a couple of hill-men with their axes and sticks. If they had been angels from Heaven I should have been less glad to meet them. I had not much voice left, but soon managed to explain my situation, and, well assured of a reward, they undertook to guide me to Malcolm-Peth, which by a short cut was not very distant. The faithful fellows

plunged into the jungle with me—one leading the
horse, the other with his arm round me, supporting
me in the saddle. Renewed confidence is in itself,
meanwhile, a cordial, and I began to allow myself to
think of drinking, which before had been a fancy
that only increased the fever and the headache.
Presently one cried, " Dekho, dekho—Sahib ! butti
hai." (Look, sir, look ! There is a lamp !) And
through the dark leaves I did really see a light
gleaming. I rode straight up to it. It was a
moderator lamp, placed upon a table in the veranda
of a bungalow, and two officers were sitting at the
table with glasses and beer-bottles before them. I
should be ashamed to say what the sight of that
beer was to me at that moment. I did not speak to
them nor salute them, but sliding from my saddle
pointed to my mouth and throat, and to the unopened
bottle. One of the good fellows, grasping the situation, drew the cork and poured out a foaming glass
of that to me then absolutely divine beverage. I
hope he forgave me for clutching the glass from
him before he had half filled it, and though to this
day I do not know his name, he lives in memory
as one of my dearest and truest friends. Do not
ask me to describe the passage of that reviving
draught into my grateful frame. Every drop seemed
a veritable elixir of life, and the odd thing was that
I was not so far gone but that the drink brought
me round as if by magic. I almost think it
must have hissed in my throat as it went down,
but I blessed the name of Bass as I shook hands

with my unknown benefactors and turned into the
well-lighted lane, where I soon found my quarters
and the pleasant welcome of anxious friends.   Once
in a lifetime to be as thirsty as that is quite enough
for anybody !

VIII

THE INDIAN UPANISHADS

VIII

THE INDIAN UPANISHADS

MEGASTHENES, ambassador of Seleucus Nicator, relates in his 45th Fragment, how that King Alexander heard of the Sage Dandamis, dwelling in the forest; and, being desirous of seeing him, how the king sent Onesicrates with this message: "Hail, thou teacher of the Bragmanes! The son of the mighty god Zeus, Alexander, sovereign lord of all men, bids you repair to him. If you comply, he will reward you with splendid gifts; if you refuse, he will cut off your head."

Dandamis, without raising his eyes from the ground, made a placid reply to the Greek envoy, in these words: "The Supreme God is nowise author of insolent wrong, but the creator of peace, of light, of life, of water, of the bodies of men and of their souls, which He receives at death. He abhors slaughter, and instigates no wars. Alexander cannot be a god, since he must die, nor master of the world, since he has not yet reached even the Ganges, where there are nations which have never heard his name. The gifts he offers me are useless; what things I prize are all here at hand—the leaves which make me a green and pleasant house, the blossoming plants which gives delicious food, and the fair water which I drink. Any other possessions appear vain to me, nor will I go to Alexander for his gold and jewels. If he shall cut off my head, he cannot touch my true life. My body will lie where it belongs, upon the earth ; my soul will go its way. Let your king seek to terrify with death those who dread it. A Brahman has no fear of that which ends life only that it may begin again."

This passage is full of deep and ancient interest. When the Hero of Macedon crossed the Indus, and overcame the kings and peoples of the Panjab, he did indeed find there certain sages invincible by his arms, and utterly indifferent to his glory. Summoned to his presence they did, in such a manner, bid the conqueror of the world rather repair to them if he wished to indulge in holy converse. In more than one case Alexander complied, and held respectful interviews with these Hindu Rishis, whom he discovered sitting under their jungle-trees, scantily clad, eating fruits and roots, but nevertheless immensely influential among the population by reason of their virtues and austerities, and absolutely free alike from the passions of life and from the fear of death ; the greatest and profoundest metaphysicians, perhaps, that humanity has ever produced.

In speaking of their philosophies I would not wish that the word "jungle," used above, should mislead any of my readers. The Indian wilderness,

rugged and desolate in many regions, is yet also
full of lovely and salubrious retreats, where solitude
is rendered charming by graceful combinations of
wood, water, and flowery thickets. I myself, when

GRÆCO-BUDDHIST SCULPTURE ON SANSHI TOPE.

shooting or riding in India, have often come upon
spots where art could add nothing to the natural
beauty of the place—the scented grass was so level,
the foliage so various and finely grouped, the air so
delicate and caressing, the views all around so calm

and fair. Acacias and neem-trees, with their blossoms
of gold and lilac, shaded the warm ground ; fantastic
and richly coloured parasites swung from the trunks
of the great sals and peepals ; butterflies like winged
jewellery flitted among the large dark leaves of the
teak and tamarind, chased in their flight by the
green and bronze bee-eaters. Gaily painted paroquets and gorgeously plumaged pea-fowl darted
through the foliage, or played in the open spaces ;
while the voices of a hundred forms of smaller woodland life forbade the loneliness of the scene to appear
oppressive. The cloudless vault overhead was
speckled with the ever-circling " Kites of Govinda,"
and echoed with their shrill cry ; while the black and
white kingfisher, the fish-hawk, and the silvery egret
haunted each pool and stream. The days are of
gold, and the nights are of ivory, in these natural
temples of the Asiatic waste, where the "gymnoso-
phists" of Alexander and Arrian—the *Maharishis*
and *Mahatmas* of Indian philosophy—meditated, to
depths of abstraction profounder perhaps than Plato
or Descartes, than Kant or Hegel, have ever reached,
upon those problems which cannot be solved by
mortal man while he lives here below, but which he
must nevertheless strive constantly to solve, if he
would give due growth and training to his soul.

These equable and passionless sages, musing so
tranquilly in the sylvan solitudes of northern India,
entertained disciples who, after long periods of
patient devotion, were eventually permitted more or
less to profit by the garnered wisdom of their Guru.

Twelve years, however, or even sometimes a longer period, must elapse, before the youthful learner would venture on so much as the indiscretion of a question. Had not the Gods themselves sate patiently round Indra for ten thousand years, before asking him as to the Great Mystery; and had they not received at length for their only answer the mystic word "OM"? At the close of his novitiate, the young Acharya was perhaps rewarded with some approximate knowledge of the text and significance of the Aranyakas—"the Upanishads of the Wood"—those subtle and mystic treatises in which the Recluses of the Vedanta had enshrined some of the speculations of their intensely concentrated minds.

The word "Upanishads" is perhaps best translated "Sessions." The idea involved in the name is certainly that of scholars listening—"seated"—at the feet of teachers. It came, however, also to imply secret or occult doctrines. Though these old Sanskrit treatises sprang from the ancient Veds, they were framed to lead the mind and heart of a philosophic student on another and higher road than that indicated by primitive hymns and Mantras. For kings and warriors, for the town and village people generally, it was still considered good enough to worship personified forces of Nature, and to perform traditional rites and moral duties. That was the *Karma Kanda*, the very excellent law of action; but the *Jnana Kanda*, or Way of Knowledge—the *Vidya para*, or perfect wisdom—stood infinitely superior; and this mysterious wisdom was taught by

hints and aphorisms in the Upanishads. They are
thus the basis of the esoteric and most occult ideas
of India, as well as the constantly active influence
controlling her external life—furnishing a guide to
her inmost feelings and beliefs, and supplying the
keys to her real mind and heart. The Upanishads
are very numerous—149 have been catalogued,—
and none but a life-long votary can possibly know
them all; yet some ten or a dozen—such as the
Chandogya, Brihadaranyaka, Isa, Kena, Katha,
Prasna, Mundaka, Mandukya, and Swetasvatara—
are especially renowned and canonical, being as
such universally studied by Hindu theologians, and
universally revered. These brief treatises are in
form partly poetical, partly condensed into abrupt,
disjointed prose-passages, where a small vein of
precious doctrine is shut into a massive rock of
rugged exposition. Sometimes, indeed, the terse
incoherence and purposed obscurity of the Sanskrit
defies comprehension, like Merlin's Book, of which
Lord Tennyson sings, that

> "One or two at most may read the text,
> But none can read the comment."

The leading ideas, however, developed in the
silence of those Indian forests from the antique
root of the Vedas, thus growing to leaf and blossom
in the inner sunshine of thought, are plain enough.
They were first enshrined in the Aranyakas, and
then fixed and finished in the greater Upanishads.
The solitude of the jungle produced three vast con-

ceptions or conclusions which have governed Hindu
life, as the elementary powers govern and qualify our
common human existence. Meditating perpetually
in that soft Asiatic quietude, and amid its countless
forms of life, these silent and unscientific observers
had reached—two thousand five hundred years
before our English Poet gave it eloquent expression—

> "A sense sublime
> Of something far more deeply interfused,
> Whose dwelling is the light of setting suns,
> And the round ocean, and the living air,
> And the blue sky, and in the mind of Man;
> A motion and a spirit which impels
> All thinking things, all objects of all thought;
> And is through all things."

Sublime and supreme pantheists, they rejected
plurality of existence as an appearance only, de-
nominating it *Maya*—"Illusion"—a phenomenal
duality of subject and object which are really in an
actual but disguised unity. They affirmed that the
only true existence was that of the *Atman*—the
Self—the All-pervading Soul—the "Para-Brahm"
who is *Sat-Chit-Ananda*, which means "All-present
Being, Thought and Joy." While all forms come,
and pass, and go, that ("*Tad*") alone endures, per-
meating all things. Thus my "Secret of Death"
has :

> "To reach to Being
> Beyond all seeming Being; to know true life,
> This is not gained by many; seeing that few
> So much as hear of it, and of those few
> The more part understand not. Brahma's Truth

Is wonderful to tell, splendid to see,
Delightful, being perceived; when the Wise teach."
"(Teach me a little, here, what Brahma is !)"

PUNDIT.

"I tell thee from the Swetaswatara!
HE WHO. Alone, Undifferenced, unites
With NATURE, making endless difference,
Producing, and receiving all which seems,
Is Brahma! May he give us light to know !"
    "He is the Unseen Spirit which informs
All subtle essences! He flames in fire,
He shines in Sun and Moon, Planets and Stars !
He bloweth with the winds, rolls with the waves,
He is Prajâpati, that fills the worlds !"
    "He is the Man and Woman, Youth and Maid !
The babe new-born, the withered ancient, propped
Upon his staff! HE is whatever is—
The black bee, and the tiger, and.the fish,
The green bird with red eyes, the tree, the grass,
The cloud that hath the lightning in its womb,
The seasons, and the seas ! By HIM they are,
In HIM begin and end."

All things live upon portions of the Central Life
and Joy. Here I invite my readers not too easily to
believe in what writers of great learning but limited
insight have said about the pessimism of Hindu
theology. "Who could breathe, who could exist,"
exclaims the Kena Upanishad, "if there were not
the bliss of Brahm within the ether of his heart?"
Inconceivable to the mind this all-comprehensive
Being is still a necessity of true thought, and
veritable beyond every other conception of reality.
"It is thought by him who thinks it not; he that
thinks it grasps it not; it is unknown to those who

fancy that they know, and known to those who
know they know it not." The highest Gods of the
Vedas are themselves temporary and insignificant
manifestations of this all-comprehending Deity ; the
meanest creature, the very blade of kusha grass,
immortally exists by his immanence, as surely as
Indra or Siva.

The next great generalisation of our Wood
Philosophers was the doctrine of transmigration.
The principle of Reality had been from everlasting
linked with a reflection, an embodiment, in the
Unreality or Maya. Portions of the Self—though
partition of it is inexplicable—become incarnated in
fleeting forms, and this divided essence goes off,
wrapped in several intermediate robes, of which the
visible body is the outermost and grossest. There
is, first, the now visible Frame ; secondly, the vesture
of vital airs ; thirdly, the sensorial Body ; fourthly, the
mental or cognitial Body ; and fifthly, the Beatific
Investiture. The Self, thus exiled, forgets its nature
and identifies itself with its *upadhi*—its outer and
lower disguise. Hence the march of all animated
life, and its countless metamorphoses. Maya, the
apparent life, is not, be it understood, non-existent,
but rather fallacious, non-comprehended, and mis-
guiding. "Things are not what they seem." All
the stir of daily life, all the pleasures and pains of
each existence following after existence, are the
imagery of a dream—shadows of the true and
eternal—from which we shall wake when due experience is complete, and from which we may awake

by the touch of Knowledge, whenever we please.
In dreamless sleep we sink back into the *Anan-
damaya Kosha*, the beatific garb of the migrating
soul. For all souls migrate, under a law of inherent
equation, implicitly governing the Universe towards
and for virtue, use and beauty; so that weal and
woe follow implicitly upon good and evil; and
"beauty is the splendour of fitness." There are
traces only of the doctrines of transmigration in
the Vedas; but in the Upanishads it becomes
prominent. Thus in the Chandogya we read—"He
whose life has been good will quickly obtain a new
embodiment as a Brahman, a Kshatriya, or a Vaisya.
Those whose lives have been evil will quickly pass
into an evil embodiment, as a dog, as a hog, or as a
Chandâla." How did this tenet arise? We find it
everywhere among even primitive peoples. The
totem-worship of Red Indians seems founded on it.
The Tuscalans of Mexico held that the spirits of
their chiefs migrated at death into beautiful singing
birds, and those of bad people into beetles, weasels,
and rats. Zulus, Dyaks, and Indian Sonthals have
ever cherished similar beliefs, which, moreover,
governed the whole social life and customs of the
Egyptians, and finds so memorable an expression in
the PHAEDON of Plato. Let us recall a portion of
that passage.

   "Are we to suppose, says Socrates, that the soul,
an invisible thing, is going to a place like itself,
invisible, pure, and noble, the true Hades, into the
presence of the good and wise God, whither, if God

will, my soul is also soon to go——or that the soul, I say, if this be her nature and origin, is blown away and perishes immediately on quitting the body, as the many say? It is far otherwise, my dear Simmias and Cebes. The truth is much more this, that if the soul is pure at its departure, it drags after it nothing bodily, in that it has never of its own will had connection with the body in its life, but has always shunned it, and gathered itself unto itself; for this avoidance of the body has been its constant practice. And this is nothing else than that it philosophises truly, and practises how to die with ease. And is not philosophy the practice of death?"

" Certainly."

"That soul, I say, itself invisible, departs to a world invisible like itself—to the divine and immortal, and rational. Arriving there, its lot is to be happy; released from human error and unwisdom, from fears, and wild passions, and all other human ills, and it dwells for all future time, as they say of the initiated, in the society of the Gods. Shall we say this, Cebes, or say otherwise?"

"It is so," said Cebes, "beyond a doubt."

If, then, the ancient Rishis of the Indian forest evolved so great an idea for themselves, we can imagine some of the reasons which suggested it. They would note amid the living creatures round them the marvels of what we call instinct, which looks like a pre-natal memory—the jungle-chicken pecking its food, distinguishing wholesome from unfit seeds, on the very day of its emergence from the

L

egg; the new-born cobra striking with an untaught
poison-fang; the butterfly just sprung from the
chrysalis, unaware of its natural enemies, but sport-
ing in the honey-cups of the flowers with immediate
intelligence. If we will see it, we have in this
doctrine of transmigration an anticipatory Asiatic
Darwinism, connoting evolution. The descent of
man implies the ascent of man. Whence did these
living things so suddenly learn how to live except
by experience garnered and gathered from previous
lives? In the inequalities of fortune, moreover; in
the imperfection of all careers, in the unpunished
injustices, the unrewarded merits, the unfinished
though unextinguished efforts, the unsatisfied aspirations of the human careers around them, these old
sages would perceive arguments for transmigration.
They would be fortified by such facts as that,
although we have all lived as babes, we all forget
our first year of infancy; but that the memory once
established, carries on during our present lives the
consciousness of an immutable "ego" through all
the physical alterations of the frame.

Yet, there would be no escape except in prodigious
ages of slow time for this progress of the exiled
"Atman" through forms; and, accordingly, the third
great and dominant conception of the Wood Philosophers was that it is good to withdraw from this
constant whirl of successive lives, and that deliverance is possible by insight, by illumination, by
reunion with the Real and Self-Existing. It was
intolerable to them to think that the never-ceasing

circle of existence must for ever turn—with its
painful pleasures and recurring pains. The splendid
elevation of their conception of God demanded as
exalted a destiny for Man, and to true insight this
recurring round of lives and passions was not worthy.
That alone is real which neither comes nor goes ;
neither begins nor ceases. And such was surely the
Self—the Atman detached from the Para-Atman,
which (as that to Maya) fictitiously limits itself to
this or that individual form, and passes through
spheres of transmigratory experience, like a sleeper
through dream after dream. It is necessary to
awake from dreaming, to escape from transmigration,
to draw back the wandering personality into the one
and only Self, as the air in a sealed jar is reunited
with the circumambient air when the jar is broken.
To the soul awakened the dream-lives become
nullities ; the higher light is veiled no more ; the
only Being that is, or ever has truly been, becomes
recognised. And even while still living in the body,
the once illuminated spirit may grow superior to
sense, and rise to become untouched by merits or
demerits. How the separated soul may thus recover
union with the universal soul is taught in the
Chahandogya Upanishad by Sandilya, who says—
"The soul is made of thought ; as its thought has
been in this life, so shall its nature be when it
departs : let, therefore, the wise man think this !
The universal soul is within my heart, smaller than
the growing spot in a grain of millet ; this is my
soul within my heart, greater than the earth, the air,

and the sky—greater than all the worlds. My soul
within the heart is Brahman, and as soon as I
depart out of this life I shall win reunion with the
Self." Again, the Brihadaranyaka Upanishad says—
" Invisible is the path—far-going, trodden from of
old—which I have discovered : the sages who know
the Atman travel along that path to Heaven. If a
man know himself to be also in this universal spirit,
what more can he need ? Being here, we know this;
and if we did not know it, it would be a great grief.
They that know the real breathing of the breath, the
real seeing of the eye, the real hearing of the ear,
the real thinking of the thought, they truly have
seen the Self. He goes from death to death who
looks on the soul as manifold. It is to be seen in
one way only."

    To explain fully that lofty way—the method of
" Moksha " or Release—would pass beyond the
limits of this article. It is, however, fairly described
as the Brahmanic antecedent of the Buddhistic
Nirvana. Its best exposition will perhaps be
found in the Bhagavad-Gita as translated in my
"Song Celestial." It is moral, let me specially add
—and not merely metaphysical. Moksha is libera-
tion from sin as well as from ignorance. The
Chahandogya Upanishad sings : " I shake off my
sin, as a horse shakes the dust from his mane ;
relinquishing my body, and finishing my duties, I
am at last born indeed." The Katha Upanishad
says : " He that hath not ceased from wickedness,
and is uncontrolled, shall not find HIM—Brahman

—by keenness of understanding." The attainment of Moksha depends first on the performance of good works without the desire of rewards. Krishna says to Arjuna exactly what Socrates declared before the judges: *"Na hi kalyanakrit kaschit durgatin tata gachchati"* (No evil can befall any one that does what is good) :—ἄνδρι γὰρ ἀγαθῷ οὐδὲν κάκον γίγνεται. Moksha is not, however, be it well understood, the recompense of virtue—a sort of season-ticket to Heaven, which by-and-by expires. It is a mental and moral state attained. The individual attaining it is said to enter into all things—to be the world, to become all life, to grow identified with good in the common good. It is attainable, as has been remarked, in this existence ; death or life makes no difference : the soul by Moksha does not become anything it was not before, but knows itself, and lives as if already bodiless. The Panchadasi says : " Partaking of the pleasures of sense as well as of bliss in Brahma, the true knower is as one who in his city knows two languages—that of the world, and that of the sacred books."

Consequently, though the pathways to Deliverance lie through good deeds, through useful lives, and all which we call " Morality," it is right knowledge which must illuminate them ; and so far Moksha is intellectual and metaphysical. The greatest of all the texts of the Upanishads is the 6th Prapathaka of the Chandogya, called the Mahârâkya or Supreme Announcement. It occurs in the dialogue of the Sage Aruni with his son Sweta Ketu, and is the

famous formula *tad twam asi*, "That art Thou."
Just as to understand the word OM is to know
Hindu ontology, so to comprehend *tad twam asi*
is to grasp the Way, the Truth, and the Life of
Hindu theology. I can now but point to the
prodigious abyss of human thought into which this
golden plummet sinks, until it truly seems to touch
bottom. *Tad*, "That," say the commentators,
denotes both the totality of things made up of the
Universal soul and of Maya its shadow, called
together the Universe, and also the Arch-Self itself,
apart from all inter-blending with phenomena.
Twam, "Thou," denotes both the totality of things
in the parts—I, each of my readers, and every
individually migrating life or mind, indwelling in
each corner of the phenomenal—along with the
pure characterless Self in each which underlies
every semblance of the Universe, and animates
every wandered fragment of the Arch-Self. Thus
the famous phrase implies, "Each soul is one with
the Universal soul."   "Thou art That," and to
know this and realise this is the beginning and
the end of Moksha, leading to a region where
"good" and "evil"—and therefore morality, are
words just as obsolete as lungs would be beyond
this atmosphere—a region where Love and Joy
and Good are one in the light of a divine Truth
and consummated Knowledge.

   Sadly I feel how little the willing boldness of my
pen succeeds in conveying within these few pages
the outcome of those placid centuries when India

sate apart from the nations—meditating. I have not
touched upon twenty great questions pertaining to
the Upanishads, and I cannot here touch. Something, perhaps, of the spirit of those wonderful
treatises may be finally apparent in this last extract
from my "Secret of Death," where the old Brahman
priest is made to say:

"If he that slayeth thinks 'I slay'; if he
Whom he doth slay thinks 'I am slain,' then both
Know not aright!   That which was life in each
Cannot be slain, nor slay!"

"The Untouched Soul,
Greater than all the worlds (because the worlds
By it subsist); smaller than subtleties
Of things minutest; last of ultimates;
Sits in the hollow heart of all that lives!
Whoso hath laid aside desire and fear,
His senses mastered, and his spirit still,
Sees in the quiet light of verity,
Eternal, safe, majestical—His Soul!"

"Resting, it ranges everywhere! asleep,
It roams the world, unsleeping!   Who is Wise
Knows that divinest spirit, as it is,
Glad beyond joy, existing outside life."

"Beholding it in bodies bodiless,
Amid impermanency permanent,
Embracing all things, yet i' the midst of all,
The mind, enlightened, casts its griefs away!"

"It is not to be seen by Knowledge!   Man
Wotteth it not by wisdom!   Learning vast
Halts short of it!   Only by Soul itself
Is Soul perceived—when the Soul wills it so.
There shines no light save its own light to show
Itself unto itself."

IX
THE TWO BRIDGES

THE TWO BRIDGES

One ought never to grudge a little help and patient sympathy to slow-minded people trudging along the road of life. It does not cost much, and oftentimes it results in far more abundant returns than mere material gifts can bring. Most gifts, indeed, demoralise, and it often seems to close observers that more harm than good is wrought by money bestowed upon people never seen, through agencies never overlooked, without that element of human contact which redeems the idle and frigid business. But if you can help anybody to help himself, that very frequently turns out satisfactory to both. A pleasant instance of it comes to my recollection connected with some early days in my life.

After leaving Oxford, and before receiving the appointment of Principal of the Government Deccan College in India, I was chosen by the Governors of King Edward's School in Birmingham as a master of the English division of that great educational institution ; and passed a brief period there. The schoolhouse, designed and erected by Barry, who built the Houses of Parliament, is of noble aspect and elevation, as everybody knows who is familiar with

Birmingham. I have never, until recently, been in
that city since the year 1856, and can therefore speak
only from distant memory of the edifice, its massive
structure, stained-glass windows, spacious class-rooms,
and the noise of busy life for ever echoing along its
front, which looks, I believe, on New Street. But
very pleasant days—albeit, no doubt, a little laborious—were those which were passed by me in that
stately building, teaching the young mechanicians
and embryo manufacturers of the city, in company
with fifteen or twenty other University men from
Oxford and Cambridge, under the kindly sway of
our amiable and learned headmaster, Archdeacon
Gifford. I became immensely attached to my two
classes, and was, if I may venture to say so, somewhat
popular in the whole school, chiefly, perhaps, because
I tried to identify myself with the feelings of the
boys, and to render their lessons pleasant and attractive, instead of cramming them artificially with verbs
and facts and axioms, as prize poultry are fed. I
used to arrange and superintend their fights when
the quarrel was a just one ; to get them out of scrapes
with the authorities whenever it was feasible; and
on a certain rather notable occasion we in concert
solemnly abolished the stick as an instrument of
education. That detestable implement used to be
duly placed on all the desks of the masters, along
with the inkstand and class-list, always to my profound disgust ; for he who cannot teach without
the stick had better get to some other business.
But the thing always lay there ; and one sultry

afternoon, when Birmingham outside was blazing like one of its own blast-furnaces, and my young brassfounders were all languid with the heat, and with the involved rhetoric of Cicero—I myself being possibly at the time· a little dyspeptic—there was a disturbance of order near my chair. "The sight of means to do ill deeds Makes ill deeds done," as Shakespeare truly writes : thus it was that I caught up my cane and gave a hasty cut upon the too-tempting back of one youth who seemed the offender.

"If you please, sir," said the boy, squirming, "I did nothing ! It was Scudamore that kicked me in the stomach, underneath the desk !"

Now, it is obviously difficult to pursue the study of "De Amicitia" quietly and satisfactorily if you be interrupted in such a manner ; and inquiry revealed that the statement was indeed true. Scudamore had demanded from his neighbour, quite illegitimately, the explanation of an obscure passage, and not being attended to, had taken this much too emphatic means of enforcing attention. Meantime, the most guilty party appeared to be myself, and having called the class up, I said to the doubly-wronged boy, who was still "rubbing the place" :

"It is I who am most to blame, for having dealt you an undeserved blow. Take that cane and give it back to me, as hard as you got it."

"Ah, no, sir," the lad answered, "I can't do that."

The whole great schoolroom was now listening, masters and all, and the scene had become a little dramatic and important. It was necessary, therefore, to go through with the matter, and I insisted.

"Jones, you must do as I tell you. I insist. It is the only way in which we can all get right again."

"I really can't hit you, sir! It didn't hurt me so very much, sir! If you please, I don't want to do it," said Jones.

"Well," I replied, "but you must obey me; and if you disobey, I am sorry to say that I shall make you write out that page of Cicero three times, staying in to do it."

Whether it was desperation at this dreaded alternative (for it was cricket time), or whether it was that the sparkling eyes of his class-fellows around him, all evidently longing to have the good luck themselves of "licking" a master, suddenly inspired Jones, I know not. What I do know is that he reached forth his hand, took the cane, and dealt me no sham stroke, but the severest and most telling cut over my shoulders. I had no idea that the ridiculous implement could sting, as it did, like a scorpion. I had never once been caned or flogged at school, nor had ever in my life received a blow of any sort which I did not promptly return. Consequently the sensation was something of a revelation, and I could well understand at last how mortally boys must hate for ever and ever the "glories which were Greece, and the grandeurs which were Rome," when they are recommended to their unwilling intellects by these cowardly and clumsy methods.

"Rubbing the place" in my own turn, I managed

to thank Jones for his obliging compliance, and then said to him :

"Break that detestable weapon across your knee, and throw it out of the window. Never again will we have anything to do with such methods here."

But it is time some reason were furnished for entitling these my present recollections "The Two Bridges." In truth, the thought of Birmingham reminded me of one afternoon, when there came to the gate of my garden in Edgbaston the boy I considered the most stupid and hopeless in all my classes. He was tall and ungainly, although good-looking; very shy and silent; docile and respectful enough, but always behind-hand with some among his tasks, and, consequently, for ever at the bottom of his form ; the sort of lad no master troubles himself about. I must confess I had given up all idea of making anything out of him, at any rate as regarded certain important lessons—a helpless, dull, unwilling, profitless dunce —so I imagined ; and thus I had reluctantly come to treat him. With him came into my garden a pretty girl a year younger, who explained that "Trotter" wanted badly to see me, but did not dare to venture alone, and so, being his friend, and living with his mother, she had accompanied him. Possibly that made me more indulgent to the hulking, stupid, silent youth; for there were great, bright tears in the girl's blue eyes, and she held the big nervous fellow by the edge of his coat, as if she feared he would run away, from shame or fright. And then she softly related how good a boy he was to

his mother, and how hard he .worked to learn his
school tasks, and how miserable he became at his
repeated failures, and his perpetual ignominy at the
bottom of the form; and how all-important it was
that he should pass a forthcoming examination, on
which his future bread and meat would depend; and
that she had accordingly persuaded him to come
straight to me, and now desired very ardently to
make me understand that "Trotter" was burning
with desire to win my good opinions, and that she
and his mother thought he could not be really
stupid, because there were other lessons, outside
geometry and what not, which he always did well;
and he had, moreover, invented two or three
remarkable improvements for a steel-rolling factory.
So I made the poor lad speak for himself, and when
he ruefully explained how he had never, for one
fleeting moment, understood any atom of Euclid,
nor why it was ever written and taught at all, with
other special difficulties in his course; certain subjects being all the time, as I myself well knew,
easy enough to him. The truth was, he was
no more stupid than the other average "Brum-
magem" boys. He was a proud, silent, well-
meaning lad, who had been vilely taught at the
beginning; for teaching is a fine art, and very few
really understand it. His humility and earnestness
melted me, as well as the tears in the blue eyes of
his little friend. I sent her home and made him
stop to tea, and that afternoon we tore up Euclid by
the roots; we divested ourselves of all the false

terror inspired in young minds by that ancient name; we went behind the old Alexandrian geometer, and found him out in his plan, his purposes, his beginnings, his fallacies, and his merits. I told "Trotter" not to be ashamed at any little personal difficulties, since King Ptolemy had boggled like himself at the foot of the "Asses' Bridge," and had asked Euclid, one day, in Alexandria, if he could not make it all a bit easier, to which the ancient mathematician replied that "there is no royal road to learning." "But there is, Trotter!" I said. "A very broad and good king's highway exists, by means of which no thing is difficult, nothing abstruse. It is just as easy to learn the binomial theorem, or Persian, or Sanskrit, or Euclid, or navigation, or chemistry, as it is to mow grass or shear a sheep. The secret is to be rightly taught, or to teach yourself rightly from the beginning, making sure of every step taken, and bearing in mind that most learning is very simple, and that most school-books do their very best to render it obscure and senseless." Well, with that we built up Euclid for ourselves. Trotter came to me privately, day by day, and we attacked that fatal Fifth Proposition of the First Book as Napoleon his enemies at the Bridge of Arcola. We surveyed it, we made coloured sections of it, so that he ended by knowing all its intricate triangles; we mapped out and marked its angles and lines, so that we came to be able to prove the theorem by colours, or numbers, just as well as letters; we worked out deductions and corollaries from it, until, like a

M

kind of geometrical Clapham Junction, or the big
railway bridges one over the other at Birmingham,
we had all sorts of supplementary propositions built
over and under it. And as he grasped the *raisons
d'être* of Euclid his terrors changed to pleasure.
The lad became the finest demonstrator in the
class, always at top for geometry. His diagrams,
charmingly drawn for him by the girl with the blue
eyes, were the envy and wonder of the form, and,
from the despondent victim of conventional and
foolish instruction, he developed, by getting use of
his free senses, into what he was meant for, a
sharp-witted inventor, with an eye every bit as keen
as Euclid's for proportion, relation, and the subtle
feeling of form. "A fine thing," I used to say to
him, "if a bald old Greek gentleman of Ptolemy's
time is to set puzzles in squares and circles and
triangles that an English boy in Birmingham can't
understand! Go to the heart of it! don't grant
him anything! don't be quite sure that the three
angles of every triangle are equal to two right
angles; and don't at all allow, until you are yourself fairly convinced, that parallel straight lines produced will never meet. Euclid could not have
made a steel pen, or electro-plated a brass cup;
and you must forget the miserable learning by rote
forced upon you by impostors who call themselves
'teachers,' and begin where Euclid began." As I
have said, the lad became confident, joyous, successful. He passed with elastic step over the
" Bridge of Asses," took prize after prize, and when

I left Birmingham was on the fair road to be head of his division in the school.

Well, that was one Bridge! As I was crossing Canada many and many a year afterwards, in the new and wonderful region which extends between Vancouver and Winnipeg, we came upon a "junction." If all Englishmen and Scotchmen and Irishmen comprehended what a magnificent imperial estate they own in that splendid country on both sides of the Rockies, I think some would not stay at home so doggedly to grow wheat at the value of its cleaned straw, and to poke about for a miserable living in the moors of the North and the bogs of Clare and Donegal. If Capital has its great resource in suspension of work, Labour has its best defence in emigration, and it is mainly the foolish blind clinging to one spot of the globe, together with the apathy of governments and colonial administrations, which has created the Irish Home Rule difficulty, and which chokes the labour market to an unprofitable point. However, all this is politics and economics, with which these pages have nothing to do. What I would say is, that we came through the superb scenery of the Rocky Mountains, past the glories of the Glacier Station, and Banff, and down the foot-hills to Regina and the prairies, right upon a very important ceremony which was impending at a large prairie town. It was to celebrate the opening of a most remarkable bridge, built over a most impetuous and unrestrainable river, and connecting in a most momentous manner for commerce and intercourse

the sister States of a great province. We had to
stay overnight at the station, and decided to be
present at the inauguration of the new bridge.

Thus it was that, having received a very polite
invitation to attend, I repaired to the residence of
the superintending engineer of the district in order
to obtain some particulars of time and place. The
house was one of those commodious, wholesome,
clean-looking abodes of wood which they raise so
quickly and paint so prettily in that land of lumber,
with all the prairie for its back garden, and a long
post and rail in front to which to tie up "any man's
horses." Inquiring at the door, I was told that the
superintending engineer was for the moment out,
but his wife, whose name I did not catch, would see
me. Looking round the walls of matchboard in a
casual manner, I spied, to my astonishment, among
pictures of various kinds, a photographic view of
King Edward's School, Birmingham, and close
beside it the Fifth Proposition of the First Book
of Euclid, with the angles and triangles done in
diverse colours, and underneath it written, "My
First Bridge." Near at hand was a truly superb
picture of the new Canadian bridge, in all its glory
of iron and timber, with the rushing forest-born river
innocuously whirling ice-slabs and slags beneath its
wide arches; while in the corner I read the words,
very neatly inscribed, "His Second Bridge." Just
then the door opened, and in there came the nicest,
brightest, most open-faced matron that can be
imagined, leading a handsome boy of ten or twelve

years by the hand. In an instant, after all these years, we had recognised each other. She was the very same girl with the blue eyes who had brought Trotter up to me in his deep woe about Euclid—and Trotter, none other than the melancholy Trotter, was the great and glad mechanical hero of the occasion, the triumphant engineer who had spanned the Red River with his world-admired bridge. "His Second Bridge!" She had proudly written it herself upon the plan, to go beside that diagram of the "Bridge of Asses"; although, indeed, my old pupil had done plenty of other wonderful engineering work before erecting that *Pons Asinorum* over the great Canadian stream. He had made a fortune, in fact; was one of the biggest men in his province; and we did not part before we had renewed old Birmingham memories in some very good Californian wine, and had pledged a cup of kindness to the good luck and firm foundations of the second of the "Two Bridges."

X

INDIAN VICEROYS

INDIAN VICEROYS

Upon an amiable Scotch nobleman has lately devolved what Lord Rosebery justly once called the "sublime" office of the viceroyalty of India. Mr. Gladstone's range of choice for a successor to Lord Lansdowne was necessarily limited, and the recommendation of the Earl of Elgin to Her Majesty for that post—following as it did upon the unfortunate nomination and abdication of Sir Henry Norman—no doubt somewhat surprised those who take an interest in the affairs of India. But it sometimes happens that such hasty and almost desperate appointments turn out well, nor could anything be of better promise than the modest and self-distrustful yet earnest words used by Lord Elgin at the Imperial Institute on the 16th of November, in the speech by which he responded to that of Lord Rosebery, who had proposed his health. There are three types of Indian viceroys which are all good in their way. One is that of the man who, like Sir John Lawrence, knows the vast country by previous long service, and is therefore the least likely to commit administrative mistakes. The second is the practised statesman, the assured master of state affairs, like Lord Dufferin, who carries to his splendid office the habits of command and the knowledge of men.   And the third may be very well represented by Lord Elgin himself, the intelligent and high-bred ruler, who is sure of nothing except of his good heart to serve faithfully India and her Empress, and who goes out willing and ready to learn from those who understand them the hundred problems of the Peninsula.   Its history is not deficient in examples of governors-general of such a kind who have borne authority excellently well in the land ; and it must be remembered in recommendation of Lord Elgin that he is the son of a viceroy whose record in China and in India was in every way noble and becoming, and who died in the Queen's high service.

It is not too extravagant to call the office of an Indian viceroy " sublime." No position in the world, not actually royal, approaches it for influence and for splendour ; and probably no extant monarch keeps up so much visible state as the representative of Her Majesty at Calcutta.   The residence which he inhabits there is stately and striking, without any great architectural pretensions.   There is a mansion almost exactly like it in England—that called Keddlestone Hall, in Derbyshire—which consists of a central building with four wings connected to the centre by galleries, in the same fashion as seen at Government House.   By a wise custom, the precincts of this viceregal palace are always guarded by picked native soldiers—Sikhs, Bengalis, Ghoorkas, or what not—and their picturesque uniforms marshal you fittingly into the suite of superb apartments. The banquet-room, all in white *chunam*, with floor of white marble, contains six fine marble busts of the Cæsars, taken from a French ship in the wars, along with a magnificent chandelier, captured at the same time, which is suspended in the ball-room. From the banquet-room you pass to the throne-room, so named from the golden chair of Tippoo, which is there ; and thence to the council-room, which contains a whole gallery of the governors-general of India. Over the second door, on the right, in the great company of Minto, and Coote and Cornwallis, Warren Hastings, Wellesley, Clive, Auckland, and Adam, the new viceroy will constantly see the picture of his illustrious father. Above the banquet and the council rooms is the magnificent hall for dancing, with floor of polished teak and panelled ceiling. As you descend the sweep of steps leading from the veranda to the beautiful gardens, trophies of bygone wars meet the eye. A long brass 32-pounder, taken at Aliwal, fronts the entrance, and on either hand are tiger-guns in bronze obtained from Tippo Sahib, with others marked by the names of " Miani " and " Hyderabad," and an especially strange-looking piece having a carriage in the shape of a dragon. When last I had the pleasure and distinction of strolling in those sunny grounds that surround Government House, brilliant with such beautiful flowers and variegated plants as one only dreams of in our climate, Lord Dufferin was walking there in the early morning, characteristically engaged in reading "Robinson Crusoe" in Persian, with his *Munshi* at his side. That was his clever and highly practical way of mastering the court language of Mohammedan India, at which he afterwards became adept enough to make a fluent and graceful speech in the tongue of Hâfiz during his interview with the Ameer of Afghanistan at Rawul Pindi. Among all our recent viceroys, Lord Dufferin was perhaps the one most admired and regarded by the native population at large. They quickly take their own measure of their rulers ; and in the perfect grace and geniality which veiled the strong will and resolute policy of this most accomplished of public servants, they saw their ideal of the *Pukka Lat Bahadur*. His never-failing brightness of manner fascinated all alike, while, if the political crisis had come in his time which is "ever impending," no abler statesman could have held and defended our Eastern Empire. I recall an instance of his pleasant seriousness. I was seated in his sanctum at Government House, bidding the Viceroy farewell, when he playfully asked me what he could do for me "unto the half of my kingdom." I replied that I had two boons to ask of him ; and the first was that, having regard to the dangerous state of things on the frontier, he would not again expose himself to the sun as he had lately done at Delhi, and elsewhere ; contracting, in consequence, a slight fever. Laughingly Lord Dufferin answered, "Well, you see, they have been sending me recently always to the Arctic regions. They packed me off to St. Petersburg as ambassador, and then afterwards to Canada to be governor-general there, so that when I received the honour of appointment as viceroy of India, I said in my own mind, 'Now I will hang myself up to dry!' and possibly I have been overdoing it. What is the second boon?" "Oh," I replied, "I want a railway to Kandahar." "Ah!" he said, slightly smiling, "I will show you something at least towards it," and unlocking his escritoire, produced the first draft of the railway now opened to Quetta and beyond.

But were I viceroy, I should like much better than my palace at Calcutta the charming country-house which he possesses eight or nine koss up the river at Barrackpur. Calcutta at the best of times is hot and flat, but under the splendid trees of that river-palace you get glorious shade and the cool airs always wafted from the water. Beneath a great tamarind tree to the south of the residence is the white marble monument of Lady Canning, who died in India while her husband was viceroy, a gentle and illustrious type of those countless Englishwomen who have shared with husbands and brothers the burden of empire in the East. In the same gardens is to be seen a splendid avenue of bamboos, making such a corridor of laced silver and green leaves and golden stems as one might go a hundred leagues to admire, with near at hand a wonderful banyan tree dropping its aërial branches from aloft into the soil and so producing a number of column-like stems, under the canopies of which a whole regiment might

encamp. By the side of that touching memorial to
a viceroy's wife, I remember that I had the honour
of a conversation upon the mysteries of such a
pathetic fate with Lady Dufferin, whose presence
and work in India the natives have had such lasting
cause to bless. I pointed to the Temple of Mahadev
on the other side of the stream, and cited to her the
Sanskrit lines in the *Bhagavad Gita*, which begin,
" *Hantâ Chenmanyatê Hantûm*," and which mean,

> " If one that dieth thinks, 'I die!' If one
> When he doth slay thinks, 'I have slain!' then both
> Know not aright! That which was life in each
> Cannot be slain, or die."

To every viceroy there is pretty sure to come
some vast task in the course of his administration.
India is an ocean the surface of which is never
always and at all places tranquil. Lord Lawrence,
after stormy duties, which included the events of
the great Mutiny, during which I was myself in
India, enjoyed a comparatively quiet spell. But for
Lord Northbrook suddenly sprang up the terrible
problem of the famine, with which dire enemy he
contended sagaciously, and on the whole successfully. It was my singular privilege to be the first
in this country to acquaint Lord—then Sir John—
Lawrence with his approaching nomination as viceroy, which had come to my knowledge as imminent
before it reached the ears most interested. I called
on him to ask, in confidence, if he would accept it
if offered, as the *Daily Telegraph* desired to sustain

his claims to the high office. Sir John had done me the kindness, in previous days, to go over the sheets of my work upon the Administration of Lord Dalhousie, and very interesting it is now to remember how I heard him, with his briarwood pipe in hand, discussing time after time Moolraj and the second Punjab war, the fields of Chillianwallah and Guzerat, the frontier problems and those that concern the huge populations of India. How beneficent our government of them is, was well shown in those dark days of the famine. No other administration could have grappled with Fate itself for the sake of the helpless natives as Lord Northbrook's did; and to a great extent we gained a victory over Death and Destiny. I prize among the few papers that I care to preserve a telegram from that able and conscientious viceroy, in which he told me that the rains had come, and the worst of the dreadful dearth was at an end. Under Lord Lytton's government perhaps the most important event was the proclamation in great state at Delhi of Her Majesty the Queen as Empress of India—*Kaisar-i-Hind;* while Lord Dufferin had upon his hands the conquest and annexation of Upper Burmah, and the temporary adjustment of Afghan affairs. Something new and surprising is sure to devolve upon Lord Elgin, and there is no need to doubt that when it comes he will sustain, by prudence, wisdom, and devotion to his lofty duty, the grand traditions of his predecessors.

Wandering in Culcutta either in those delicious gardens of Government House, or under the sacred

fig trees of Barrackpur, or haply among the peaks
and precipices of the official highland capital at
Simla, the thought of an Englishman must often go
back to the small and humble beginnings of all this
splendour and power. If we will trace the special
river of history to its source, it may be demonstrated
that the grandeur which Lord Elgin goes out to
assume derives itself entirely from a doctor's prescription.   In 1636 A.D. the daughter-in-law of Shah
Jehan, and favourite wife of Sultan Shuja, Nawab of
Bengal, who was the second son of the Great Mogul,
lay sick of a malady beyond the skill of the Mohammedan *hakims.*   Distressed at the danger of one so
fair and precious, the Nawab called to his aid the
surgeon of the East-India Company's ship *Hopewell,*
by name Gabriel Boughton, a clever young doctor,
who, although not allowed to see the beautiful face of
his royal patient, all the same effected a perfect cure.
The grateful prince asked him to name his own fee ;
whereupon Boughton begged for and obtained a
firmán, granting permission to the East-India Company to trade throughout the dominions of the Great
Moguls, and giving them land to build a factory,
which factory has since grown up to become the
stately city of Calcutta.   Those who best know the
intervening incidents of that brilliant story of
growing empire will be the last to assert, as some
ignorant persons do, that our Eastern Empire has
been founded on fraud and wrong.   Its story,
properly told, is full of the high enterprise, and
mainly honourable efforts, which belong to the

general history of England; and there is little or
nothing for an honest Briton to be ashamed of in all
that wonderful record which stretches from Gabriel
Boughton's prescription to the approaching entry of
Lord Elgin into his capital. The time has now
come when India must be regarded as an inseparable
and indispensable portion of the British Empire.
The task committed by Providence to the English
race of repaying the debt of the West to the East by
giving good government and profound peace to three
hundred millions of Indian people, and thereby protecting the modern up-rise of Asia, is a task not nearly
completed, but rather demanding a century of quiet
continuance. It is therefore before all things necessary that the British people should comprehend the
Imperial importance of India, and be very resolute
amid all political changes, not to suffer for one
moment that the strong hand of the Queen's viceroy
in Calcutta shall be weakened by ignorant theorists,
and the breathless benevolence of globe-trotting
politicians.

XI

UNDER THE SUNSHINE

XI

UNDER THE SUNSHINE

In the dark December weather of these islands, when the days are so short, and influenza stalks unchecked, the thought naturally turns to those happier countries that have no winter. Which is the nearest of them? I think the answer to that would not be the Riviera, where the mistral often blows, and the shaded side of a street will be as cold as Clapham Common; nor Italy, nor Spain, except in its most southern regions. The shortest road to the sunshine is to go to Algiers, where, although the climate is not so good as that of Egypt, the wanderer may be fairly certain of fine weather. Among my memories is that of a journey suddenly taken from London to the capital of French Africa. The snow was lying thick in the streets of our beloved but dingy metropolis. The doors of houses and shops were blocked with great drifts of it. Cabs and omnibuses toiled along in the deep blackened slush, and an eager and nipping north wind broke off the long icicles and chilled the stoutest wayfarer in spite of wraps and fur coat. The mail steamer across the Channel had snow upon its deck and paddle-boxes, and the snow whitened all France north of Paris; nay, even to the south of

that city snow-drifts covered the Forest of Fontaine-
bleau and the plane trees down to Lyons with fairy
frost-work. When the guard opened the door of the
coupé-lit to ask for tickets, the breath of passengers
in the warm interior, suddenly condensing, fell in
flakes of snow, and the grim winter hung about us till
the olive trees of Provence were reached. We caught
the Friday night boat at Marseilles, where already
the sun was shining upon a sparkling sea, and it was
warm enough for the Zouave soldiers whom we carried
with us to sleep upon the deck. The boat was a
slow one, but in about thirty hours we saw Algiers
rising against the Atlas Mountains, a steep white
city, presenting an appearance from the sea as of
some vast merchant ship with all her canvas set ; and
entering the harbour we found the winter entirely left
behind us. A glowing blue sky bent over the bright
landscape near and far, and that same afternoon we
were plucking ripe oranges in a garden of the suburb
of Mustapha Superieur, though the slush of London
was hardly yet dried upon our walking-boots. Nowadays, with improved train and steamboat accommodation, and good "connections," one might, I
suppose, pass from London to Algiers in about fifty
hours. It is, on the whole, the shortest road to the
sunshine.

All this was, however, a long time ago ; so long
ago that Marshal MacMahon, who has lately died, was
at the time Governor-General of Algeria, and I had
the honour to make his acquaintance in connection
with an earthquake which had shaken and devastated

ALGIERS HARBOUR.

P. 198.

the district round about the city on the very day of
our arrival. One of the first sounds, indeed, which
met our ears on landing was the cry of the newspaper boys calling out "Demandez le *Moniteur
d'Algerie.* Gran, tremblement de terre. Nouvelles
très interressantes." Algiers itself had not seriously
suffered, although some of its buildings were shaken ;
but the country in the vicinity exhibited many marks
of the recent shock, and the town of Blidah especially lay almost entirely in ruins. We went out to
see them, in company with his Excellency and staff,
and a most curious spectacle did the place present.
Half the houses were cracked from top to bottom.
The steeple of a church had been twisted round and
out of the perpendicular, so that the stone angel on
the top of it was very much in the attitude of Mr.
Gilbert's aluminium effigy surmounting the Piccadilly
Fountain. Whole streets of houses of the colonists,
built, as they were, of round stones from the river-
bed, had crumbled into the roadway, and the greater
part of the population was encamped under canvas,
up and down the thoroughfares, or in the plain.
The soldierly presence of MacMahon, with his
brilliant staff, seemed to bring new spirits to the
unfortunate people ; and I could not but admire his
cheery and gallant manner among them. Little did
we dream at the time that he would be a central
figure in such a terrible catastrophe as Sedan, and
rise to hold the destinies of France in his hand as
President of the Republic. But to this hour I well
remember the singular grace and courtesy of his

bearing. We had to return from the scenes of disaster by an omnibus running to the station, which was half full of French washerwomen when we entered it. The pretty deferential style in which MacMahon lifted his gold-embroidered *kepi* to those *blanchisseuses*, and meekly took a crowded corner seat among his female subjects, stamped itself on my mind as an example of high manners. In wandering about this desolate town I entered a schoolhouse where a French professor was still busily engaged in lecturing to a class of advanced French students, with the sunlight shining through the cracked walls and open roof of his little *lycée*. I asked permission to listen for a while to the lecture, which was upon the Odes of Horace, and a copy of the Latin poet was lying on the professor's desk. When he said to me that, notwithstanding the earthquake, he was still trying to do his duty, I opened the volume, with a bow to the professor, at Ode iii. of Book III., and pointed the attention of the pupils to those lines about the " upright and resolute man," "si fractus illabatur orbis, Impavidum ferient ruinæ."

> " If the world were shattered to fragments,
>   Its ruins would strike him unmoved."

It was delightful to see how pleased the brave schoolmaster was with the little classic compliment.

Even in Algeria, however, during December it was easy enough to find the winter again, if you went up into the Kabyle Mountains. I think I was never colder in all my life than on a little excursion made to Fort Napoleon, as it was then called. In descending from the highlands, a bitter blizzard was abroad, and I and the driver of my *calèche* were caked with the driving sleet from head to foot. We got some hot coffee at the cottage of a colonist just in time to prevent us from freezing solid. The poor people were suffering from fever, and spoke of their little house as a *maison de misère;* and in those days, indeed, Algeria was far from prosperous as a dependency. I had with me an Arab of the country, named Ahmad, who gave a very signal proof of the fidelity of even the humblest Mohammedans to the tenets of their religion. It was the time of Ramadan, the great fast, during which none of the Faithful may taste food, or even smoke, between sunrise and sunset. It had been a day of hard and wearying travel, alternately very cold and very hot, and Ahmad was much fatigued, like his master, plus the fact that he had taken no coffee at the stopping-place. When we got into the plain, near a place called Tizi-ouzu, I bought some oranges, and as there were still several leagues to traverse, I offered some to Ahmad, who was green with fatigue and hunger. When he declined, I rather maliciously pressed them upon him, wanting to see how sincere he would prove.

"Eat, Ahmad," I said, "the sunset-gun will soon go, and there is nobody hereabouts to blame you."

"No, sir, no," he replied; "Allah will know

and blame me. We may not eat till the sun is down."

There was no touch of pride or exclusiveness in the poor fellow, for when we got into the inn, and I was consuming rice and boiled chicken in bed, to keep warm, Ahmad sat on the floor at my side and ate the bones of the chickens, as well as what was upon them, like a house-dog at the foot of the couch.

That same spot, Tizi-ouzu, has two recollections for me. Perhaps to-day it is a big town : at that time it was a desolate little hamlet on the skirt of the Desert, and I think I never felt more lonely than during my first night there, with no society but that of Ahmad. On the second day matters brightened, for I made the acquaintance of some officers of the small French garrison, and we not only dined well at mess, having among other dishes some wild asparagus, but attended an Arab wedding in the evening, where, after music and dancing, the bride walked round the circle of guests, each of whom wetted a small coin of silver or gold in his mouth and stuck it upon her forehead. And the next day I saw in the little Court of Justice, what for its picturesque *dénouement* might be called a *cause célèbre*, if Tizi-ouzu had any legal chronicles.

A young and handsome Turco soldier was up before the mixed tribunal, charged by an infuriated native with having violated the sanctity of his house and made love to the man's wife. Everybody in the small court was very excited, and it seemed to be indeed the case that the young soldier, who had for some time back been a friend of the family, had pushed the privileges of this friendship much too far. The rules of enlistment were different then from what they are now, and many of the native peasants were glad to get the French pay and food, under a temporary engagement of local service. Something like the following dialogue took place in this little Court:

Plaintiff: "The justice of my lords is praised in all the world; but see how this dog despises it. He comes by night-time to the house of a friend, in his absence, having designs upon his wife."

Female Defendant: "By your life, my lords, my husband is a fool, and this thing is not so."

Plaintiff: "I have given him *kibab* and millet cakes every other day, and this woman lies. But for the majesty of the Court I would beat her on the mouth with my slipper."

The Court to the Young Soldier: "What have you to say to this charge?"

Soldier: "By Allah! it is a false charge. This man is foolish, as the woman sayeth, and has a wife too good for him. It is true that I owe him gratitude, and am not of those who would forget it."

Plaintiff: "Tell the honourable Court, then, if you can, and if you dare, why you were behind my wife's curtain when I came suddenly home. Was not this so?"

Soldier: "Yea, it was so! But there was no sin."

Plaintiff: "No sin! Oh! By Al-Hakk, the Truth! will the Court still listen to the tongue of this dog? Let them question that wicked woman."

. The Court to the Wife: "What do you say to this?"

The Wife: "May the heads of my lords be protected, the soldier speaks the truth. There was no sin at all, and my husband is but a braying jackass."

The Court: "Nevertheless, a man alone with you, not your husband—this surely must be explained."

The Wife: "It cannot be explained; yet was there no sin."

The Court: "If there was no blame, make that good to us and to this man."

Plaintiff: "They cannot make it good, I say. Give justice, my lords."

Upon this there ensued much hubbub in the crowd, everybody apparently being of the opinion that the silence of the two incriminated parties was not only very suspicious, but impudent and insulting to the Court, the judgment of which, probably a very severe one, was now on the point of being delivered. The plaintiff had already been foiled in two attempts to get near the soldier, and they had taken away the knife from his girdle, fearing extremities. The female, a good-looking peasant-girl, was standing, sullen and troubled, but had quietly sidled up within reach of the young soldier.

Order was with difficulty restored in the little hall of justice, and the native assessor had nearly got through the decree of imprisonment which he was going to give to the injured husband, while a French officer was reading the sentence of suspension and other penalties against the silent defendant, whose face was yet curiously placid amid all the confusion.

Suddenly everything was altered by the action of the woman, who broke from her attitude of reserve, and volubly addressed the Court.

"May my lords allow speech to their slave. This, my husband, who hath brought shame and calamity on us, is an ass, and the son of an ass. I will make his face black with the truth, since the truth must be told. This soldier here did, indeed, come, and hath ofttimes come, into my chamber. The mother of him is a poor woman who had no means to live, and the friend in past days of my own mother. For her sake he hath taken the French money, and put upon him the French soldier-clothes, that he might have wages of service to give to her who gave him birth. But all this was a secret between us, because"—and here she stepped up closer to the prisoner—"because it is not lawful that one should serve under a false name, nor call himself a man when he hath nothing of man except a brave heart. See, now, my lords, and thou, too, that dost slander thy true wife, whether there was sin between me and my mother's friend's child when he came by night asking a drink of milk." Abruptly at these words she laid her hand on the upper buttons of the tunic of the young Turco, and with a violent gesture tore the garment off. Then in the midst of deep silence the truth was revealed—the Turco was a woman; and after a moment's silent amazement, the case broke up in such laughter, and cries, and pleasant amazement for everybody but the husband, as could rarely be witnessed in a place of justice. Tizi-ouzu, under the sunshine of the Atlas, is always coupled in my mind with that strange ending to a village divorce case.

XII
JUNGLE KINGDOMS

XII

JUNGLE KINGDOMS

PART I

THE WAR BETWEEN MAN AND BEAST

WE say to each other, with good reason, that "Man is lord of the creation." If this be a boast, it is a true one, and the rest of the animated world, had they reason and speech, would, each in their separate tribes, wild or domesticated, perceive and allow it. Yet few of us realise by what small steps and chance advantages we came to planetary sovereignty.

Do you reflect, as you take up the leaf of this volume between your finger and thumb, to do me the honour of reading about Indian wild beasts and serpents, that you have just exercised the one great physical act of our organism which made us "man," and placed in the human hand the sceptre of our little star? The hand! All the secret of the advancement of the race lies in that opposable finger and thumb by which you have just turned this page.

The arts, the sciences, the machinery and manufactures of ancient and modern times; the subjuga-

tion of nature by "genus homo," and the submission
of the kindred but hopelessly outstripped "peoples
of the wing and hoof," mainly depend, if Darwinism
be true, on this fact that man alone can properly
pinch.

True it is that certain of the anthropoid apes
possess in some degree the same faculty. But the
index finger and the face of the thumb are not brought
together in quite the same exact and instinctive way,
as anybody may see who watches monkeys hunting
each other for fleas. As often as not, they will prefer
to catch the object with their lips, and if they use
the paw, they pinch with the second joint of the
forefinger.

The tree-climbing apes, *ateles* in America, *colobus*
in Africa, *hylobates* in Asia, are either thumbless, or
their toes partially cohere, so that their so-called
hands and feet are mere grasping-hooks. These poor
relations of man have spoiled their early chances by
walking on their outside palms or knuckles, as the
orang and chimpanzee do, or crooking them perpetually round the branches of trees. Mr. Hornaday's
" Mias " always slept with its fists clenched.

" Some ancient member of the great order of Pri-
mates," writes Darwin, " owing to a change in his
manner of procuring subsistence, or some alteration
in surrounding conditions, modified his habitual style
of progression, and thus was rendered bipedal." In
other words, our primeval ancestor one day stood
erect, and stayed there ; by that act rescuing the
wonderful plan and mechanism of his hands from

the ruinous toil of walking and climbing, and commencing the development of them in the direction
of the craftsman, the hunter, and the artist.

The relatively stupendous inventions of flint
weapons, of the spear, and of the bow followed, with
that immense achievement of fire ; and man, with a
lighted stick and a hand to carry it in place of a
paw, became the veritable king of the earth. Speech
and social combinations, slowly ensuing upon these,
completed his coronation.

Yet how different might have proved the outcome
of natural selection ! The peoples of the sea, particularly the amphibians, who command two elements, might well have won the prize. If the
whales, which are mammals, had only banded together, who could have dared, against their will, to
dwell on the seashore or to launch boats ?

If the birds which, by transforming reptilian fins
into wings, gained dominion of the sky, had learned
to talk, and perhaps to turn the double-spur, which
we see upon *Palamedea cornuta*, into a sort of extra
hand, what could have prevented the roc and
dinornis, the moa, the ostrich, and the condor, from
possessing the globe ?

Man has prevailed, thanks largely to that marvellous hand which Sir Charles Bell has called " all
instruments in one," and the planet has become his
real estate ; but not without dispute and rebellion,
even yet !

The victory is won, but the battle of nature still
sullenly goes on in certain quarters of the globe

to an extent not easily realised by those who dwell in the populous cities of England or of the American Republic. In the latter, indeed, men have almost too severely pushed to its issues the triumph of man.

Men have well-nigh exterminated not only the rivals, but the wild neighbours and companions of our earthly existence. That grand creature, the buffalo, is gone from the vast plains of the West, more to be regretted than the red man, who is apparently on the road to disappear with it; and to anybody accustomed to other countries, with their teeming life of forest and field, it is sad to see how empty the American landscape has become of furred and feathered beings.

In a journey taken lately through nine thousand miles of the United States, I did not notice from the windows of the train more than a score or two of wild birds; and although, no doubt, it was winter-time, and the migrants were away, it was too painfully plain that wood and meadow in America have been nearly depopulated. In England one would observe more wild life in one day's journey than there in a month's travelling.

In India, as in many parts of Africa, animal life swarms. The reasons are different, but the result, in the enriching of the interest and variety of nature, is the same, and lends an extraordinary enhancement to every retired landscape.

There are hundreds of miles of railway journeying in India where you may watch from your car the monkey-people, dwelling in safety and pleasure by the

side of the track. All along the line, for instance,
in Guzerat and parts of the North-west, the "four-
handed folk" sit in the wayside trees or trot about
the millet-fields, or gather in sententious groups near
the well, amusing, harmless, respected.

Herds of the graceful black antelope gallop over
the yellow plains within view, stopping still now and
then in their lightsome procession to gaze with little
show of fear on the passing express.

Throughout Rajpootana there will be seen, almost
in every patch of garden, bevies of the lovely wild
pea-fowl, the male bird shining like a jewelled Rajah
in his panoply of purple, gold, and green, and the
peahens pacing meekly along with their splendid
lord. The thickets are full of pretty gem-necked
doves and bright-winged birds ; and, with no enemies
except the kites and hawks for ever wheeling in the
sky, a whole separate world of innocent beauty and
happiness goes on, in fact, at the side of the prolific
humanity everywhere visible.

Even in the crowded cities of India, among their
thickest and busiest bustle, the jungle creatures
make part of the population. You will see the
monkeys sitting observantly on the ridge-tiles of the
shops, up and down the door-posts of which the
lively, striped palm-squirrels scour. From end to
end of the street clouds of green paroquets fly
backward and forward, screaming loudly ; and on the
trees by the temple hundreds of "flying foxes"—the
large bat called *Pteropus Edwardsi*—hang by their
feet and hooked wings, like large black fruit.

But these are the friendly creatures of wood and
wild, which the peculiar customs of the Hindoos
have rendered safe and fearless. A Hindoo does not
kill for food or for sport ; and, as the amicable animal
world has found this out, you witness in most parts
of Hindostan the charming spectacle of peace firmly
established between man and the lower creation.
Birds, beasts, and fishes are secure from slaughter,
and after their invariable fashion, repay this with a
glad attachment to man, who is as a god to them.

In many a city or village you may observe seed-
boxes set up for the birds, and citizens going daily
forth to feed the monkeys. But for the most part the
Hindoo just lets things alone, and lives side by side
with the birds and beasts, having a particular reverence for some among them, such as the peacock,
the Hanuman monkey, and in certain places the
snake.

Only where the Mussulman and the European
come is this " peace of God " broken. The Mohammedan has little regard for animals, and the English
sahib is usually an eager sportsman ; so that bitter
are the feelings often engendered in a native village
when the young officer or the soldier-recruit, out
of ignorance of the Hindoo's reverence for them
rather than a bad heart, kills the sacred peacock or
the local monkeys.

Sometimes mischievous little Muslim boys will go
along a row of shops in an Indian city with a cage
of small birds, offering them at an easy price to the
Hindoo " Setts," as they sit among their rice and

grain, and, in case of refusal, wringing the necks of the small prisoners. I have often seen a tradesman, who would not lose a cowrie-shell if he could help it, give a whole handful of pice to buy the birds and set them all free.

This brings me to my subject, the war still waged between man and the wild beasts in India. Partly in consequence of the abstinence from flesh-food which Buddhism has taught to Brahmanism, partly because of the natural and physical features of the Indian Peninsula, and partly from the fact that to carry firearms without a license is forbidden by government, the number of wild animals is always very large there.

In the United States, if a farmer or pioneer loses his life by a grizzly bear, a catamount, or a rattlesnake, all the newspapers would be full of it. But listen to the death-roll of one year in India, due to this same unfinished war between man and his carnivorous competitors !

The official returns of the deaths due to wild beasts among the inhabitants of India show that in 1891 the total of natives, men, women, and children, who perished from *feræ naturæ*, including venomous snakes, amounted to twenty-three thousand eight hundred and seventy-two !

Here is a whole army of mankind destroyed by what we must call " the enemy," and albeit the conflict can have but one end, and these unreconciled and irreconcilable foes of our race must finally disappear, still it arrests the imagination most forcibly

to find what a costly warfare yet goes on between
civilisation and the jungle kingdoms. Nor let it be
supposed that the year 1890 or 1891 was excep-
tional.

That tremendous destruction of twenty-three or
twenty-four thousand lives is about the average
of late years for all India, and has increased rather
than diminished during the bygone ten or fifteen
years. For comparison on this point I will take the
official reports of the year 1877-78, which give us
twenty thousand two hundred and fifty-six human
lives destroyed by wild beasts and serpents during
those twelve months.

Allowing for deaths which never come to official
knowledge, for especially bad years when tigers and
wolves and the like lose their natural food and prey
more boldly than usual upon man, and for other
reasons which make these returns always understate-
ments, we may roughly conclude that two millions
and a half of India's people have perished by the
teeth and claws and fangs of the warriors of the
jungle in the last century.

If tigers and leopards and serpents wrote history,
with such figures as these before them, we could
hardly expect the savage chroniclers to allow that
the war was as good as concluded between man and
his forest rivals for the lordship of the earth.

Of course the issue is not doubtful. These
astonishing records of slaughter are really but the
dropping fire of a finished conflict. The great
carnivora live everywhere doomed to extinction, and

must pass at last from the catalogue of nature, unless they can change their habits and become herbivorous. But if to these returns of loss of human life in India we could add the death-roll of the scores of thousands of African, of Asiatic, of South American natives, who year after year meet their doom in rencontre with the denizens of the wilderness and the wood, the fact that these jungle kingdoms exist, and do seriously dispute the sovereignty of the earth with its real lords, would be still more emphatically brought home to the minds of my readers.

There are islands of the sea, as is well understood, so entirely occupied by oceanic birds that man is unknown there, and the boobies and penguins do not even move at his approach; and there are many tracts in India which belong so exclusively to wild elephants, leopards, wild boars, and jungle creatures generally, that most of the beast-people have never even set eyes upon a man or woman.

I have known in India villages to be seized and occupied by tigers, and a post-road was more than once so grimly guarded and patrolled by a couple of hungry man-eaters, that nobody dared to pass that way for a week or two.

In the next portion of this article I will analyse these strange and terrible death returns, and try to explain, from a close and considerable, though by-gone acquaintance with Indian wild creatures, how it is that all these human victims perish.

PART II

CHARACTERISTICS OF THE CONFLICT

It hardly matters which year's record we take for an analysis of the great and deadly warfare being perpetually waged between mankind and the wild beasts in India. There is, in truth, a curious regularity about the annual returns as regards' the number of casualties attributed to each destructive animal. Of course in every year by far the largest number of deaths are set down to venomous serpents.

For example, in the year just elapsed, out of the nearly twenty-four thousand deaths put down for the total, more than twenty-one thousand were ascribed to poisonous snakes! So, too, in the year 1877, which I have recalled for comparison, nearly seventeen thousand deaths, out of the total number of twenty thousand, were registered to those deadly reptiles which abound in the peninsula, and constitute, as of old, the curse and peril of many an Indian paradise.

I shall talk about snakes at the close of these remarks, and will deal now with the much smaller, but still very considerable, number of human lives destroyed by the carnivora of Hindostan.

These, in the year 1877, amounted to thirty-four

hundred and forty-four, and were distributed among our jungle enemies in the following proportions :— Wild elephants slew thirty-three; tigers killed eight hundred and sixteen, most of them in Bengal and Assam ; leopards, panthers, and cheetahs made victims of three hundred, and bears disposed of ninety-four. Wolves are set down for the large total of eight hundred and forty-five, and hyænas for thirty-three. Other animals, including all not mentioned in the above categories, figure for the serious score of thirteen hundred and twenty-three.

Here are the thirty-four hundred and forty-four deaths, duly distributed, and we will proceed to examine them a little from the point of view of jungle life.

The wild elephants are entered upon the battle-list for the same number as the hyænas, but these majestic brutes suffer a certain wrong in being placed at all upon the catalogue of man's enemies. Herbivorous, placid, pacific, the herds of wild elephants which still roam the thick forests of the Anamullees, the Assam hills, and the Terai, live now protected by law, and are from time to time driven by official hunters into *keddahs*, to be captured and trained for government service. In such work, occasionally of necessity dangerous, or by the unexpected onset of a " rogue " elephant in close jungle, or by the sudden bad temper of a tame elephant in time of " must," these three dozen lives must have been lost.

In the wild and tame state alike elephants are
subject to moods of fierce gloom and savage morose-
ness, during which they need to be chained up, if
domesticated ; and if free, they will separate themselves from the herd and retire to some forest
sanctuary, where it is death to disturb their massive
melancholy.

Sometimes, again, a herd will break at night-
time into a little village of the woods, and for
love of sheer mischief crash and smash through
everything, ruining huts, gardens, and fences, and
trampling into a jelly one or two miserable
villagers.

This tale of thirty-three casualties is made up in
some such ways ; but when one sees the thousands
of trained elephants employed everywhere in India,
and knows that almost all the wild ones will come,
sooner or later, under the iron hook of the mahout,
it is hardly just to reckon this sagacious beast
among those which war against mankind.   It is
rather like ranking accidents on railways with the
deplorable and guilty returns of murders and man-
slaughters.

Next on the roll of woodland warfare comes the
tiger, who must, indeed, be called and considered
man's declared enemy.   Between that royal tyrant of
the jungle, wearing his splendid and terrible robe
of black and gold, and the feeble, intellectual biped
in thin muslin, whose existence he can terminate
with one blow of his mighty paw, there is no peace,
and can never be.   So savage, so irreconcilable, so

bloodthirsty, so strong is he, that one exclaims with Blake :

"Tiger! tiger! burning bright,

.   .   .   .   .   .

Did He, who made thee, make the lamb ?"

Cruelty and cunning are personified and embodied in that lithe and powerful form of deadly grace and vigour ; and a royal tiger in his native thickets is one of the most glorious and dreadful sights in nature.

If I were a painter I would try to put into colours a sight I once saw in the Indian forest—from a safe position, of course—where a tigress lay at ease in an open patch of reeds, while her two cubs tore to pieces a big peacock which their grim mother had killed, playing wantonly with the broken jewellery and ruined loveliness of their prey. The shining coats of that wild family group, the yellow reeds with strong bars of shadow imitating and reproducing the gold and stripes of the tiger's regal dress, the scattered and shattered purples and blues of the beautiful bird, made up a picture of such wonderful tints and such horrible charm and awful grace, that I have never forgotten its effects.

To understand the eight hundred and sixteen deaths registered against tigers, it must be known that there are three classes of the grand beast in India. There is what may be styled the respectable and orderly tiger, who gets his living in an orthodox manner, feeding upon deer, wild pig, small animals, and occasionally upon chance carrion, if better food be lacking. These are generally the strongest and best-looking animals.

Ranging a district well-stocked with sambur, buck, ravine-deer, the spotted axis and boar, they exercise all the slyness and stupendous force and speed which they possess to surprise and seize their prey; and get lusty and sleek. They help rather than injure the agricultural people, by keeping down the antelope and other cervine plunderers, who break into and damage the crops, as well as the wild pigs, who do so much harm rooting and grubbing. They carefully shun man and his abodes, lying very close in their sylvan dens by day, and coming forth into desolate regions at night, like the nocturnal cats that they really are.

Like cats, too, they have delicate feet, and hate to be obliged to tread the ground, baked hard and burning by the summer sun; so that in the hot weather sportsmen will never get even these strong brutes to travel far away from shade and water.

The next description of tiger is the cattle-lifter. He and his ill-tempered but splendid wife and cubs are beasts which have discovered how much easier it is to strike down a cow from the villager's grazing herd than to stalk and seize the quick-bounding antelope, or tough and pugnacious boar. Where such tigers range there is never any safety for the kine.

The Hindoo lad—clad in nothing but his loin-cloth and turban—has taken out the cattle to some open pasture skirted with a forest of bamboo-patches, or intersected by a nullah lined with long grass and korinda bushes. The hot day has gone by quickly; the cows are finishing their evening bite; they spread out less timidly than in the morning along the edge of the thicket, or where the grass tastes sweetest by the rim of the water-course. The boy is completing the basket of twigs which he was weaving, and thinking that the sun is low enough for the drive homeward.

Suddenly, from some unsuspected bush or clump to leeward, there is a flash as of yellow lightning, a short, ferocious roar, and the tiger, who has been watching his prey for hours, springs upon the neck of the nearest cow, drags it backward with such prodigious strength as ofttimes to break the vertebræ, or else with a tremendous blow of his fore-limb—all sinew and muscle—tears open the arteries of the throat and grips the windpipe between his dagger-like fangs.

The herd and the herdsman fly; the robber-beast, when his victim is dead, drags it a little way inside the jungle, and sucks some of the warm blood, leaving the carcass then for a more leisurely meal, which he and his striped household will make, if all is quiet, when the night has fallen.

Here is where the tigers wage very successful warfare indeed upon man. It will seem incredible, indeed, to safe and careless ranchmen in the Western States to hear of the devastation caused in India by cattle-lifting tigers. Leopards, hyænas, and wolves kill a good many among the herds, especially calves; but the tigers are the arch

raiders, and in the past year, 1891, they slaughtered
in the mode described the larger part of sixty-four
thousand five hundred cattle. In the year 1877, to
which reference for comparison of different periods
has been made, the total number of cattle killed by
wild beasts was fifty-three thousand one hundred
and ninety-seven.

In the long conflict waged on man by the jungle
kingdoms, this is some of the booty carried off by
the enemy.

The third class of tiger is the dreaded man-eater,
to whom must be assigned most of the recorded
human deaths. Sometimes this destructive species
develops out of the cattle-lifter. Watching the
grazing cattle, and being, perhaps, balked of his
prey by the courage of the herd-boy, who, particularly with buffaloes to help him, will now and then
shout at the tiger and frighten him, the brute has
learned how simple a thing it is to crush the naked,
soft, brown body of this youthful lord of creation.

After that it learns to prefer the flesh of man, and
will invade the village at night to pick up some
hapless sleeper lying on his "charpoy" for coolness
outside the hut; or will take up a station on the
country road where the postman passes with his
letter-bag and jingling staff, or the peasant slowly
drives along his bullock-cart.

There have been times and places when and
where a pair of these strong tigers, with cubs to
feed, have driven all the people out of a village, to
devour at leisure the old and sick in it; or have

taken possession of a temple, after eating up the priest.

But the professional man-eater is usually an old and worn-out tiger, whose limbs are no longer equal to the swift rush which must be made upon the black buck, or bara-singh; whose teeth cannot easily grip and tear the tough hide of the wild boar; whose claws are worn down, and his once brilliantly painted coat turned dull and mangy. Yet he has the old, fierce appetite, which cannot be stayed upon frogs and lizards, rats and young monkeys, or such meat as the jackals and hyænas leave.

Some evil afternoon, blinking in the sunlight near the well, famished and sick, he sees the slender, graceful Hindoo girl come for water with the brass lota balanced on her head. The wind brings the scent of her warm flesh; the wicked brute crouches flatter and flatter in the long grass. The early, instinctive dread and reverence of mankind are strong upon the spirit of that striped old assassin, but the craving for food is stronger. As she stoops to lower the rope there is a hoarse cry, between a cough and growl; she knows herself lost before the heavy pad with the blunt claws falls upon her soft neck; she is dead in the very moment of her agonised cry, " O Shiva! Shiva!"

The cruel brute drags her gentle body into the bushes, and his feast upon it converts him into a man-eater. Henceforward he will be the pest of the district, waylaying women and children and solitary men; until the shikarry of the region, or a passing

P

Englishman, puts a bullet into his brain or heart, and sets the people free of their scourge.

Leopards are down on the list of destructiveness for three hundred human lives, and bears for ninety-four. The Indian leopard is as dangerous, if cornered or suddenly come upon, as it is beautiful in its shape and markings ; but will scarcely ever venture to attack a man, except in self defence. It will run great risks to secure a kid or a dog, and it will pounce upon children, so that probably most of the murders put to its account in this red schedule are of native boys and girls who have strayed near some tree on a limb of which the big spotted cat was watching.

It kills also herdsmen protecting their flocks, and women walking alone through the jungle, but wages no aggressive war, like the tiger, upon man. Sometimes it will let him alone in a curiously respectful way.

My eldest son, the author of "Phra, the Phœnician," while coffee-planting in the Wynaad Hills, was cutting some initials on a tree trunk in the forest. A strange shadow, swinging back and forth, intercepted his light ; and looking up to find the cause he saw a large panther lying on the branch over his head, whose long tail, slowly and sullenly oscillating, cast the shadow which had interrupted his task. My son had only a white umbrella as a weapon, and quietly retreated, keeping his eyes fixed on the yellow orbs of the beast, which snarled and spat like a cat, but suffered him to depart in peace.

As for the "butchers' bill" set down to the bears, that must have been incurred almost wholly in hunting them. An Indian bear, entirely frugivorous, asks nothing except to be let alone, albeit in defence of cubs, or when wounded, it becomes a very dangerous enemy. In the year under notice nearly thirteen hundred of these animals were killed, against ninety-four human lives ; but for the nearly fifteen hundred tigers shot or trapped, eight hundred and sixteen men, women, and children were slain by the great striped cat, so that the outcome of the combat was not very unequal.

Wolves and hyænas are credited with eight hundred and forty-five and thirty-three slaughters, respectively. The first item appears large—it would be found to consist almost wholly of native children, caught up and carried away. The Indian wolf is very dangerous in this respect, prowling about villages and wells, and pouncing, if occasion offers, on the unprotected baby or the tiny, toddling, naked child playing in the dust.

It is a gaunt, grey, hungry-looking brute, smaller than the European variety, and would never have the courage to attack a man.

I retain a singular recollection from my hunting days in India, of an occasion when two wolves joined in the chase with me, and made themselves very serviceable. I had wounded a black buck, and was following it on horseback, when the two wolves took up the pursuit, and for three or four miles we went along in this way, the wolves chasing the antelope for me like hounds, and eventually pulling it down. Then they retired snarling as I rode up, and sat at a distance on their haunches ; nor did I think it fair to empty my rifle at them, since they had been so useful.

The deaths set down to hyænas are naturally few, and these again would consist of cases of sick people and little children. The Indian hyæna is a mean, foul prowler after dead meat and carrion, of no courage, and heavy in movement ; savage, and commonly styled "untamable." But this last epithet is inaccurate.

When in India, during 1859, I shot a she hyæna, and took her two new-born cubs home to rear. They grew up famously, and became as docile as puppies, so that when half or three parts grown I could take them out safely for a walk, unchained. Both came to a melancholy and violent end, having developed with their molar teeth a taste for native babies. But my jungle pets proved that no animal is really "untamable," if it be treated with constant and consistent kindness.

Under the head of " other animals " we find thirteen hundred and twenty-three deaths entered for the year which I am noticing. This would appear large if one did not remember the immense population of India, her vast regions, and the long catalogue of wild creatures which are embraced under this category.

The rhinoceros, the bison, the jungle buffalo, the crocodile and the alligator, lynxes and cheetahs,

Guzerat lions and wild boars, have contributed to the heavy score which runs up the total of human lives destroyed to the serious amount already stated. To this we must add the destruction of useful and valuable cattle, in order to perceive what India loses in one year by the jungle kingdoms.

I will close this section with a *per contra* statement of the dangerous animals destroyed in India during 1878. The returns differ a little each twelve months, but not in a marked degree. There are in ordinary seasons about sixty thousand licensed native hunters, carrying firearms. These, with the sport-loving Englishmen and the wild people— Bheels, Todas, Mhars, and the like—who kill many *feræ naturæ* with arrows, spears, and traps—furnish the following list of reprisals :

The number of tigers destroyed in British India during 1878 was 1496 ; of leopards, 3237 ; of bears, 1283 ; of wolves, 5067 ; of hyænas, 1202 ; and 1 elephant ; of other animals, 10,501. Total animals, 22,487. Snakes, 117,928.

PART III

SNAKES

IT has been noticed already that the proportion of deaths caused by all the other denizens of the jungle put together is small compared with the deadly mischief done by venomous serpents. Last year in India, while twenty-four hundred and sixty natives lost their lives by wild beasts, the men, women, and children of the land killed by snakes reached the prodigious total of twenty-one thousand one hundred and forty-two. And if we glance back to the year selected for comparison, 1878, it will be seen that the casualties by snake-bite were nearly seventeen thousand.

Rewards are regularly given by the Indian Government for the heads of poisonous snakes when brought in; and reference to the statistics will show that in this way, during the year recalled, there was paid about one hundred thousand rupees. In 1890 the native "shikarries" got payment for fourteen thousand six hundred and four wild beasts destroyed, and for more than half a million snakes, the upshot of all which is to show that this jungle war goes on from year to year, with very little real victory on one side or the other; the wild side, if anything, having rather the best of it.

Even with that enormous population of British India of which I have spoken, it is a terrible return of deaths by venomous serpents only—more than twenty-one thousand! What would be thought in the United States if, taking the same ratio, more than four thousand citizens annually perished in the same fashion by rattle-snakes, copperheads, moccasins, and the like?

You would try to exterminate the plague, and in comparatively open country like the States this might be effected; but India is full of jungle, waste, and thorny thickets, a paradise and nursery for reptiles in almost every district. Moreover, there are difficulties of custom and religion to encounter.

The ancient worship of the Nag, the serpent, is still a very strong tradition in many parts of the peninsula. Millions of Hindoos would rather kill a relative than a snake; and I have known villagers to raise up, and reverently to bury or burn, the body of a cobra-de-capello found dead, as if it were one of themselves.

The objection to take away life, too, among the chief castes of the Hindoos, applies to poisonous reptiles as much as to the gentlest of domesticated creatures; so that you may see a cobra regularly domiciled in an Indian hut, inhabiting either the roof or the foundation, quite undisturbed by the family. In such cases it is remarkable how familiar and harmless the gruesome lodger becomes; he appears and disappears, doing no injury except to the rats;

and the people will set a daily bowl of milk for him, and call him "Uncle."

All the same, some dark night, if he is gliding over the floor when one of the bare-footed inmates is about, and the hapless boy or girl or man or woman should tread upon him, the terrible fangs snap and prick, and that Hindoo will be a corpse within an hour or two. The bite of a fresh cobra is certain death.

A sepoy soldier of my acquaintance put his hand into a hole of the thatch over his hut door to take out the key. A cobra had hidden up there during the poor fellow's absence, and bit his hand. In an hour and forty minutes I saw that strong man lie cold and pallid, the mark upon his hand no bigger than a pin-point might have made!

The cobra-de-capello—the hooded snake—is the most common of poisonous serpents in India, and causes most of these deaths. It haunts gardens, compounds, and the neighbourhood of houses, being found even in the suburbs of great cities like Bombay and Calcutta. Water and rats are its probable attractions, both of which it finds near human abodes; and you must expect, if you live in India, to see more than once a cobra coiled up in your bath-room, or perhaps have even to shake one out of your boot.

Everybody there goes through some sort of adventure with snakes before he has sojourned long; but being well shod, as Europeans always are, they seldom or never get bitten. It is the bare-footed, bare-legged native who suffers, unintentionally treading upon the coiled-up serpent, or laying hold of a branch or tuft of grass where one is concealed.

The cobra, however, terrible as he knows himself to be, never really wants to attack. He will evade light and fighting if he can ; it costs him weakness and perhaps pain to expel the poison, and when not alarmed or angry, he will put up his hood and pretend to strike a dozen times at the serpent-charmer's hand without ever elevating his poison-fang.

Many of these jugglers and " samp-wallahs," who carry cobras about, know this, and play with those which have fangs and poison just as carelessly as with fangless snakes. I have satisfied myself over and over again as to that fact, having seen a cobra from a basket kill a goat with one stroke, after having delivered many pretended attacks upon the back of his master's hand.

Any one who desires to know about the venomous reptiles of India will find full information in the " Thanatophidia " of Sir J. Fayrer. There are worse snakes than even the cobra-de-capello haunting the jungle. One of them is called by the western Hindoos " foorsa," and is of the deadliest nature. Its scientific name is *Echis carinata*, because it has along its sides rows of peculiar ridged scales, which grate when they are rubbed together, producing a low, evil, ominous sound, something between a rattle and a hiss. It is the whisper of death for him who fails to heed it !

One passing nip from those needle-like fangs of the " foorsa " is enough ! The victim succumbs after sharp agony, passing to stupor, during which, it is said, the serum of the blood oozes out from the eyelids, the finger-nails, and any old wound. I have never seen that, but I remember well the excited ejaculation of my Mahratta attendant one day when, hunting antelope in the plains, I passed close by a small snake coiled in the sun. He saw it, and cried out, "*Khurbardar, saheb! Us ka chaya marenga!*" (Take care, sir! The shadow of that snake can kill you!)

Stooping down on one occasion to gather, what I thought, a beautifully-shaped and marked little stick lying in the hill-path, it suddenly curled and wriggled away out of my reach. It was a foorsa, and had I touched its tail, the chances are I should not have lived to take any lunch that day.

Snakes are far more intellectual and gifted than those know who have never lived with and studied them. They have strong affections, and the male serpent, who may generally be known by his smaller size and brighter colours from the female, will lie for hours, nay for days, by the side of his dead wife if nobody disturbs his mourning.

They learn in captivity to distinguish persons, and are capable of real attachments, especially toward some individuals, who appear to possess a strange and subtle affinity for them, like Elsie Venner's. They must possess, as Darwin argues, some sense of beauty, otherwise how were developed those wonderful and lovely colours which we see upon certain serpents, notably the coral snakes of South America,

which are a rich red, with black and yellow trans-
verse bands ; and the bright green and bronze of the
Indian *tragops dispar?*

In the eternal conflict between these subtle
enemies and man, he has some odd allies.   Pigs,
wild and tame, kill snakes of all kinds; so do
pea-fowl, which are kept in gardens for this purpose
all over Rajpootana.   And there is a specially constructed little creature, the mungoose, which rambles
over nearly every region of Hindostan, and hates
snakes as cordially as if he knew all about the
garden of Eden and the mischief done to the whole
world there.   This is an ichneumon, with bristly fur
of pepper and salt colour—*Herpestes griseus* is his
scientific name, if I remember ; and whenever the
little animal comes across a snake, he leaves it dead
if he possibly can.

The natives pretend that, when bitten, the
mungoose knows where to find a certain grass
which is an antidote to the poison, but this is a
fable.   He trusts to his extreme agility in assailing
a cobra, and perhaps also to the hard and bristly
coat which he wears, through which it would be
difficult for the snake to drive his fang.

Such, then, is a cursory statement of this long-
continued and not yet concluded conflict which
in many countries, and most notably, perhaps, of
all in India, is waged year after year with changeful
fortunes.

XIII

A FISHERMAN'S WIFE

A FISHERMAN'S WIFE

It was a curious old golden signet which she was wearing, as a kind of keeper to her wedding-ring—my fisherman's wife—sitting at the window of her cottage, which looked over the grey and green waters of the German Ocean. If I had not asked how she came by it, I should never have known a great many new points about those two grand industries of our seas—long-lining and beam-trawling; for the question led to talk about the ways and fortunes of fisher folk, and to one or two very interesting cruises in the smack, on board of which the husband of my pleasant landlady sailed as mate. His port was a well-known naval and maritime station on the eastern coast, where two inland rivers flow forth together into a common estuary, forming a commodious harbour, next to Grimsby, one of the greatest places for landing cod along our shores. Her fresh young face was tanned like a red barge-sail by the east wind, and alight with health; and her well-made, though not unsoiled, fingers, were twinkling among the hooks—she was helping the business of her "man" by laying the "snoods" or loops for a "string" while the little boy at her knee was getting whelks out of the shell

for bait. But, perhaps, it ought to be explained
what "long-lining" is, and, should the description
of the splendid fishing which it sometimes furnishes
make shore-keeping anglers jealous, let them remember what the North Sea is often like in winter.

For it must be winter when you catch the cod
upon what is variously styled round the British
shores, the long-line, spiller, spilliard, bulter, or
trot. The season, at least the best season, runs
from November to March and April, and thus for
the most part the lines are now being coiled away
at the fishing port I speak of, and in others besides.
Anybody can follow this business with fair success
who has a stout craft, a good crew, and a full knowledge of the tides and sea-grounds, as well as an
acquaintance with the habits and swimming-times
of the fish, particularly cod. To these must be
added a hardy indifference to the dangers and furies
of the winter sea ; but the cost of outfit or of repara-
tion is nothing like as heavy as that of trawling, so
that one need not be a wealthy owner, or a company,
to go " long-lining."

A first-class " string," or set, may consist of fifteen
dozen lines, each forty fathoms long, or 240 feet,
so that the entire string may measure as much as
eight miles in length. Fancy preparing, coiling,
and baiting such a line, compared with the Thames
angler's tiny thread of gut or horsehair ! On each
of these 180 portions are suspended by short lines
or " snoods " twenty-six hooks, which make a total
of more than 4500. It takes so long to get so many

NORTH SEA TRAWLERS.

P. 240.

hooks baited that some of the work is ofttimes done, as in the case mentioned, by the women and boys at home, and the rest is finished while the boat is being sailed out to the fishing waters. Mussel makes possibly the most attractive bait, and is the easiest to procure, but it will not stay upon the hooks like the tough whelks, which are, therefore, taken for this purpose in great quantities by means of hoop nets. The prepared lines are very carefully coiled away, and the armed hooks laid regularly in trays, for it would be very bad if they fouled when the " string" was being paid out at sea. You must have daylight for the work, both in veering the long line and hauling it in, so that the usual custom is to "shoot" about daybreak, in order to keep enough of the brief winter sunshine to take off your captures. The tide and wind serving, and the "string" being ready, the smack is put under easy canvas, with the breeze on her beam, so as to be able to keep a straight course ; and as she goes quietly but merrily along, tray after tray of the lines is reeled away overboard, until three or four miles of string—perhaps more—lies along the waves. Every now and then a little anchor and cord is dropped over to hold the string steady, and each mile of it with the two extremities are marked by buoys carrying a staff on which flutters a flag. It is best to "shoot" at half tide, and so to let the hooks take all the chance there is until flood, when the hauling on board commences. Ah ! then, sometimes, truly amazing is the sport which these hard-working smacksmen obtain—interesting even to them, to the

Q

land-fisherman exciting beyond all his river-bank
experiences. The foresail is lowered ; the smack
comes to the wind, and makes short boards back
again, along the miles of submerged " string," hauling it in "hand over hand" as the little ship beats
to windward. There will be a length or two with
nothing but dangling hooks—which must all be
carefully laid away as the line comes in—then a
codling or two and many untouched baits ; then
stripped hooks again, then, perhaps, a big fish ; and
afterwards, possibly, a whole file of the big green
and grey cod, fighting like small whales, as the
stress on the line lifts them into the foam of the
sea, with great, astonished goggle eyes and shiny
tails threshing among the snoods. It wants a quick
eye and a strong grip to unhook the great fellows
when they thus come in thickly together, and a
smart hand is needed to pass them adroitly down
into the well of the ship. But before putting them
there a sharp "pricker" must be run into the air-
bladders of the poor finny captives, for their sounds
become inflated by their struggles upon the hook,
and they would otherwise flounder helplessly upon
the top of the water. Sometimes the dog-fishes,
which are the chief enemies and rivals of the fisher-
folk, find out the take, seeing or hearing the great
cod flopping upon the snoods ; and then too often
there will only be left the head and bones of a fine
twelve or twenty pound fish upon the hook. Times
have been, when the water was clear and the dog-
fish plentiful and on the rampage, that almost every

cod, ling, tusk, and haddock has been eaten away
from the lines in this piratical manner. The fish
which have died, or are likely soon to succumb, if
not otherwise unfit for the market, will be flung into
the ice-hold. But if the shoot has proved lucky,
and the cod and haddock come in well, and pretty
numerously—say seven, eight, or ten score of size-
able ones—it is fishing with a real meaning! fishing lordly, magnificent, and stirring! to watch the
" string" tauten like a harp cord with the weight
of each big, shining, suspended prisoner, glittering
under the waves like a bar of silver before he comes
" golumphing" out of the crest of the roller, spatter-
ing it into sea-cream with the last desperate flap of
his tail.

Such is "long-lining," and thus is the major portion of the cod-fish captured which come to London
tables, to figure there as " cod's head and shoulders,"
or " fried cutlets." The fisherman's wife knew,
what is not by any means of universal knowledge,
that you can manufacture out of cod's head a soup
almost, if not quite, as good as the best calipash.
Chefs and connoisseurs are beginning to find this out,
and to place it on fashionable menus as " Yorkshire
turtle." After the live cod are brought into port,
they are generally stored in large wooden chests,
made with open sides, and holes in the top and
bottom, to let the water flow in and out. This keeps
the fish in good condition, sometimes for as long as
a fortnight. It is rather a disturbing scene for one of
pitiful nature to observe what happens when a chest

of fish, holding perhaps fifty or sixty, is wanted for market. It is hauled up alongside a vessel till the water drains away; and then a fisherman goes in among the struggling creatures, throwing them out one by one upon the deck. Another man seizes the fish behind the gills with his left hand, and with the right deals it a sharp and heavy blow with a short oak stick on the nose, killing it directly, after which the whole lot passes as "live cod" into the truck for Billingsgate.

The gold ring which the fisherman's wife wore upon her marriage finger had upon it a St. Andrew's Cross and a foreign inscription—"So DNYA NAH DEN'N "— which, I think, is Russian for *From one day to another*. Nothing would induce her to part with it, nor was this to be wondered at when you heard the odd story of how she came by it. It was in the days of her early married life, and things were not going very well with the honest mariner—her husband— who had just been appointed mate of a smack. But their luck turned from a single fortnight of fine weather in the winter of 1864, when the fish were particularly plentiful, and news had come in from the " long-line " grounds causing every skipper to want to put immediately to sea. The *Good Intent* was unluckily short-handed, even after every man and boy that could be got at had been mustered; and, consequently, brought up from her girlhood to the water, my landlady, Mrs. Bates, forthwith volunteered to sail with her husband to tie the " snoods " and help arm the hooks. On the second day out they had a wonderful stroke of luck, with only three miles of long-line down. Almost every hook for half the length had upon it some sort of fish, and besides eleven score of cod, the boat came back full of many extra sorts, and made a splendid market. The skipper picked out a fine fish as a present to the brave petticoated hand that had done the ship and the voyage such good service; and, strange to say, in cleaning that cod she found inside it something like the remains of a finger wearing an outlandish-looking gold ring. It may very likely have been that the voracious fish had nibbled it away from the floating body of some poor Muscovite mariner; but there it was, she said, come to her as a sea-present in this unheard-of manner on the day of the best luck and the best ship's wages they had ever taken. And so she wore, and always meant to wear, that Russian ring, with its significant inscription, " From One Day to Another," which does not by any means fit in badly with the fisherman's life and the vicissitudes that he and his must encounter in reaping the harvest of the sea.

XIV

AN ENGINE OF FATE

XIV

AN ENGINE OF FATE

It is written in the Koran that among the things known only to Allah are the place, the time, and the way in which every one will die. Nor is there any decree more benignant in all the laws of human life than that this useful and merciful veil should be for ever suspended between our weak eyes and the stern outlines of the inevitable. But an incident occurred at the time of my Indian service, wherein, if it was not exactly known that any particular person was fated, it was known only too well and bitterly that cruel death was impending over many persons absolutely unconscious of their peril. I am willing all the more to recall the melancholy event in order that honour may be done to the memory of a most eminent and remarkable man, Mr. Edward Howard, the Director of Public Instruction in the Presidency of Bombay under the government of Lord Elphinstone, and immediate Chief of the Educational Department, he being therefore my official superior and directing genius of the Bombay University and of the Deccan College, of which I was then president. Few abler public men than my accomplished friend had ever served the Indian

Government in that important department. I had
the honour to assist him in sweeping away the old
perfunctory and absurd system of half-and-half education, and in substituting for it in the Indian colleges
the better and sincerer methods of Western teaching.
Bright, erudite, and resolute of will, he animated all
our work during the years of the Mutiny, and afterwards received, deservedly, the larger portion of the
praise which was bestowed upon our labours by the
Governor in Council. Alas! then, in the moment
of his success and high appreciation, an evil destiny
condemned him to die suddenly, by the most trivial
oversight, and in a manner tragic enough to deserve
commemoration.

In bygone travelling from Bombay to Poona we
used to ascend and descend the Ghâts, the mountain-
range dividing the Concan from the Deccan, either on
foot or by *gharries*, while the coolie women toiled up
and down the steep road, carrying boxes and port-
manteaux on their shapely heads. But during my
time that railway line was built which now carries
the traveller by daring gradients up the black slopes
of those beautiful hills, twisting and turning back-
wards and forwards among the groves of bamboo,
teak, and banyan. At the top of the highlands was
a great rest-station, near Khandala, where the
ponderous engines were cleaned and recoaled for
the inland journey to Poona or through Kampoolee
to the coast. Very picturesque are the Indian
railways, with the names of the stations painted in
three different characters ; the long hedges of aloe,

prickly pear, and milk-bush ; the green parrots and
long-tailed shrikes perching on the telegraph wires ;
the villages and village people seen upon the way,
and the chattering crowd of passengers taken up
and put down at every station.   It was an astonishing
social phenomenon to note how quickly and gladly
the Hindoos took to the "fire-carriage."   Even the
Brahman priests decided—fortunately for the companies and the government, which had guaranteed
interest—that pilgrimages might be performed by
means of third and fourth class carriages, so that the
population joyfully used the line, and many natives
sought employment upon it, quickly acquiring the
knowledge and habits of Western working men.

Now, to understand the hard fate of my respected
chief, something ought to be known about the ways
of railway people with their engines.   Little do
most folk think, when they dismount from a train
and go about their business, what a deal of labour
has to be gone through "to groom and to stable"
that iron steed which has brought them so swiftly
and safely.   The engine exteriorly appears little
affected by the journey; but when the driver has
finished his trip he must take her to the coaling-
stage, and will not leave her there, if a good man,
without thoroughly inspecting all her machinery.   He
enters her in the repair book, and if anything has
to be done, such as washing out the boiler, he must
write that down.   Next, the washing-out men must
blow the steam off, and let all the water out from
the iron stomach of the " Fire Horse," and then she

ought to stand for six hours to cool, before new coal
and coke are put upon the tender and fresh water
into the boiler.   Also the "bar-boy" must creep
through the fire-hole door with torch-lamp and
scraper, to put the fire-bars in their proper places,
and to clear the fire-box and the arch of "clinkers,"
and ashes.   Then the "cleaner," with cotton waste,
oil, and tallow, must rough-wipe the "motion,"
clean the wheels and the bottom of the boiler as
well as the fire-box, both back and front, the chimney
smoke-box and door; and afterwards the framing.
Lastly, the bright work must be burnished with
bath-brick and water, and rubbed with a dry cloth
till the brass is like gold and the copper like sunshine.   It takes eight to ten hours to clean and
"fettle" an engine properly, and then the "turner"
examines, coals, and puts "her" away, each engine
standing in its stall, like a harnessed horse, ready
for the driver when he comes again to take charge
of the monster.   At that time the engine will
be in steam for him, the fire having been lighted
two hours before his arrival; and these men get
to know their engines and the ways of them better
than a carman knows his cart-horse, or a skipper
his smack.   Engines differ in their behaviour quite
as much as horses or ships, and the custom was,
and to a great extent is still, to entrust an Indian
locomotive only to the white man's hands.   It needs,
indeed, a courage as iron as the metallic Levia-
than itself—although that courage becomes at last
mechanical—to grapple with the fierce strength and

DOWN THE GHÂTS. *P.* 252.

fiery moods of these creations of man's ingenuity. But subordinate posts, of course, are and were filled by natives, especially in the cleaning-sheds; and a slight oversight on the part of a Mahratta "bar-boy" cost the lives of my old chief and of many others beside.

He was to travel down by the night express from Poona on important official business, and had with him, indeed, our last reports on the Condition of Education in the Deccan. Full of life, full of honour, full of high and useful plans for the intellectual good of the country, which was then rapidly recovering from the tumult of the Great Mutiny, he took his seat in the comfortable first-class carriage, protected by a double roof against the heat of the sun in the daytime, and luxuriously fitted for sleeping accommodation by night. To provide something less business-like than the Reports, he had taken with him a French novel and the last number of *The Quarterly Review*. But perhaps—who knows—he had some presentiment that this was to be his last journey. We had been conversing not very long before about Indian astrology, which is, of course, entirely believed in by the people of Hindostan, and indeed reduced to an exact science. In my own college there were no such things as certificates of birth. Every student brought with him upon admission a *janma patra*, or "natal paper," in which was represented the aspect of the stars when he commenced existence, with various calculations of "houses," "planets," "ascensions," and "trines,"

displaying the days which would be lucky and
unlucky for him, and when it would be well to
commence studies, to marry, to travel, and to buy
or sell. Idle as it appears to a Western mind, the
respect paid to these papers of the "Joshi" is very deep
in India, and over and over again astonishing instances
have occurred of correct predictions and timely warn-
ings resulting from them. Edward Howard had
been going into the subject a little, and had caused
his own horoscope to be drawn, not altogether to
his satisfaction, as he laughingly said, since the old
" Joshi" had told him to be careful about a certain
train and locality, with other particulars which escape
my memory. Truly a " glassy essence " is human life,
when to such a man, on such important business,
in possession of such a plenitude of physical and
intellectual power, the casual mistake of a careless
native could be the touch of the finger of *Yama*,
God of Death.

What happened was this. A certain heavy engine
had been brought into the rest-station on the top of
the Ghâts, where she had been cleaned, and coaled,
and oiled, and put into steam, to go on the up-line
to Poona. One of the last things to do is to see
that the regulator works in good order, without any
indications of leaking, for, if there be, the engine will
show it when at rest, with the cylinder-cocks open.
The hapless native who gave the last polishing touch
on the foot-plate must have set the regulator open,
after the boiler had been filled up. The tender-
brake had been taken off in order to move her to the

coal stage, and not put on again ; and the locomotive
was in, instead of out of, gear. So, charged to be the
instrument of Fate, that night she moved quietly out
by herself from the shed, and took the open points
on to the main line. The pointsman saw an engine
go slowly by his box, and supposed it was being trotted
out for a run to fill the boiler, as is often done when
the line is clear. He was wondering why she did
not return, when the driver, coming for his engine,
found her gone. The full horror of the situation
swiftly broke upon their minds. Here was a ponderous locomotive, with fires newly lighted, boiler
full, furnace in quick draught, and regulator open,
going away faster and faster upon a down grade
towards the express train coming up on the same
metals westward. It was inevitable that she would
tear along, gathering fresh speed at every mile, until
she dashed into the utterly unwarned engine of the
passenger train from Poona. Telegraphic communi-
cation was not perfect in those days, but there
were means of conveying signals, and the affrighted
officials made use of them to send a message east-
ward to an intermediate station in some such words
as these : "Loose engine running away, main line,
no driver; throw her off the line if possible with
sleepers, trucks, or anything." And the answer came
back : "Too late. Engine just passed, fifty miles an
hour. Must run into the express." And there, in the
Indian night, the people at Lanowlie waited in horror
and dismay, knowing as plainly as if they stood at the
spot how the fugitive engine was thundering and flar-

ing down the long incline, racing under the unseen
fingers of Fate as no human driver would have dared
to send her along; while impelled by this same
resistless hand of Destiny the crowded Indian train,
loaded with precious and innocent lives, and among
them that of my unfortunate chief, was swiftly labour-
ing onwards to meet the runaway. No more awful
interval of terror could well be imagined than thus
to know how infallibly the catastrophe was preparing,
and how utterly helpless on this side and on that
everybody was to make the slightest effort to avert
the deadly crash.

It came at the point that had been calculated.
Flying round a curve, the driver of the express
suddenly saw in front of him the furious run-away
engine, and almost before he could touch the brakes
—which were afterwards found reversed—and shut
off his steam, the mad truant smashed into the train,
killing its driver—who did not leap, like the fire-
man—shattering both locomotives into a chaos of
ruin, and hurling off the line carriage after carriage
of the Poona train in a frightful confusion of twisted
metal-work, splintered wood, and bleeding men and
women. Under the fragments of the first-class coach
my hapless friend was found, his head crushed almost
out of recognition, and *The Quarterly Review* in his
hand, half severed by the flange of a wheel. They
talk still along that line of the fatal night when
the God of Death rode the runaway engine, and
killed so many people with the " fire horse " of
the " Feringhee."

XV

IN THE STONE TRADE

K

XV

IN THE STONE TRADE

A HUNDRED times over, when I was living in Japan, I used to wish that Mr. Ruskin could have sojourned in that country. If there be any passage in his works touching upon the arts and customs of the gifted and industrious people of the Empire of the Rising Sun it has escaped my memory. I do not know what his judgment has been or would be upon the wonderful impressionist sketches of its painters; the delicate, faultless *netsukes* of its ivory carvers; and the fanciful patterns of its dyers and weavers. But certainly nobody would ever have sympathised more with some of the common popular tastes of that nation. For example, there is no race on the globe that has such a liking for stones. By stones, I mean nothing dressed, sculptured, or squared by architect or mason, but the rough, rugged fragments of cliff and mountain, in working out which to their outlines and inscriptions the elements have been the only craftsman. The captious may say, " How can you like mere stones?" and before talking of my friend the Japanese rock-dealer, I will let Mr. Ruskin answer such a question. Here is a passage from " Modern Painters " : " There are no

MINIATURE ROCK AND TREE.
Actual height of rock, 13 inches.

natural objects out of which more can be learned
than out of stones. They seem to have been created
especially to reward a patient observer. Nearly all
other objects in Nature can be seen, to some extent,
without patience, and are pleasant even in being
half seen. Trees, clouds, rivers are enjoyable, even
by the careless; but the stone under his foot has for
the careless person nothing in it but stumbling; no
pleasure is languidly to be had out of it, nor food,
nor good of any kind; nothing but symbolism of
the hard heart and the unfatherly gift. And yet,
do but give it some reverence and watchfulness, and
there is breadth of thought in it, more than in any
other lowly feature of all the landscape. For a
stone, when it is examined, will be found a mountain in miniature. The fineness of Nature's work
is so great that into a single block, a foot or two in
diameter, she can compress as many changes of form
and structure on a small scale as she needs for her
mountains on a large one; and, taking moss for
forests and grains of crystal for crags, the surface of
a stone, in by far the plurality of instances, is more
interesting than the surface of an ordinary hill, more
fantastic in shape, and incomparably richer in colour."

With the spirit of this passage every Japanese
would agree, though he would express his appreciation differently. There must be many among ourselves who have often admired the attractive effect of
crags or slabs of rock breaking up through the green
turf or heather on the side of a Welsh or Scotch hill.
Somebody has called it the "bones of the earth"

showing through the skin; but the effect is rather one of living beauty and rich, healthy contrast: the grey crag has so many colours upon it; the turf and flowery plants nestle round its base so closely, and the lights and shadows upon the little world which it represents have such various suggestions. That is what the Japanese also admire, rejoice in, and reproduce in their gardens. They have too fine a taste, too cultured a sense of Nature, to put there what we call "rockeries"—hideous agglomerations of slag or broken bricks, or specimens of ore impossibly approximated. What they take pleasure in is to imitate the way in which Nature herself breaks a carpet of mountain green with a boulder harmoniously slanted, providing on it all sorts of nooks and shelters for small creatures to live in and for the sunlight to play upon. Ten times better it will be if, instead of a naked stone, the fragment of mountain which they borrow for their little garden is not only natural in its roughness and colour, but covered still with those native growths of mosses and lichen which only the pure open air produces. And if you want to know how Nature can play jeweller with a piece of hillside, and why the Japanese will sit and look at it for hours amid the azaleas and irises of a small city garden, read once more what Mr. Ruskin says about these mosses and weather-stains: "They will not conceal the form of the rock, but will gather over it in little brown bosses, like small cushions of velvet made of mixed threads of dark ruby silk and gold, rounded over more subdued

films of white and grey, with lightly-crisped and
curled edges, like hoarfrost on fallen leaves, and
minute clusters of upright orange stalks with pointed
caps and fibres of deep green and gold, and faint
purple passing into black, all woven together, and
following with unimaginable fineness of gentle
growth the undulation of the stone they cherish,
until it is charged with colour, so that it can receive
no more, and, instead of looking rugged or cold or
stern, as anything that a rock is held to be at heart,
it seems to be clothed with a soft, dark leopard skin,
embroidered with arabesque of purple and silver."

This, again, is exactly what a Japanese householder
thinks and feels—albeit he cannot put it as elo-
quently as the author of " Modern Painters "—and
because he has such artistic imagination, every tiny
back garden in Tokyo contains among its floral and
artificial ornaments slabs of natural rock, judiciously
placed. Marvellous are the illusions produced by
them with the aid of those dwarf trees that the
Japanese gardener knows how to grow and train.
It is absolutely magical to see what lovely landscape
effects the *uyekeya* can obtain out of an ox-cartload
of big stones and a few of these stunted plants. He
will create for you, with his dwarf pines and micro-
scopic bamboos, upon a few square yards of soil, what
looks like leagues of wild or cultivated country, if,
like himself, you will "make believe" while you
smoke, and sip the fragrant *sake*. There shall be a
stream and water meadows and rice fields, perfect,
though each no bigger than a chess-board ; a moun-

tain tarn, with carp in it and gold fishes and tortoise,
shall appear; a flying bridge, a glittering waterfall,
and a range of Liliputian but lovely mountains.
Accordingly, rocks are an article in much demand,
and Tokyo, being an alluvial plain, without anything
of the sort at hand, numerous dealers exist in the city
whose business it is to bring in from the mountains
and to supply to their customers these indispensable

TOBAKO-BON, PIPES, AND SAKI BOTTLES.

adjuncts of Japanese horticulture.   Great round
stones from the bed of the river, and square or
oblong slabs, of moderate size, can be had cheap
enough.   But if you will go into something impos-
ing for dimensions, or remarkable in colour and
material, there are rocks in the *Ishiya's* yard that
will cost you from one to two hundred *yen*—say,
ten or twenty pounds.   Learned treatises exist

which teach how these rocks should be planted in
the gardens, and what plants should be disposed
near them ; how you should build the *ishi-bashi*,
or bridge of stone ; how should stand the *ishi-bâmi*
or tablet bearing an inscription ; where should be
placed the *ishi-doro*, or stone lamp-stand. Rocks
that have a hollow in them are much valued for
ame-no-ishi, or natural basins ; and stones with a
vein in them, *ishime*, may be of high value if the
marks lend themselves to any fancy, religious or
poetical, of the stone-cutter.

How I came to know anything about this trade
in Japan was by attending one day at the Court of
Criminal Justice in the Japanese capital. A batch
of prisoners—eleven in number—were to be brought
up for sentence, and the two presiding judges, with
the usual courtesy of their class to a foreigner, made
me sit between them upon the bench. Ten of the
prisoners were men guilty of various offences against
the peace of his Imperial Majesty the Mikado, one
or two among them, the most voluble in their pro-
testations of innocence, being ruffians who had
broken into houses at night, in the usual style of
Japanese burglars, with a naked sword, and arms
and legs greased to render themselves difficult of
capture. Six or seven of the group had already
come before the majesty of the law, and received
judgment, varying from six months to as many
years of imprisonment, when the only woman of this
" gaol-delivery " was summoned, and stood before us
with downcast face. I noticed with pleasure that

while the men's hands were all tied with a cord held by the policeman in attendance, the woman was not thus humiliated, although I should remark that even in the case of the male prisoners nothing could exceed the courtesy between them and the police officers. They bowed to each other on every possible occasion, and it was amusing, as the constables re-roped their villains, to have them say, "I beg the honourable pardon," and hear the criminal respond, "What is this, sir! that I should mention it?" The woman's delinquency was recited from a written paper lying before the judge. She had come from the country to Tokyo hoping to get employment there, because the people with whom she lived had been unkind to her. Finding no work, and becoming moneyless, she had at last reached such a point of hunger that she had ab-stracted some *mochi*, little cakes made of bean-flour, from a bakery, and was taken in the act of eating them in the neighbouring temple-court. The senior judge awarded her imprisonment for a month, with six months' police supervision to follow, and also a money-fine, not very heavy, but quite beyond any hope on her part to defray. She had been asked if she had any plea to offer, and her answer, given in a humble whisper, was, "My hunger had become great. I did not know what I was doing. What the honourable Personage says is all true. I have nothing to speak." The Bench nodded its head, and a policeman with blue spectacles and a steel sword made her a little bow and marched her off to gaol.

I had been touched by the demeanour of the woman, and asked permission from the judge to pay her fine. After consultation with his colleague, who said it was unusual, but in nowise unpermitted, leave was given me to discharge the small sum; and while Justice retired to its lunch, the prisoner was again sent for that I might speak with her. She returned, still in charge of the polite constable, expecting, no doubt, to get something worse than before, and was astonished to find the foreigner alone on the Bench. Then ensued this brief conversation:

"Have you ever stolen *mochis* before, O Haru San?"

"Never, Danna Sama; but I was so hungry."

"Shall you steal them again when you come out of prison?"

"Next time I would rather die; but I shall have no chance, for I cannot pay the fine, and so I must stay always in gaol."

"Have you any friends in Tokyo to speak to your character?"

"There is only one, my uncle, who works for a rock-dealer, at No. 101 Imaicho, Azabu."

"Would he pay your fine?"

"Ah! He is too poor! He is only a *ninsoku*, a 'leg-man,' who brings the stones in from the hills to make gardens."

"Well, then, your fine is paid; here is the receipt, and when you have done your month come and see my daughter, at this address, which I give you, and we will try to find something for you to do."

I have not written the real name of my *roya no-onna,* or "prison-woman," because she turned out splendidly, and is at this moment as good and worthy,

MINIATURE GARDEN.

and trusted a house - servant as any in the establishment which received her. She did not fail to present herself in my house at the expiration of her sentence, still wearing the dress in which she was made prisoner, and sadly reciting the miseries of her incarceration. Japanese policemen are very dutiful and polite, but Japanese prisons are serious places, and Japanese justice never trifles. But she came out with a good-conduct paper, and having renewed her garments at the *Kimono* shop—not an expensive thing in Japan—I took her for counsel and help to an English Archdeacon of my acquaintance, one of those noble and devoted Churchmen who, by their piety, learning, and simple Christian love, do more good in a quiet way than dozens of diplomats and professional missionaries. It was a good deal like illustrating in action Sydney Smith's axiom that A never sees B in distress, but he wants C to do something for the case. However, my kindly friend was a man of as much resource as virtue. He found for poor O Haru San the chance she needed. The young woman herself, glad of the opportunity, behaved with such fidelity and devotion that my friend's wife took her, after a few months, into her own service, and when, at my second visit to Japan, after more than a year's interval, I entered that house in Shiba, the Musume who opened the sliding door was no other than O Haru San herself, radiant with health, neat as an ivory *kanzashi*, and as pleased to see me as I was pleased and proud to see her, and to find what fair treatment and kindness in that exemplary household had effected to change a prison-bird into an honest and happy girl.

It was in connection, therefore, with the *roya no-onna*—the prison-woman—that I went one morning to the rock-seller's, at Azabu, and learned a good deal more than I knew before of the mysteries of his trade. At the gateway a bullock waggon, with three strong oxen harnessed to it, had just brought

down an immense slab of black stone, and a lame
elderly Japanese, who turned out to be O Haru's
uncle, was preparing the ropes and levers to transfer
the huge mass into his master's stoneyard. The
old fellow had had a foot crushed some time ago in
the hard and dangerous duty which occupied him.
But he was an honest man, well-esteemed by his
employer, although very poor, and the character he
gave to his niece, helped out by new particulars of
the sore straits which had driven her to do wrong,
enabled us, without much difficulty, to get the police
supervision removed. The number of women who
commit crimes in the empire of Japan is not much
more than seven or eight per cent. of the total of male
criminals. They are, without doubt, the most law-
abiding of their sex in the whole world.

XVI

THE TRIUMPH OF JAPAN

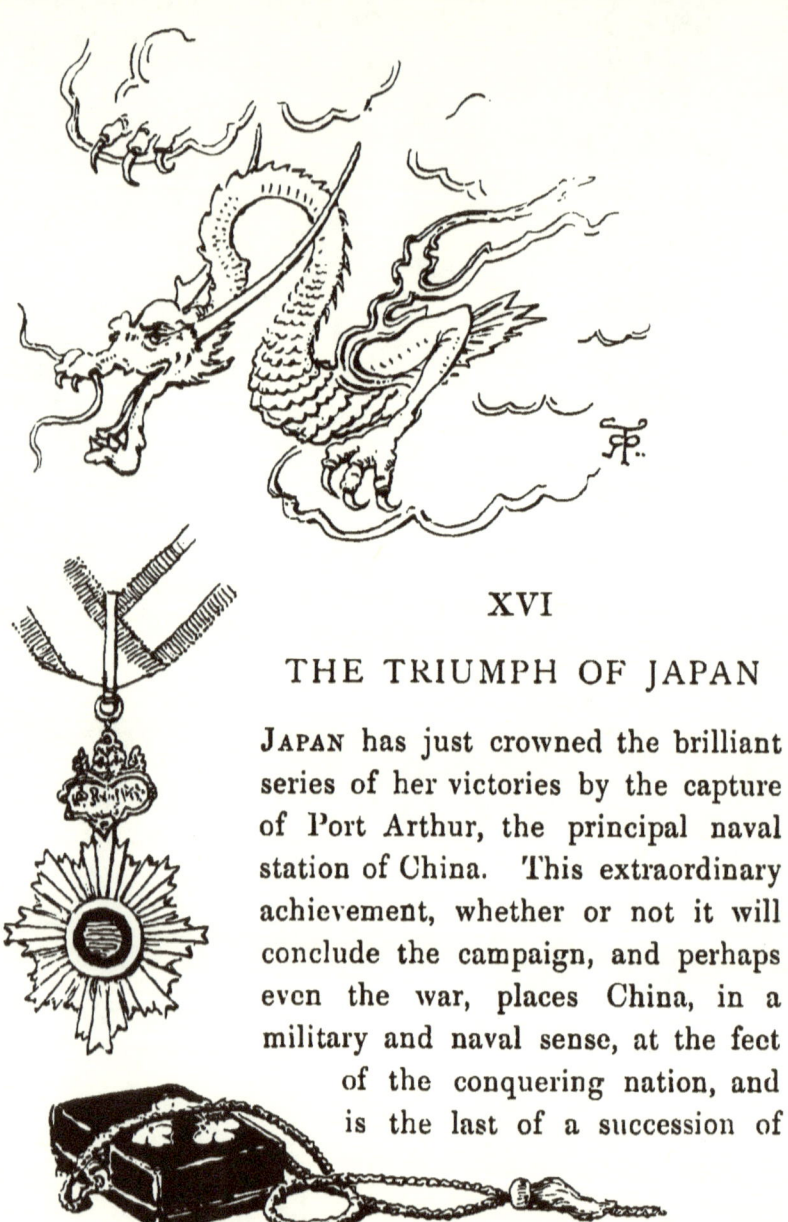

XVI

THE TRIUMPH OF JAPAN

JAPAN has just crowned the brilliant series of her victories by the capture of Port Arthur, the principal naval station of China. This extraordinary achievement, whether or not it will conclude the campaign, and perhaps even the war, places China, in a military and naval sense, at the feet of the conquering nation, and is the last of a succession of

warlike movements planned with the utmost skill, and carried out with wonderful sagacity, energy, and valour. The result may well seem astound-

273   S

ing to those who did not know the true Japan,
and who took their notions of the temper of its
people from superficial observers. Accomplished
as this series of triumphs has been within less than
four months, it is indeed calculated to satisfy, if
not to surprise, those even who best understood the
spirit and resources of the Mikado's country, and
the high intelligence with which the Japanese
Government and its subjects had prepared themselves for such a crisis in the national history.
I shall endeavour in this paper to furnish some
reasons why the present outcome of the conflict was
to be surely foreseen by well-informed persons from
the commencement ; and I may do this with a better
grace, because when the war was breaking out I
ventured to write in the *New Review*, and elsewhere, that the troops and ships of China would
not be able to stand before those of Japan anywhere, or at any time, in anything like equal
numbers and strength. That was in the hour when
almost all Western critics of the war were saying
that, whatever slight successes Japan might at
first obtain, the " sombre strength " of China would
eventually overwhelm her, and when even Mr.
Curzon did not fear to affirm that the war was being
entered upon chiefly to please the parliamentary
Opposition of Tokyo.

The fact is, that until recently the Western mind
generally cherished an entirely erroneous idea about
Japan and the Japanese. Its conception was derived from such sources as M. Pierre Loti's clever

but superficial " Madame Chrysanthème," and from
various similar publications by "globe-trotters"
who had seen and understood no more of the
country than *flâneurs* or curio-hunters can get at.
Mr. Gilbert and Sir Arthur Sullivan have also something to answer for, by reason of their lively mis-
representations of Japan in the comic opera entitled
"The Mikado." Yum-yum and Pitti Sing were
accepted as types of the Japanese woman, and it is
one example out of many of the errors which per-
vaded the amusing piece that the "Kimono" of
those young ladies were crossed over their bosoms
from right to left. Never by any chance is the
graceful robe in question thus worn, except at death,
when it is the custom to fold the garment for the
first time in that way, it being arranged during life
always from left to right. The Mikado himself,
together with Pooh-Bah, with the Ministers and
the *mise-en-scène* generally, were all of them equally
ridiculous to a Japanese eye, and the piece could
not be produced in Japan partly on this account,
and partly because of the gross disrespect offered
in it to the growing empire and its sovereign.
Signs of the same mistaken notions have been
almost everywhere visible in the English Press,
whether serious or comic. *Mr. Punch*, at the first
great victory of Ping-Yang, had a cartoon representing "Jap, the Giant Killer," proudly trampling upon
a colossal Chinaman ; and in all quarters might
be read expressions of wonder and occasionally of
disappointment, that "little" Japan should make

such headway
against the pro-
digious Middle
Kingdom. But
Japan is not little,
measured by any just
standard. Even *Whi-
taker's Almanack*
might have informed
these ill-equipped
public instructors that
the empire — which
comprises no less than
4200 islands, nearly
150,000 square miles
in area—has a popu-
lation of over forty-one
million souls — more
than the number of
those dwelling either
in the British realm or
in France.
This popu-
lation is as
homogeneous as a sack of
rice. A native of Hakodate
or Sendai talks with the
same tongue as one of Kioto
or Nagasaki, wears the same
clothes, and cherishes the
same loyalty to his "heaven-

RICE.

born " sovereign and the same patriotism towards Dai Nippon. Only one-thirteenth part of the empire, meanwhile, is under cultivation, the rest consisting of mountainous ground, either barren, or forbidding tillage, and the keeping of flocks and herds, because of a prickly bamboo-grass which grows everywhere and spoils the pasture. Being at heart a Buddhist country, flesh-meat in any case has never become popular in Japan, although it has been found that for the army and navy beef and mutton are needed to correct the exclusive fish and rice diet of the land. For myself, I think that, if the hillsides were steadily burnt off, good grass might be produced, and oxen and sheep be some day seen all over Japan. At present the latter familiar animal is so rare in the islands that I have paid a sen at a village-show to see a sheep in a cage, exhibited as a great novelty.

In a word, Japan is no globe-trotter's playground of undersized, frivolous people, living a life like that depicted upon the tea-trays and screens ; but a great, a serious, and a most civilised nation, having a history extending over 2500 years, obeying an unbroken dynasty dating its origin from only a hundred years short of the time of the foundation of Rome, and deriving from its isolated position in the North Pacific a solidity and unity only possible to island-empires. Japan has borrowed from China many important elements in her religion, her arts, and her customs ; but it is the greatest mistake to speak of

the two countries in the ordinary style as if their
character and type were at all identical. Japanese
features give evidence, no doubt, of a large Mongolian
element in the native blood, but that blood has been
subtly tempered by Nature with a considerable ad-
mixture of the Malay and the Kanaka, the resulting
blend being one producing special gifts and extraordinary qualities. The pure Japanese language has
nothing in common with Chinese, from which, however, it takes to-day, for colloquial and literary
purposes, a large proportion of words and phrases.
Yet no Chinese vocable ever steals into Japanese
poetry, which appears, therefore, musical and graceful
beyond the reach of the harsh celestial tongue. The
first point, consequently, to have in mind while con-
templating the otherwise amazing social, civil, and
military advance of Japan, is her ancient and strictly
indigenous civilisation, during the vast prolongation
of which the Japanese, unseen and unknown by the
outer world, developed certain entirely special
national qualities and national arts, the former of
which render them one of the strongest peoples in
the world potentially, while the latter place them
absolutely at the head of mankind for several valuable
traits and social superiorities. The revolution of
1868, so radical and thorough-going that the Japanese
themselves style it O Jishin ("the honourable earthquake"), must not by any means be taken as the
starting-point of the modern empire, although it
forms the beginning of the present era of Meiji, and
marks the moment when Japan entered into the

Western system. Rather must it be clearly understood that, like a skilful gardener who grafts a new rose or a new apple upon a healthy and well-established stock, so did Japan adapt the scientific and civil achievements of the West to an Eastern root, already full of vigorous life and latent forces. The "globe-trotters" who come and go, and write their light appreciations without even learning the language, or seeing more than what a guide can show them, forget to speak of the extensive public services established, in the network of railways, in the perfect postal arrangements, the telegraph, electric lighting, educational, medical, and sanitary departments; and they did not, and could not, know, as closer students knew, how the Japanese—earnest, exact, and artistic in all things—had carried into the organisation of their army and their navy that same conscientious craftsmanship and minute fidelity as to details which you see all over the land wherever a carpenter fits a plank, or an artist carves an ivory *netsuke*, or a Japanese lady ties up a present for her friend, with the inevitable red and white string, and the *noshi*.

My own eyes were opened when I was out, by the Emperor's gracious invitation, with the imperial troops in 1890 during their three days' military manœuvres in and around Nagoya. A civilian must not pretend, of course, to judge of soldiers, but one who had seen many other armies, European and Asiatic, could at least form reasonable conclusions, and mine, after that experience, were very firmly fixed as to the reality of the fighting strength of Japan. The

sturdiness, cheerful spirit, and willing obedience of
the regiments would have struck the most careless
eye. The Emperor, who loves his army to a degree
that sometimes almost made the navy jealous, was in
our midst, soldiering in earnest like the rest, with
nothing to distinguish him in the smoke and bustle,
except the embroidered cloth of purple silk with gold
chrysanthemums laid upon an ammunition-box for
his lunch, and the golden scabbard of his Masamune
sword. In marching, the soldiers laid aside their
barrack boots to slip their feet into the *waraji*—those
sandals of cord worn everywhere through the country,
in which they can walk all day long. I will be bound
that the path of the army through Corea and
Manchuria is at this day marked by scores of thousands of such discarded foot-gear which the Japanese
pedestrian flings aside when worn out, or throws into
a tree as an offering to the God of Travellers. The
spirit of the men was admirable. I saw the wheel
of a heavy field-gun crush an artillery-man's foot;
but the gunner did not utter a word nor leave his post
until an officer, perceiving the blood running from his
sandal, and finding the man's foot broken, sent him
to the rear. In the march homewards from those
beautiful hills covered with lilac azalea blossom,
where the mimic battle had raged, the gentle and
cheerful demeanour of " Kintaro "—the Japanese
" Tommy Atkins "—was most remarkable. He was
polite and friendly with everybody in the towns and
villages ; sober, orderly, contented ; and evidently
loved his duty. Like the Turkish troops, those of

Japan live upon what would seem to us next to nothing. Cold boiled rice and pickled slices of the gigantic white radish called "daikon" suffice them, at any rate until they can get to a bit of fried fish; and the delicate cup of weak tea— the universal beverage of the land— satisfies their simple taste as completely as it does that of the rudest labourer among this strangely refined race.

In Japan, unlike China, it is held noble to be a soldier, and indeed a great number of his Majesty's marines are the sons of "samurai"—what we should call here "esquires." The police of the capital and the Imperial Guard are in like manner largely recruited from the upper classes of Japan, dispossessed of their feudal privileges by the revolution. In consequence, these Japanese regiments are not only well-recruited, but splendidly led by officers educated in warlike science; and the contrast is strong indeed between such fearless lieutenants, captains, and colonels,

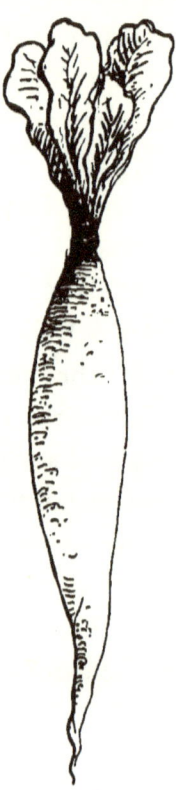

"DAIKON" RADISH.
(*Raphanus sativus*).

who rejoice in getting back to their old chivalric life, and the Chinese generals and commanders, with spectacles and long silver finger-nail guards, carried into the field in sedan-chairs with opium-pipes in hand instead of swords.

As for the Japanese navy, it has "made its proofs" in a style which renders praise superfluous. With her extensive coasts and universal habit of fish diet, Japan had early come to be encircled by a hardy breed of fishermen and sailors from whom any government could pick a superb *personnel* for warships. An old law used to forbid the building of any boats or junks beyond a certain tonnage, which was meant to keep the people to themselves. But all that exclusiveness became frankly abandoned at the beginning of Meiji, and when the present war commenced the Emperor had a splendid, though unfinished, navy at command, together with a whole fleet of passenger steamers owned by Japanese companies, which he could requisition. In the society of my friend Captain Ingles, R.N., who was chief adviser for many years to the Imperial Japanese navy, I saw and heard many a proof of its efficiency. There was a warship—I think it was the *Naniwa*—came to moorings at Kobe during the naval manœuvres there. No sooner was she fast than an order was conveyed to her to put to sea again immediately, to take part in certain sudden evolutions. From the time when she took up her berth until she cast off again and steamed seaward the interval elapsing was so brief and the smartness shown so perfect, that my professional friend observed, " We could not beat that in the British navy ! " As an example of the thorough way in which Japan went to work to create this fleet—the dimensions of which she intends to double in the next ten years—

it may be mentioned that, when commencing its establishment, she engaged an entire British ship's company, from the commander to the cabin-boys, in order to "coach" every grade of her officers, cadets, and companies in their respective duties. Rank by rank the Japanese thus moulded their own blue jackets upon our British type, while they so studied and mastered the arts of musketry and gunnery, that perhaps the best rifle now carried by any troops is that invented by Colonel Murata for the army of his Imperial Majesty; and the sanguinary record of the Yaloo River has amply proved that they knew how to profit by the warlike productions of Elswick and of Krupp.

As for this quarrel between Japan and China, it is, historically, an old one, and, twice at least before now, the *hi no maru*, the "sun-flag" of Nipon, has been carried to victory over the hills of Chosen. The Empress Jingo Ko-go successfully invaded that peninsula about the date when our Saxons first landed in Britain; and Hideyoshi, the dwarfish, six-fingered, but famous Taikun, subdued and would have annexed the land but for his sudden demise. In 1269 A.D., after a first disastrous attempt to plunder the Japan coasts, that renowned warrior, Prince Kublai Khan, made a descent upon them with many hundreds of ships and scores of thousands of fighting men. The memorable event is the Armada-story of Japanese history, and the land has never forgotten either its perils or its glories at that epoch. Aided by a mighty typhoon, the islanders

managed to shatter and disperse the argosy of the
Chinese conqueror, and cut off thousands of the
invader's heads, after the barbarous fashion towards
prisoners then prevailing, which China would still
follow, though Japan has long ago adopted the
Geneva Cross, and astonishes her pig-tailed enemies
by tenderness and humanity towards the wounded
and captives.   A nobleman of ancient lineage brought
to me, when in Japan during 1889, a very curious
painting of Kublai Khan's invasion and defeat,
which had been executed some two or three generations after the battle.   It was done with much skill
and spirit upon thin leather, and extended, when
unrolled, to a length of many yards, while attached
to it was a faded silk flag of the Tartars, and a wisp
of horse-tail from a Tartar banner.   I might have
bought the relic, and, indeed, greatly wished to become its possessor, for nothing was more interesting
than thus to behold faithfully depicted the soldiers of
" Xanadu," and the battalions of the early Japanese
emperors in " their manner as they lived."   But I
perceived it was a veritable " Bayeux tapestry " for
Japan, and therefore sent the owner with it to the
palace, where I believe his Imperial Majesty was
pleased to purchase the antique scroll for his own
archives at a very gracious price indeed.   I have
alluded, however, to Hideyoshi, Kublai Khan, and
the Empress Jingo, not to go into the annals of
Corea, but merely to indicate that this international
feud between Japan and China is one of very long
standing, and that Corea has been ofttimes before a

THE WIND GOD OF JAPAN.   *P.* 285.

bone of contention. There are ignorant observers of the present extraordinary Asiatic episode who talk and write as if Japan, in her new strength, had looked about for a likely enemy and for a plausible dispute, and had found them quite by accident in the Chinese Court and the Corean Question. The proclamation of the Chinese Emperor at the outbreak of the war, when he called his enemies " vermin," *Wojin*, and commanded, a little too lightly, their "extirpation," should teach a better insight. It was an old and inevitable quarrel.

War is a terrible evil, and I myself am just as sorry for those who have suffered on the Chinese as on the Japanese side. But very little pity is due to the mandarins, the officials, and the worthless court of the unwieldy Middle Kingdom. Statesmen naturally desire to see some sort of government survive at Pekin, and reasonably dread the chaos which may follow if the Manchu dynasty should collapse, and 350 millions of mankind be thereby temporarily without any authoritative head. But the utter feebleness and failure which China has exhibited— the disgraceful incompetence of her officers, and the cowardice of her soldiers and sailors—is but the condemnation written large of the miserable Central Government first of all, and then of a civil and social system which, if it does disappear, did not deserve to survive. Under the cruel, corrupt, and barbarously opportunist regime of Pekin, founded as it has been upon the immoral moralities of Confucius, patriotism and honour, faith and loyalty, with almost all the manly virtues, have been, reign after reign, crushed out of the hearts and souls of the ingenious, industrious, patient, and obedient people of China. In the fortunes of the present war the world beholds—if it will look deeper than to what satisfies shallow critics—the immense significance of dominant national ideas. We have suddenly found ourselves gazing upon a prodigious collision between powers founded on Confucianism and Buddhism respectively—since, behind the disgraceful defeat of the troops and ships of Pekin lie the unspirituality, the narrowness, and selfishness of the old Agnostic's philosophy, while behind the successes of Japan are the glad and lofty tenets of a modified Buddhistic metaphysic, which has mingled with the proud doctrines of Shintoism to breed reverence for the past, to inculcate and to produce patriotism, loyalty, fearlessness of death, with happiness in life, and above all, self-respect. It is this last quality which is the central characteristic of the Japanese men and women, and round about which grow up what those who do not love the gentle and gallant race may call " vanity," and many other foibles and faults. Self-respect, which Buddhism teaches to every one, and which Confucius never taught, makes the Japanese as a nation keep their personal honour—except perhaps sometimes in business affairs—as clean as they keep their bodies ; and has helped to give them the placid and polite life, full of grace, of charm, and of refinement, which contrasts so strongly with the dirty, ill-regulated, struggling, atheistic existence of

the average Chinese. Self-respect—*mizukara omon-
zuru*—has also largely given them their brilliant
victories of this year; that temper of high manhood,
the "law unto themselves," which Confucianism has
taken away by its cold and changeless unbeliefs
from the otherwise capable, clever, and indefatigable
Chinamen.

In a word, the picture passing before our eyes of
unbroken successes on one side and helpless feebleness and failure on the other—which was numerically
much the stronger—is a lesson for the West as well
as the beginning of a new era in the East. It teaches,
trumpet-tongued, how nations depend upon the
inner national life, as the individual does upon his
personal vitality. The system under which China has
stagnated was secretly fatal to patriotism, loyalty,
faith, manhood, public spirit, and private self-respect.
In Japan, on the contrary, those virtues, rooted
anciently in her soil, have never ceased to blossom
and produce the fruit that comes from a real, serious,
and sensible national unity. In the Chinese journals
we read miserable accounts of corruption, defalcation,
duties shirked, and discipline replaced by terrified
cruelty. Take up any Japanese newspaper of the
present campaign, and you will find reports of private
subscriptions and donations sent in ship-loads to the
army and navy; the Japanese men, eager to share in
the maintenance of their flag; the Japanese women,
volunteering for service in the field hospitals, or
toiling at home to prepare comforts for their brave
countrymen. One town in Ehime prefecture unani-

mously abjured the use of tea that they might raise
funds to send gifts to the regiments in Corea. Another
in Fukushima resolved to set aside the drinking of
sakë till the triumph of Japan was complete, the
money saved being forwarded to the army. The
villagers of Shizuoka went *en masse* to the top of
Fuji San to pray for the success of the armies of
Japan. In fact, the whole land, from the Emperor to
the lowest *ninsoku*, or "leg-man," has been consoli-
dated by one great heart-beat of national effort, and
the consequence is that the vast, unwieldy, inarticu-
late mass of Chinese strength has gone down before
the flag of Japan like rice before the harvest knife.
If there be indeed a "little England Party" among
us, it should, while taking note of the splendid victories which have raised Japan to the first rank of
Eastern Powers, ponder the subjoined extract from
a Tokyo journal :—

"The representatives of the *Taigen Koho*, or
'Strong Foreign Policy Party,' now in Tokyo, held
a meeting on the 16th instant at the offices of the
party, and discussed the policy to be pursued in the
approaching session of the Diet. They arrived,
according to the *Jiji Shimpo*, at a resolution that
peace must not be made with China until an agree-
ment can be come to with her securing the permanent
tranquillity of the Orient. They further determined
that no expense must be spared to achieve the above
result, and that ample supplies must be voted ; and
further, that since national unanimity is essential in
a crisis like the present, all petty subjects of dispute

with the government should be laid aside, and no voice of censure should be raised so long as the country's honour and interests are fully guarded. The spirit displayed by these politicians is deserving of all applause; but in truth the heart of the Japanese nation is so thoroughly enlisted in this struggle with China, that we may look for displays of loyalty on all sides."

As to the instances of splendid valour which have irradiated the story of the war, I could fill pages with what have reached my own personal knowledge. The Japanese soldiers have fought throughout with that bright courage which is so different to the reckless despair of Li Hung Chang's braves, and which comes from intelligence, patriotism, and happy faith. Before each action the sailors tidied themselves up, that they might die clean and neat, "like gentlemen." Over and over again the wounded stole up on deck from the cock-pit to join once more in the glorious battle. The victory of such a race in Asia is the victory of enlightenment and civilisation against barbarism and exclusiveness; and the policy of wise English statesmen henceforward will be to maintain and improve the friendship happily established by the Revised Treaty of this year between the two empires of Great Britain and Japan.

Nor is there any good reason for Englishmen as Christians to grudge to Japan her sudden elevation to high rank and influence in Asia. I have spoken above of Buddhism as the root from which her civil virtues and her gentle social manners have sprung. But it is

T

WATER GATE OF TEMPLE, MIYA SHIMA,
ISLAND OF ITSUKU.

the country of all others where the ethics—if not the doctrines—of Christianity have found, and will find, the most ready reception, and where the active instinct of the people for "whatsoever things are of good report" has already opened the way to a time when Japan may become Christian in all but name, and, possibly, even in that also "Christian."

XVII

LOST AND FOUND

XVII

LOST AND FOUND

Now and then, in the strange vicissitudes of human life, people have experienced, in some sudden joy, something of what the feeling may be when all the past rolls away, and, as Lady Constance says in Shakespeare's play of " King John," " We shall see and know our friends in heaven." An instance of this comes to mind which happened at a London dinner-table in the year, as I think, of 1880. It befell in a good house, with a charming hostess of high rank, and an excellent *chef;* nor was anything further from the minds of the happy and friendly guests on the memorable evening in question than that such a high-spiced dish of romance could possibly mingle with the menu. Nothing, in fact, could have been more pleasantly ordinary than the occasion of the feast, nor more genially matter of fact than the character of those partaking of it. Her kindly ladyship, the hostess ; one or two statesmen and men of letters ; a middle-aged dame or two of fashion ; and the indispensable commingling of some pretty and clever girls—without whose presence a graceful banquet degenerates into a gross repast—these, together with an old Indian general

and his adopted daughter, composed the company.
Among those whom I have ventured to call middle-
aged sat one that would have been notable anywhere
for the faded, yet still commanding, beauty of a countenance in which a profound melancholy clouded,
without concealing, the tenderness and refinement
of a rare and noble nature. The silver threads of
approaching age were very visible in her masses of
dark hair, but she was comely, and, indeed, attractive,
in her evening of life, specially possessing a softness
of voice which seemed partly due to the gift of birth
and partly to some ever-remembered sadness. If, indeed, one had noticed more curiously beforehand all
the circumstances of that dinner-party, no ear could
have failed to have been struck by the strange simi-
larity between the " timbre " of this charming lady's
voice in conversation and that of the very handsome girl sitting by her side—the general's adopted
daughter. To hear them speak one after the other
was really like hearing the same string of a harp
twice vibrating, or the same soft chord struck in the
minor key of the piano. But the impression produced by such an identity of vocal organ was naturally
a transitory one, and in other respects the elderly
lady and the bright-eyed girl at her side in no way
resembled each other, except by the colour of their
hair, which—silvered, as has been remarked, in the
locks of the widow—were night-black and glossy as
the wing of the raven in those of the younger
woman. Chance alone and the hospitable decree
of our noble hostess had brought these two thus

side by side at a London dinner-table—if, indeed,
there be such a thing as chance. No one present
could guess what a startling incident was to befall ·
that evening before the ladies rose to leave the
dining-room, and least of all the jovial, garrulous,
white-haired general, who, after his usual style, was
gaily chattering, his lively reminiscences, indeed, leading to the astounding but happy catastrophe.

The conversation had somehow turned—probably
under the gallant veteran's guidance—to the subject
of the Indian Mutiny of 1857, and he was narrating,
between the entrées and the "roast," how he had
assisted at the taking of the town of Calpee by the
British relieving force under Lord Strathnairn—then
Sir Hugh Rose. There is nothing more absorbing
than the story of a battle told by one who has taken
part in it. All outside accounts of engagements
by sea or land recounted by professional historians
appear to me practically worthless. You cannot
gather from the pages of Livy how Trebia was
really won, or Thrasimene, or Cannæ; and all the
learned disquisitions upon Ramillies or Malplaquet
or Waterloo leave you still helplessly wondering
why, if Marlborough "refused" his left, the enemy
did not also "refuse" his right; and wherefore one
side allowed the other side to outflank them when the
game seemed just as easy for this party as for that.
But the man who has been in a battle knows at least
his own fiery corner of it, and the aged general
was precise as Thucydides and graphic as Napier or
Macaulay, while he kept those about him unusually

inattentive to the delicacies cooling before them, and
even distracted more than one fair young listener
from the pretty things whispered in her ear by her
cavalier. Properly, even so respected a guest ought
not to have talked so much about battles—at least,
before the dessert; but "chatted food" is not unsalu-
tary, and a good diner-out understands how to eat
while he listens. The general himself managed
cleverly enough to interlard his warlike chronicle
with woodcock trail upon toast and a supreme cut
of Southdown mutton. Yet he himself permitted
the "épinards aux croûtons" to pass when he got
to the critical point in that famous day—May 22,
1858—of the great Indian conflict.

"I tell you, madam," he said, addressing himself
to the silver-tressed lady, whose attention had somehow become entirely riveted upon his narration,
"Sir Hugh Rose won the city and the success of
that campaign with nothing but an opera-glass. It
had been frightfully warm weather. The sun, from
rising to setting, was like a great red-hot cannon-ball
in a sky of copper, for it was the height of the dry
season. The men suffered far more from the sultry
atmosphere than from the enemy; and we lost,
indeed, many a good fellow that afternoon by sun-
stroke. Sir Hugh himself was three times down on
the ground with the terrible solar radiation, but a
regimental 'bhisti' on each occasion poured the
contents of a 'mussuk' of water over his head and
neck, and brought him round. We had beaten the
Pandies, and they were retreating helter-skelter

down the long hillside to the gates of Calpee, in full view of the advanced companies of our victorious but very exhausted column. Somebody handed a field-glass to Sir Hugh, who steadied himself on his horse, and took a long look at the swarming rebels pouring into the gateway."

The silver-haired lady here cut the old soldier short by ejaculating, "You are speaking, sir, of the Ganesgunj Gate, I think, by the Palace of Sing Dev?"

"Yes, madam," replied the general; "you seem to know the place?"

The lady sighed and nodded, while the general went on. "Sir Hugh Rose was the politest man in the world, but, I must also sorrowfully add, one of the greatest swearers in the army since the time of Uncle Toby in Flanders, and I cannot repeat to you the exact words he used as he clapped the glasses together and exclaimed to the chief of his staff, with some language which made the hot air blue, 'By ——, we shall have the city and everything else, if we only look sharp.' In a moment the camel corps was called up—a body of about 250 men, still pretty fresh. The camels were made to kneel, and two infantrymen, in some cases three, scrambled, armed, on to their backs. They were then ordered to pelt away, as hard as the camels' legs could go, to the gate of the city, and to throw themselves, upon dismounting, on to the straggling mob of the fugitives. We artillery men," said the old soldier, "gave the rebels pepper from either flank with our field-guns, until the camels got too close, and then it was a sight to see how the turbaned rabble scattered to this side and that, as the four or five hundred infantrymen flung themselves into the gateway, and triumphantly entered and captured the entire city."

"It is all most interesting," said the hostess; "but, general, you must really try these 'bouchées à la reine.'"

"By Jove! I beg a thousand pardons, Lady ——, but Jhansi there, my daughter, knows too well that you never can stop me if you once set me off on that hillside in front of Calpee."

The silver-haired lady had meantime totally forgotten dinner during this belligerent narrative; but her attention at its last point became quite painfully fixed. "Might I inquire why you call your daughter, general, by that Indian name?" she asked.

"Do you not think it pretty?" he queried.

"Certainly; but how came you to choose it for her?"

"Well, ma'am, the fact is, she was my 'loot' in that day's business. I was told off with some guns to hold a post outside the city by 'the travellers' bungalow,' near to the 'Eighty-four Domes,' and the first thing we saw there was an English girl baby lying alone and crowing on a 'charpoy' in the bungalow. She was as bare of clothing as the back of my hand—you need not blush, Jhansi!—and nothing near or far appeared to tell how it came there, or to whom it belonged, except a string of

beads with a little golden cross attached to it. My
late wife and I were childless; we took care of the
small creature, first for charity, and then for love;
and now Jhansi there, named after that bloody gateway, has grown to be the same to me, and was the
same to Maria in her time, as our own daughter."
The handsome girl cast a look of evident affection
at the veteran, reddening prettily to find herself the
observed of all observers at the table.

But what on earth made the silver-haired lady
now catch her breath and her gentle face turn so
deadly white as she said to her fair young neighbour,
looking upon her with eyes singularly fixed, "Where
is that necklace of beads? What was the colour
of them?"

She answered, "They were blue beads—children's
beads, which I could not wear now. My old Indian
ayah takes care of them for me. She will be coming
here soon with my wraps. If you please, she shall
bring them to show you."

"Yes, yes!" exclaimed the lady, "please send and
tell her to bring them."

A servant was despatched with the message, and
an attempt was made to continue the dinner; but
nobody could fail to notice the strange absorption
and emotion of the lady, from whose eyes presently
tears were seen to run, while, through the falling
drops, every now and then she glanced again at the
embarrassed aspect of the young girl. In a few
moments, unable longer to contain herself, and
conscious of the distress which her agitation was

causing among the guests, she began to speak in
those tones which were so curiously the echo and
symphony of Jhansi's soft voice, " Forgive me, Lady
—— ; what the general has told us makes me remember too sadly what happened to my husband and
me in that dreadful time of the Great Mutiny. We
lost our only little child in the North-West. The
servants were to bring it up to the Hills from Mhow,
and I was at a distance with my husband—who
afterwards fell, alas! near Gwalior. Our people
were all killed or ran away, and we never heard nor
could hear of the child, one of very many English
babies who disappeared in the same sad way during
the great troubles. But what did you do, general,
with your little Jhansi in the midst of the fighting ? "

"My wife, madam," said the old soldier, "was
going to England, and took the child with her. We
made a thousand inquiries in India and at home,
but there was no sign or token to be had of
Jhansi's parentage, and, as you say, scores of little
ones were lost or abandoned at that time."

Nobody now was eating, nobody drinking, nobody spoke a word ; all were watching the serious,
wrinkled face of the general, the eager, pallid
anguish of vanished love evoked upon the widow's
countenance by these painful memories, and the
wistful look of the pretty, black-haired damsel, who
found herself thus uncomfortably a central object
of interest.

Suddenly turning towards her, " You do not, I

suppose, dear," said the widow, " remember a single word of Hindostani ? "

" No," interposed the general, " she could but just lisp—a tiny bit of a thing, some fourteen months old."

" 'There was one word though, papa, you used to say I knew, 'Dilkoo! dilkoo!' and you told me it must be meant for 'dilkoosh,' 'Heart's delight,' which I had perhaps heard the native servants saying to me."

" No, no, no ! " broke forth the widow. " Oh Lady ——, forgive me, but my heart is full of a terrible and precious hope. General, that was the pet name by which my dead husband used to call me, and our little child did catch the sound of it, and would sometimes try to repeat the word when she wanted her mother."

At this juncture the old Indian ayah crept into the room, beckoned from the door by the general. She held in her little brown, withered hand a string of blue beads, from which depended a small gold Maltese cross. The general took the necklet, and, with an expression of profoundest respect and breathless curiosity, passed it across the table into the eager grasp of the widow, whose eyes still roamed over the face, and head, and figure of the graceful girl at her side.

The moment she received the trinket, she turned the cross round and pulled out one of its golden arms. From the small hollow thus revealed she drew a tiny scrap of paper, on which something was written in very small characters. Then she rose from her place, amid the intense attention of all the company, and, with a look on her gentle features never to be forgotten by those who witnessed it, exclaimed, "I think that God has this night given me back my child. Oh! if you are mine, as I believe, for Heaven's sake! let me see your foot—here! now!—your right foot. General, on our baby's right foot the third toe was missing."

At another time, the remark and the request would have sounded like the *dénouement* of a transpontine melodrama; here it was immortal Nature and Celestial Truth. Nobody thought it bold or unusual when the beautiful girl—beside herself with tender emotion—stooped, drew from her right leg the satin slipper and the silk stocking, and placing a pretty little ivory-white foot on the seat of her chair, displayed in the eyes of all the birth-mark which was the sure and convincing sign that there had indeed been witnessed by those present on that evening one of those real dramas of human life which outdo fiction.

What followed, with its wild delight and passionate explanation, cannot be here described. Those present alone could give an idea of the close of that amazing evening. One of the guests had the curiosity to read the little text written on the paper revealed from inside the cross. It ran : "In heaven their angels do always behold the face of My Father Which is in heaven."

XVIII

BUDDHA-GYA

BUDDHA-GAYA.   P. 305.

Entrance arches before restoration.

XVIII

BUDDHA-GYA

I would to-day, in these columns (*Daily Telegraph*), respectfully invite the vast and intelligent British public to forget, for a little while, home weather and home politics, and to accompany me, in fancy, to a sunny corner of their empire, where there centres a far more important question, for the future of religion and civilisation, than any relating to parish councils or parish pumps. I will, by their leave, tell them of beautiful scenes under warm skies; of a temple fairer and more stately, as well as more ancient, than almost any existing fane; and will also show them how the Indian Government of Her Majesty, supported by their own enlightened opinion, might, through an easy and blameless act of administrative sympathy, render four hundred millions of Asiatics for ever the friends and grateful admirers of England.

We will spread the magic carpet of Kamar-az-zaman, told of in the "Arabian Nights," and pass at once upon it to Patna, the busy city beside the Ganges, some 350 miles by rail from Calcutta. The closing days of March are hot there, and the river glitters as if it were molten gold under the fiery sun. We will not stay accordingly to inspect the indigo

factories ; or to visit the wonderful *Golah*, where
140,coo tons of rice can be laid up ; nor the government opium factory, where enough of that most
useful and benign drug is stored to put the whole
world to sleep. We will take train from Bankipore
for Gaya, only fifty-seven miles away, and having
rested in that town for the night, we shall have
ordered carriages to be ready at break of day to
convey us four *koss* further—some seven or eight
miles—into the hills which hereabouts jut across
the valley of the Ganges.

I said you should see beautiful scenery, and surely
this is such. The road, broad and well made, runs
between the Gaya Hills on the right and the bright
slow-stealing stream of the ancient Nilájan on the
left. The mountain flanks are covered with cactus,
wild indigo, and korinda bushes, showing a little
temple perched upon almost every peak ; while down
on the flat, and especially along the sandy levels
bordering the river, green stretches of palm-groves
are interspersed with sal and tamarind trees, the
undergrowth being long tiger-grass and the common
but ever-lovely ground palmetto, *chamærops humilis*.
The air, deliciously cool before the sun rises, is full of
birds abroad for food—crows, parrakeets, mynas, the
blue-winged rollers, the green and scarlet " hammer-
smiths," black and white king-fishers, bee-birds,
bronze and emerald, with graceful silvery egrets stalk-
ing among the cattle. Later on, when the sky grows
warmer, you will see clouds of lovely butterflies
among the flowers of the orchids and poisonous

ASOKA PILLAR AT TIRHOOT.   *P.* 307.

datura, with sun-birds and dragon-flies skimming
along the blue and pink lotuses in the pools. The
people whom we meet upon the road are dark-skinned
patient peasants going with their products to Gaya
and Bankipur, while those whom we shall overtake
will be mainly pilgrims of the day, wending their
way to the immeasurably holy place towards which we
also are bound. For, see! they also at the fifth mile
quit the main track, and turning to the left by a less
excellent but still carriageable road, which winds
under the now welcome shade of the jack-trees and
mangoes, are making for that most sacred spot of all
hallowed places in Asia, towards which our own
feet and thoughts are bound.

It is here! Beyond the little village of mud huts
and the open space where dogs and children and
cattle bask together in the dust, beyond the Mahunt's
College, and yonder great fig tree which has split with
its roots that wall, twelve feet thick, built before
England had ever been discovered, nestles an abrupt
hollow in the surface, symmetrical and well-kept, and
full of stone images, terraces, balustrades, and shrines.
It is oblong—as big, perhaps, altogether as Russell
Square, and surrounded on its edges by small houses
and buildings. From one extremity of the hallowed
area rises with great beauty and majesty a temple
of very special style and design. The plinth of the
temple is square, with a projecting porch, and on
the top of this soars to the sky a pyramidical tower
of nine storeys, profusely embellished with niches,
string courses, and mouldings, while from the trun-

cated summit of this an upper pinnacle rears itself, of graceful form, topped by a gold finial, representing the amalaka fruit. A smaller pyramidical tower stands at each corner of the roof of the lower structure, and there is a broad walk round the base of the Great Tower. Over the richly-worked porch which fronts the east a triangular aperture is pierced, whereby the morning glory of the sun may fall through upon the gilded image seated in the sanctuary within. That image, you will perceive, is—or was—of Buddha, and this temple is the holiest and most famous, as well as nearly the sole surviving shrine, of all those eighty-four thousand fanes erected to the Great Teacher by King Asoka two hundred and eighteen years after the Lord Buddha's *Nirvana*.

Yet more sacred even than the cool, dark sanctuary into which we look, to see the sunbeams kissing the mild countenance of the Golden Buddh inside ; more intensely moving to the Buddhists who come hither, and richer with associations of unspeakable interest and honour than King Asoka's stately temple, or even those stone railings carved with mermaids, crocodiles, elephants, and lotus flowers, which the king himself commanded, and which still surround the shrine, is yonder square platform of stone, about a yard high from the ground, out of which a tree is growing. That is the Maha Bodhi tree—in the opinion of superstitious votaries the very original Bodhi tree, miraculously preserved—but more rationally that which replaces and represents the ever-memorable shade under which the inspired Siddartha sate at the moment when he attained *sambuddhi*, the supreme light of his gentle wisdom. It is a fig tree—of the *ficus Indica* species—with the well-known long glossy leaves. Its stem is covered with patches of gold leaf, and its boughs are hung with streamers of white and coloured cloth, while at its root—frequently watered by the pious with sandal oil and attar of roses—will probably be seen sitting a Brahman priest of the Saivite sect intoning *mantras*. You will hear him say, "*Gaya! Gaya Sirsa, Bodhi Gaya*," for though he is praying on behalf of Mahratta pilgrims, and does not know or care for Buddha, the ancient formulas cling to the spot and to his lips. And, beyond all doubt, this *is* the spot, most dear and divine, and precious beyond every other place on earth, to all the four hundred million Buddhists in China, Japan, Mongolia, Assam, Cambodia, Siam, Burma, Arakan, Nepaul, Thibet, and Ceylon. This is the authentic site, and this the successor-tree, by many unbrokenly cherished generations of that about which my "Light of Asia" says :

> "Then he arose, made strong by the pure meat,
> And bent his footsteps where a great Tree grew,
> The Bodhi tree (thenceforward in all years
> Never to fade, and ever to be kept
> In homage of the world), beneath whose leaves
> It was ordained the Truth should come to Buddh,
> Which now the Master knew ; wherefore he went
> With measured pace, steadfast, majestical,
> Unto the Tree of Wisdom. Oh, ye worlds
> Rejoice ! Our Lord wended unto the Tree !"

There is no doubt, in fact, of the authenticity of

the spot. The four most sacred places of Buddhism are Kapilavastu (now Bhūila), where Prince Siddartha was born; Isipatana, outside Benares, where he first preached; Kusinagara, where he died; and this site marked by the tree, whereat "in the full moon of Wesak" 2483 years ago he mentally elaborated the gentle and lofty faith with which he has civilised Asia. And of all those four, the Tree-Place here at Buddha-Gaya is the most dear and sacred to Asiatic Buddhists. Why, then, is it to-day in the hands of Brahman priests, who do not care about the temple, except for the credit of owning it, and for the fees which they draw? The facts are these. Until the thirteenth century—that is, for more than 1400 years—it was exclusively used and guardianed by Buddhists, but fell into decay and neglect, like other Buddhist temples, on the expulsion of Buddhism from India. Three hundred years ago a wandering Sivaite ascetic visited the spot, and settled down, drawing round him gradually the beginning of what is now the College of Priests established there. So strong have they since become in ownership, that when the Bengal Government in 1880 was repairing the temple and its grounds, and begged for its embellishment from the Mahunt a portion of Asoka's stone railing which he had built into his own house, the old Brahman would not give it up, and Sir Ashley Eden could not, or did not, compel the restoration.

The Buddhist world had, indeed, well-nigh forgotten this hallowed and most interesting centre of

THE BUDDHIST CHIEF PRIEST—SRI-MANGALA WELIGAMA OF PANADÈRE.

P. 311.

their faith—the Mecca, the Jerusalem, of a million
Oriental congregations—when I sojourned in Buddha-
Gaya a few years ago. I was grieved to see Mahratta peasants performing " Shraddh " in such a
place, and thousands of precious ancient relics of
carved stone inscribed with Sanskrit lying in piles
around. I asked the priest if I might have a leaf
from the sacred tree.

"Pluck as many as ever you like, sahib," was his
reply, "it is nought to us."

Ashamed of his indifference, I took silently the
three or four dark shining leaves which he pulled
from the bough over his head, and carried them with
me to Ceylon, having written upon each the holy
Sanskrit formula. There I found them prized by
the Cingalese Buddhist with eager and passionate
emotion. The leaf presented by me to the temple
at Kandy, for example, was placed in a casket of
precious metal and made the centre of a weekly
service, and there and then it befell that, talking to
the gentle and learned priests at Panadurè—particularly to my dear and wise friend, Sri Weligama—
I gave utterance to the suggestion that the temple
and its appurtenances ought to be, and might be, by
amicable arrangements with the Hindoo College and
by the favour of the Queen's Government, placed in
the hands of a representative committee of the Buddhist nations.

I think there never was an idea which took root
and spread so far and fast as that thrown out thus
in the sunny temple-court at Panadurè, amid the

waving taliputs. Like those tropical plants which
can almost be seen to grow, the suggestion quickly
became an universal aspiration, first in Ceylon and
next in other Buddhist countries. I was entreated
to lay the plan before the Oriental authorities, which
I did. I wrote to Sir Arthur Gordon, Governor of
Ceylon, in these words : " I suggest a Governmental
Act, which would be historically just, which would
win the love and gratitude of all Buddhist populations, and would reflect enduring honour upon English administration. The temple and enclosure at
Buddha-Gaya are, as you know, the most sacred
spots in all the world for the Buddhists. . . . But
Buddha-Gaya is occupied by a college of Saivite
priests, who worship Mahadeva there, and deface the
shrine with emblems and rituals foreign to its nature.
That shrine and the ground surrounding it remain,
however, government property, and there would be
little difficulty, after proper and friendly negotiations, in procuring the departure of the Mahunt
with his priests, and the transfer of the temple and
its grounds to the guardianship of Buddhists from
Ceylon and elsewhere. I have consulted high
authorities, among them General Cunningham, who
thoroughly sympathises with the idea, and declares
it entirely feasible. . . . I apprehend that a certain
sum of money might be required to facilitate the
transfer of the Brahmans, and to establish the Buddhist College. In my opinion, a lakh of rupees
could not be expended by any government in a more
profitable manner."

Sir Arthur, who had just been exploring Buddhist remains in Ceylon, was very well disposed to the idea. Lord Dufferin warmly received it, at Calcutta; Lord Connemara, in Madras; and at that time, if only the Home Government had been more alive to a grand opportunity, it would have been easy to make satisfactory terms with the Brahmans, and to have effected the transfer of the holy place to a representative committee—at one stroke delighting and conciliating all Buddhistic Asia.

But two or three years passed by, and while the idea was spreading throughout Asia, and a large society had become established with the special purpose of acquiring the guardianship of the sacred site, the Mahunt grew more exacting in his expectations, and clung closer to the possession of the temple. The letters which I received from the East showed that the old Brahman had memorialised the government, in his alarm or avarice, and that local authorities had for quiet's sake reported adversely to the negotiation. I think the Mahunt was a good man. I had never wished any but friendly and satisfactory arrangements with him. Yet if you walked in that spot which all these scores of millions of our race love so dearly, you would observe with shame and grief in the mango groves, to the east of Lilajan, ancient statues plastered to the walls of an irrigating well near the village Mucharin—identified with the "Muchalinda" tank. Stones carved with Buddha's images are to be found used as weights to the levers for drawing water. I have seen ryots in the villages

surrounding the temple using beautifully-carved blocks
as steps to their huts. I have seen three feet high
statues in an excellent state of preservation, buried
under rubbish to the east of the Mahunt's baradari.
A few are plastered into the eastern outer wall of
the garden along the bank of Lilajan ; and the Asoka
pillars, the most ancient relics of the site—indeed,
"the most antique memorials of all India"—which
graced a temple pavement, are now used as posts of
the Mahunt's kitchen. To rectify this sad neglect,
and to make the temple, what it should be, the
living and learned centre of purified Bhuddism,
money was not, and is not, lacking. If the Home
Government had seen its way to make the Hindoo
Abbot well-disposed, I could have commanded any
sum which might have seemed fair and necessary.
But the idea was too intelligent for the official
grasp, and the golden moment went by.

Nevertheless, Asia did not abandon its new desire,
and I received so many, and such pressing, communications, that I went at last to the then Indian Secretary of State, Lord Cross—always intelligent, kindly,
and receptive—and once more pleaded for the great
restoration.

"Do you wish, Lord Cross," I asked, "to have four
hundred millions of Eastern peoples blessing your
name night and day, and to be for ever remembered in
Asia, like Alexander, or Asoka, or Akbar the Great?"

"God bless my soul, yes," answered the Minister ;
"how is that to be done?"

Then I repeated all the facts, and produced so

happy an effect upon the Indian Minister's mind, that he promised to consult the Council, and to write— if the idea was approved—to Lord Lansdowne. In due time the Viceroy replied that the idea was legitimate and beneficial, and that so long as no religious ill-feeling was aroused, and no pecuniary grant asked from the Indian Treasury, the Calcutta Government would be inclined to favour any friendly negotiations. Thus the matter stood at my last visit to the East, when I was astonished and rejoiced to find how firmly the desire of this restoration had taken root, and how enkindled with the hope of it Ceylon, Siam, Burmah, and Japan had become. The Mahá-Bodhi Society, established to carry out the scheme, was constituted as follows :—

MAH-ÁBODHI SOCIETY.

Patron.
LOZANG THUB-DAN-GYA-TCHO, Grand Láma of Tibet.

President.
Right Rev. H. SUMANGALA, Pradhána Nayaka Mahá Sthavira of Ceylon.

Vice-Presidents.
The Ven. THE TATHANABAING, Mandalay, Burmah.
Right Rev. SHAKU UNSIYO, Tokyo, Japan.
THE FANG TANG, Yung-Ho-Kung, Pekin, China.
The Ven. VASKADUVÈ SUBHUTI, P.N.M., Ceylon.
The Ven. V. SRI SUMANGALA, Ceylon.

Representatives.
Siam—H.R.H. Prince Chandradat Chudadhar, Bangkok.
Japan—S. Horiuchi, Esq., Indo-Buseki Kofuku Kwai, 1 Hachigo, Shiba Park, Tokyo.

Japan—The Secretary the Society of Buddhist Affairs, Jokojoji, Teramachi-dori, Shojo Sagaru, Kioto.

Ceylon—G. P. Weerasekera, Esq., Assistant-Secretary Mahá-Bodhi Society, 61 Maliban Street, Colombo.

Burmah—Moung Hpo Mhyin, K.S.M., Secretary Mahá-Bodhi Society, 5 Commissioner's Road, Rangoon.

Burmah—Moung Hpay, Extra-Assistant Commissioner, Thayetmyo.

Arakan—Chan Htoon Aung, Advocate, ⎱ Secretaries Arakan Mahá-
Htoon Chan, B.A., B.L.,   ⎰ Bodhi Society, Akyab.

Chittagong—Krishna Chandra Chowdhury, Secretary Buddhist Aid Association, Raozan, Chittagong.

Darjeeling (India)—Láma Ugyen Gyatsho, Tibetan Interpreter, Secretary Mahá-Bodhi Society, Darjeeling.

Calcutta—The Secretary Calcutta Mahá-Bodhi Society, 20-1 Gangadhur Babu's Lane, Bowbazar, Calcutta.

California—Philangi Dasa, Editor *Buddhist Ray*, Santa Cruz, California, U.S.A.

New York—Charles T. Strauss, 466 Broadway, New York, U.S.A.

France—Baron Harden Hickey, Secretary Bouddhique Propagande, Andilly par Montmorency, Seine-et-Oise, France.

All communications to be addressed to H. DHARMAPALA, General Secretary Mahá-Bodhi Society, 29 Baniapooker Road, Entally, Calcutta.

The purpose of the Society was thus stated :—

" 'The site where the Divine Teacher attained supreme wisdom, now known as Buddha-Gaya, is in middle India, and to his followers there is no spot on earth more sacred than the Bodhimanda, whereon stands the Bodhi-tree—

" ' Never to fade, and ever to be kept
In homage of the world, beneath whose leaves
It was ordained the truth should come to Buddh.'

" At this hallowed spot, full of imperishable associations, it is proposed to re-establish a monastery for the residence of Bhikhus representing the Buddhist countries of Tibet, Ceylon, China, Japan, Cambodia, Burmah, Chittagong, Nepal, Korea, and Arakan. We hope to found, also, a college at Buddha-Gaya for training young men of unblemished character, of whatsoever race and country, for the Buddhist Order (Sangha), on the lines of the ancient Buddhist University at Nálanda, where were taught the 'Maháyána and also works belonging to the eighteen sects.'

"The study of Sanskrit, Pali, and English will be made compulsory on all students. One or more Buddhist scholars from each of the Buddhist countries will in time be attached to the staff of teachers.

"To carry on this great and glorious works of Buddhist revival, after a torpor of seven hundred years, whence dates the destruction of Buddhism in India, the Mahá-Bodhi Society has been organised, and the promoters solicit sympathy and generous support all the world over."

To give some faint idea of the interest felt in this matter even among such remote communities as those of Japan, I will speak of a scene in Tokyo still vivid in my memory. Last summer, in the Japanese capital, the Buddhist High Priest, with certain of the fraternity, begged me to come to the temple in Atagoshita and speak to the brethren about the Holy Places in India, and especially upon the prospects of acquiring for the Buddhist world the guardianship of the Temple of the Tree. In the cool, dark inner court of that Japanese tera the priests and their friends sate on the white mats in concentric circles,

eagerly listening while I told them all about that three
or four hundred miles of Indian country lying between
Busti in Oudh and Buddha-Gaya in the Lower Pro-
vinces, which is the Holy Land of the " calm brethren
of the yellow robe." I spoke of the birth-place and
death-place of the Gentle Teacher, and showed them
pictures which I had myself taken of the ancient
building at Isipatana, outside Benares. The hot day,
beating upon the hillside beyond the temple garden,
shone upon the scarlet azaleas and the lotus-buds in
the garden-lake, and rendered it warm enough, even
in that vast shadowy apartment, for a constant flutter
of fans, while now and then a young priest from the
outer circle would glide away for drinking-water.
But when I came to paint for them that site of the
stately temple—which, from its hollow beside the
Buddhist-tree looks over the hill of the "Thousand Gardens," and marks the spot where the whole
religious history of Asia was transformed, and its
manners for ever stamped with the merciful tenderness and indestructible hopes of Buddhism—those
hundreds of priests and novices sate like rows of
little children lost in a fairy story. The fans were
laid aside ; the shaven heads were craned forward
in intense desire to hear every word ; old men laid
their hands to their ears, and young ones leaned
towards me with clasped palms, to learn all about the
Tree, and the Temple, and the broken statues, and
the Hindoo priests who do not care for the spirit of
the place, and who ought, in a friendly way, to yield
it up, on proper conditions, to Buddhist guardian-

ship. Every man present would have given all he
possessed, I think, to help towards such an end.
As for their unworthy guest, they lavished upon me
marks of pleasure and gratitude ; they spread me out
an outrageously elaborate feast-table in the temple
pavilion, and sent with me back to my lodgings
servants carrying presents of books and boxes of
beautiful Japanese silks and embroideries. Since
then the High Priest writes to me thus from
Tokyo :—

"After your regretted departure from Japan the
Indo-Bussiki Kofuku Society has not been idle, and
now I am glad to inform you that we are trying to
buy a certain piece of land near each of the sacred
sites according to your kind advice to us. Mr.
Dharmapala, of the Mahá-Bodhi Society, is doing
all he can to help us in India ; and if everything
goes as intended, a certain number of Japanese
monks will start for India within this year."

Thus is this new and great idea spreading, and the
world will not be very much older, I think, before
Buddhism by this gateway goes back to its own land,
and India becomes the natural centre of Buddhistic
Asia. For the moment I am sorry to say the movement has sustained a check. After a friendly cor-
respondence in Sanskrit between the Mahunt and
myself, matters were looking fair for an arrangement,
when — against my wish — hostile measures were
commenced between the Mahá-Bodhi Society and
the Hindoo monks. Mr. Dharmapala, the energetic
secretary, whose enthusiastic services to the cause

can never be sufficiently praised, and the example of whose generous efforts ought to make him beloved throughout Buddhistic Asia — thought proper to place in the temple a very precious gilded image of Buddha, sent to his care from Japan. The Mahunt's people ejected this, not without violence, and a series of lawsuits began. We gained the favourable decision of the resident official, and of the Suddar Court; but the High Court of Calcutta, by a judgment which I must respectfully declare erroneous and untenable, reversed the decree, so that after an expenditure of more than one hundred thousand rupees, and the bravest labours on the part of my excellent friend, Mr. Dharmapala, the policy of appealing to law has failed.

I am, however, quite certain that my own policy of appealing to Reason and Right, and of relying upon friendly negotiations with the present Hindoo tenants of the shrine, will and must eventually prevail. It is a fixed purpose of my mind that these shall prevail, and the first really enlightened Viceroy who takes up this question, will discern its huge political importance, and assist me and my friends to obtain success. I suppose there are some people who will ask, why should the British public take any concern in such a movement? But such will be of much the same calibre as those who go about inquiring, "What is the British Empire to Battersea?" Apart from the immense historical, religious, and social importance of Buddhism in Asia, here is an opportunity for the Government of India to gratify and conciliate half that continent by the easiest and least costly exercise of goodwill. The Mahunt and his college will, no doubt, have to be bought out, and rather expensively, now that delays and misguided judgments have made him master of the bargaining. But if an enlightened Minister and Viceroy will, as they may, facilitate the arrangement, all must end well, and grateful Buddhists would furnish whatever cash is requisite. No orthodox Hindoos will be wounded in sentiment, because, by strict truth, the Mahunt, as a Brahman and follower of Sankarácharya, goes against his shastras by keeping control of a Buddhist's temple. However, it brings him so much personal dignity and so much money, that these things must be compounded for, no doubt; yet a well-disposed collector and a far-seeing government could find a score of pleasant ways to make him willing to give up his tenure. There is no room left me to dwell upon all the happy consequences which would flow to the Indian Viceroyalty and to India herself from the goodwill so created in Burmah and Siam. Buddhism would return to the place of its birth, to elevate, to spiritualise, to help, and enrich the population. It would be a new Asiatic crusade, triumphant without tears, or tyranny, or blood; and the Queen's administration would have the glory and benefit of it. The *Hindu* of Madras, a leading native journal, writes: " If there is anything in the intellectual and moral legacies of our forefathers of which we may feel proud, it is that sublime, pure, and simple conception of a religious and moral system which the world owes

x

to Buddha. Educated Hindoos cannot hesitate in helping Buddhism to find a commanding and permanent footing once more in their midst, and to live in mutually purifying amity with our Hinduism itself." Here is indeed, for an enlightened British Indian Minister, "a splendid opportunity."

XIX

THE "GARDEN OF REPOSE"

XIX

THE "GARDEN OF REPOSE"

VISHRAMBAGH, "the Garden of Repose," was the name of the Government College Building in the city of Poona, of which I had the honour to be appointed Principal at the age of twenty-two. A hundred memories, most of them dear and delight-ful, cling to that ancient Indian edifice and to the work I did there. The Deccan College, as it was called, formed with the Elphinstone College, which was in the capital of the Presidency, the University of Bombay; and my colleague in that city was Sir Alexander Grant. Between us we constituted the University, and had in the two colleges the flower of the native intellect of Western India; but my own charge was the more interesting, Poona being the centre of the Deccan, and drawing to itself students from all Maharashtra. There were about five hundred collegians at the Vishrambagh, which was a mediæval palace of the Peishwas, the former kings of the country, situated at the heart of the city, in a quarter named Sunwar-Peit. It has since perished by fire, but in its time was a picturesque structure, containing three large courts paved with basalt, and surrounded by galleries enriched with

exquisitely carved teak-wood arches. The class-
lecture-rooms, corridors, and audience-chamber or
Diwan-Khana, were similarly embellished with
beautifully carved pillars and arches, and in the

POONA.

heart of the building a green garden spread, full of
palm trees, bananas, papaw, orange and lemon bushes.
When all the students were present about the class-
rooms and corridors, in their white dresses and many-
coloured turbans, the *coup d'œil* of my college was

really charming, and a great deal of serious work
went on there ; for Hindoos are earnest pupils, and
uproar or turmoil is as rare in Indian lecture-halls
as in a Japanese school or university.

Day after day I used to ride down to the college,
through the main streets of the city of Poona, either
inside a palanquin or in my own bullock-car, drawn by

BANGLE SHOP, POONA.

two gigantic, high-humped white bullocks, christened
Krophi and Mophi, after the two famous hills in
Herodotus. It was never possible to be weary of that
ride, and even now I recall its sights and sounds with
a fond fidelity of recollection. The green lanes of the
cantonment ; the great tank where the buffaloes wal-
lowed ; the temples of Hanuman and Durga, covered

with fantastic paintings; the Gosavis' Asylum; the
guard-house with the armed sentries; the cloth and
grain and tobacco and bangle shops; the firework-
maker, the wheelwright, the huts where they wove
cloth, or carded cotton with the string of a great
twanging bow; the blind old woman begging on the
bridge; the Mussulman butcher with a few ounces of
chopped-up meat on a plantain leaf for his stock-in-
trade; the monkeys sitting on the shop roofs; the
crows and green parrots darting up and down the
streets; the flying foxes, hanging by scores upon the
great silk cotton tree; the broad Moti Chowk, or
Pearl Street, crowded with buyers and sellers; the
great stone bull (Nanda) in the middle of the road—
I know them all still as I know Piccadilly, although
it is thirty years since day by day I traversed that
ancient Mahratta city.

College opened at ten o'clock; but there was no
real need for the Principal to be punctual, because
the Paharikaris, or gate-watchmen, did not slide the
ten wooden beads which marked that hour across the
wire of the time-board until I appeared, and from the
same event, indeed, the city quarter respectfully took
its daily time. Then there were lectures and studies
until one o'clock, the hour of tiffin, which meal used
to be spread for me in a pretty apartment, formerly
occupied by the Queen of the Peishwa, looking upon
the green garden and the tank, and adorned with
the same exquisite teak-wood carvings. It was the
time of the great Indian Mutiny, from the troubles
and perils of which Poona itself was not exempt;

and I laugh to remember how Rama, my servant, used always to lay by the side of my plate a loaded revolver, which it was the general custom to carry. But I was soon on such good terms with my students and the towns-people, that one afternoon I put the offensive little weapon into the soup-tureen, as a sign that I wanted it placed on the table no more, and that was the last I knew of my armed lunches. The life was immensely amusing. The students were keen to learn, and, for those who understood human nature, eminently manageable; at the same time, it needed constant vigilance to be on one's guard against certain foibles which characterised some among them. For example, there were a number of important scholarships to be decided, and I was well aware that in preparing examination papers I could not absolutely trust the integrity of my clerks and printers. I wrote out, therefore, and gave to these people one whole set of papers, but had another and a different set privately printed in Bombay, and it was that second series which was issued on the eventful examination morning, to the consternation, I fear, of certain young gentlemen who had provided themselves at considerable cost with the earlier set. One was obliged in this way, against one's will, to match craft against craft. Every first of the month, for example, two officials from the Treasury would come down to the Vishram-bagh bearing upon their shoulders large bags full of rupees, which were for the payment of the scholars, native professors, teachers, and European staff of the

college. By ancient custom these coins were shot out
in a heap upon the marble pavement and distributed,
in the Principal's presence, through his carcoon
Ananda, to the various recipients ; the natives among
them always chinking every rupee on the stone before tying it in their girdles. But some would be
absent or ill, and in course of time large sums of
silver money would naturally collect in the college
chest, the accurate amount of which was both difficult
and tedious to check. It was my habit to have the
chest emptied now and then on to the stones, that
we might see all was right, which was invariably the
case. Yet, feeling how much blind reliance must be
reposed upon Ananda, I sent him off one day to fetch
some papers, and in his absence dropped from my own
pocket on the shining heap a rupee. When he returned and went over the counting he reported to
me, as a most singular circumstance, that there was
one rupee too much in the *hisab*, and, without saying a word to him, I felt well justified afterwards in
trusting that carcoon.

A large part of the studies of the college were
devoted to Sanskrit, and we had a strong staff of
learned Brahman pundits, who sat in little rooms
on carpets, with next to nothing on, deciphering old
manuscripts. Of these latter the college possessed
a very rich collection ; and never shall I forget the
joy manifested by that great scholar, the late Dr.
Martin Haug, who had joined us from Germany,
when I introduced him to the dusty treasure-chamber
of those black classics, and told him they were all

at his disposal. It was like Dominic Sampson, of Sir Walter Scott's novel, when the great library was made over to him and he uttered the exclamation, "Prodigious!" I recollect a singular proof of the immense learning of that same worthy Orientalist. We had ridden down at daybreak to the water's edge, where the Parsees were worshipping the rising orb of morning, and one of them, a priest, was reciting a prayer in Zend. Martin Haug asked him if he understood what he was repeating. The priest replied that he had no idea of the meaning, but they were sacred words handed down from immemorial antiquity. The doctor then slowly and correctly repeated the invocation, and translated it to the Zoroastrian, who was naturally astonished, for it was indeed remarkable that a young German student from Leipzig should know more about his own ritual than the fire-worshipper himself. Among my native teachers were some very capable men, like Krishna Shastri Chiploonkur and Kero Punt, with minds as receptive as could be found in Oxford or Cambridge. Among my students, too, were brilliant young men, who might have distinguished themselves in the front rank at our universities. I especially recall three Parsee brothers, the Pudumjis, all of whom—Dorabji, Sorabji, and Nowroji—have since become leading men in the Presidency. There was also my own especial favourite among the Brahmans, Baba Gokhlë, who died too young for his great capacities to bear full fruit. In conducting the studies of such pupils I learned more than I could teach, and

I think of them still with an endless affection and regard.

At four o'clock in the afternoon Luximan, the Mahratta ghorawallah, used to bring my white Arab to the college gates, and in the cool shadows of the sinking sun I rode back to the cantonment. It was impossible not to make a great many pleasant acquaintances among the shop-people along the route, and curious to see how caste conflicted with the charity which is universally inculcated by the Hindoo religion. In thirsty weather wayfarers of low rank would naturally ask for a drink of water. The

A SET OF LOTAS.

Brahman or Purbhoo householder could not let his brass and copper vessels be defiled by their touch, so he established a little bamboo spout in front of his abode, and the thirsty men or women would put their lips to the end of it, while the householder poured in water at the top. I came myself into a slight difficulty one day in this respect. Cantering my horse rather too sharply round a corner, his withers caught the shoulder of an old Hindoo lady who was proceeding to the temple with an offering, and sent her spinning to the ground, where she lay in a swoon. I was much distressed at the accident, and, jumping off my horse, raised the grey-haired dame from the earth, and gladly found that she was uninjured and merely shaken, but faint. The thing wanted was water; and seeing some Brahman women coming down the street with lotas of water on their heads, I asked for some, and, being refused, promptly helped myself, in order to succour the old lady, who quickly recovered. But the next day a deputation of vexed and voluble Hindoo women came to the college to represent that the " Principal-Saheb," by taking and using their lotas, had made them no longer serviceable to Brahmans, and I was obliged to furnish a new set before they would forgive me.

If I could tell one-half the humours of that daily double transit through the great Deccan city, it would be seen how interesting and charming in many aspects the domestic life of Asia is; although there would be many other things to mention besides domesticities, more grotesque and amusing, perhaps, than moral. Sometimes, again, there came sad and anxious seasons when cholera raged in the city. The streets would be blocked with mourning people while the dead were being carried out to the burning-grounds. Our own quarter suffered severely on one occasion, and my classes became almost decimated. The Hindoo students repaired to me at last in a body, and asked permission to go all together to the shrine of the goddess of that particular disease—to make propitiatory offering. I had on the college staff a worthy Scotch professor, who regarded the proposal as shockingly heathenish, and wished me to refuse;

but knowing the value of mental impressions at such a time, I compromised between science and orthodoxy, and said that if they would all give me their word to boil every drop of water before they drank any, and to take every morning five drops of hydrochloric acid in their drink, I would not only consent, but give them twenty rupees towards the expenses of the pilgrimage. It is notable that the cholera disappeared shortly after the pilgrimage —but privately, I never believed this was due to the goddess.

Closely connected with the " Garden of Repose " is the one and only artistic triumph of my career. I have always been fond of painting and sketching, but in an entirely unprofessional way. There came upon us, however, a great day in the history of India, when, the Mutiny being at an end, and the country restored to peace and order, it was decreed by those in authority that the government should be handed over from the great East-India Company to Her Majesty the Queen. Never shall I forget the banquet given by the Governor of Bombay in Kirkee, at which he read aloud to us the State paper ordaining this change, and announcing the demise and disappearance of that renowned Company Bahadur, " which we all had had the pride and honour to serve." There were generals and brigadiers at table that evening who, while Lord Elphinstone spoke, brushed from their eyes something that was not a fly or a gnat; and His Excellency's speech was received in a mournful silence, till the mention of the Queen's

name at the close of it brought back a certain loyal
cheeriness. In the daytime, on the maidan, there
had been a great parade of victorious troops, under
Sir Hugh Rose—the famous 25th Native Infantry
among them, which had gained so much distinction in the campaign of the North-West. When
these brave fellows returned to Poona—the heroes
of Jhansi, of Calpee, and a score of other fields—
we had collected two or three thousand rupees to
make an entertainment for them, and I was deputed
to consult the native officers as to what they would
best like. Western heroes would have wanted a
good feast with plenty of liquor, but these temperate
warriors were unanimous in desiring a really good
nautch dance. So we erected immense tents on the
parade ground, and hired from the neighbouring
cities, at immense expense, all the professional
female stars whom we could secure; and those
eight hundred men sat all the quiet night through
in the tents smoking, eating their betel-nut, and
watching the endless movements of the Nautchnees,
and listening to their songs.

But as to this my artistic triumph, of which mention has been made. On the evening of that memorable day the city of Poona was to illuminate, and it
suddenly struck the educational staff of the Vishrambagh that something conspicuously loyal ought
to be done by us. Fireworks, lamps, and torches we
could, of course, command, but the bangle shops and
coppersmiths and dyers would do as much as that,
and we were looked to for something striking by all

the quarter. Accordingly I volunteered, a little too rashly, to provide a special feature for the demonstration of peace and loyalty. Taking the largest table-cloth in my bungalow, which happened to be of damask spotted with roses, I stretched it tight upon the matting, and, preparing a sufficient quantity of transparent colours, set myself to reproduce, with unskilled loyalty, an effigy of her beloved Majesty the Queen from an illustration in my possession. The roses in the margin were painted red and green, and in the centre was designed a full-length image of the Sovereign with royal robes and crown and sceptre, nine or ten feet in length. The outline having been made and reasonable correctness achieved in details, the great object was to get in some brilliant colour effects ; and there was, in truth, no sparing of crimsons and purples, of amber and green and blue, in rendering Her Majesty as gorgeous as the greatness of the occasion warranted. When it was all finished and dry, the rude but sincere work of art was rolled up and carried down to the " Garden of Repose," where it was tightly stretched upon a screen of bamboo, framed with mango leaves and lotus flowers. A large quantity of buttis—oil-lamps —was arranged behind it, so as to throw a strong light through the transparency, and when evening fell those in charge erected this production outside the façade of the college amid the coloured lights and lamps elsewhere disposed. That night, after dinner, I had an artist's desire to see how the improvised picture looked in its new position, and, mounting my horse, I rode into the city, which was very gay with illuminations and holiday crowds. On coming near the Vishrambagh the throng of people thickened so much about the approaches that my horse could make no way. I rode round, therefore, to the street of the coppersmiths, but here also the squares and lanes were blocked with towns-people all apparently trying to get to the college. I asked what they were so anxious to see, and twenty voices answered, " Taswir ! taswir ! It is a picture of the Maharani in the Sunwar-Peit." When the spot was reached at last my gaze fell upon a spectacle which, for the moment, might have made a Rubens proud, a Raphael vainglorious. Her Majesty, upon my tablecloth, shone gloriously forth in such magnificence of hués—I will say nothing of design and draughtmanship—that a stained-glass window in a cathedral with the sun shining through would be quiet in comparison. The good folks had never beheld any such presentation before. They forgave, in an ecstasy of popular pleasure, the defects they did not perceive ; and for many hours there were constant shouts of " Taswir ! taswir !" among the crowds flocking to the spot, and a perpetual stream of them flowing past the gates of the college and crying, " Wah, wah ! Shabash !" and " Maharani ki jai." If I could have been guilty of artistic vanity, the cup of popular favour was filled for me as a painter that night. It had got abroad that the " Principal-Sahib" was the gifted author of this prodigious production, and no President of the

Royal Academy could for the moment have held
a prouder position in the art world.   I was positively glad to get away and retire from my undeserved
fame to the obscurity of private life ; but as for the
people, they would have stayed there all night loyally
admiring the Queen's multi-coloured majesty, if a
judicious order had not been issued towards the
small hours to extinguish the lamps and roll up
the picture.   It took our dhobi—the Hindoo washer-
man—weeks and weeks to get the last glories of
those colours out of the tablecloth, but to the end
it retained some faint tints to recall the great occasion, and to make me secretly regret that this must
be my first and last artistic success.

XX

THE SWORD OF JAPAN

XX

THE SWORD OF JAPAN[1]

A GREAT Shogun of Japan, the famous Iycyasu, left it written in his testament that "the girded sword is the life of the Samurai." The sword was, indeed, even more than this in ancient Japan. It became the central point in the morals and customs of the land ; the badge of honour and the token of chivalry ; a special and sacred weapon around which grew up the grave, punctilious manners of the lords and knights of Dai Nippon, whose politeness— exquisite, but rigid as the steel they bore—had to be imitated, and was imitated, by the lesser people. The civilisation of a country always crystallises round a few fundamental habits of that country. The manners and morals of Japan may all be traced to the sword, the tea-cup, and the paper house. The first has made the people serious, fearless, punctilious in mutual demeanour ; the second has created their identical habits, their sobriety and sociability ; while those perfectly transparent abodes of paper and panel, common throughout Japan, where " no secrets are hid," have forced upon them

[1] Many particulars in this paper are derived from Dr. Lyman's learned treatise on the subject.

a Greek simplicity of domestic behaviour, with a modesty, naturalness, and absence of *mauvaise honte* unparalleled elsewhere. The sword has been now for ever laid aside in public by the gentlemen of Japan—obeying in this, with wonderful good sense, a sudden and difficult edict. But the signs of its ancient cult linger deep to this hour in the minds and ways of the people, and it may be worth while to speak a little of the bygone importance of the Japanese sword.

The sword-maker who forged the finer blades for the Samurai and Daimio—the barons and knights—was no mere blacksmith. He ranked, indeed, first of all craftsmen in the land, and was often appointed lord or vice-lord of a province. He did not enter on his grave duties lightly. When he had a blade to make for a great Japanese gentleman, the Katanya abstained for a whole week from all animal food and strong drink ; he slept alone, and poured cold water every morning over his head. When the forge was ready (and no woman might so much as enter its precincts), and when the steel bars were duly selected, he repaired to the temple and prayed there devoutly. Then he came back to his anvil and furnace, and hung above them the consecrated straw-rope (*shime-nawa*) and the clippings of paper (*yohei*) which kept away evil spirits. He put on the dress of a court noble, with the *e-boshi* and *kami-shimo*, tying back his long sleeves with a silk cord. Only after many ceremonies, when the five elements— fire, water, wood, metal, and earth—were well con-

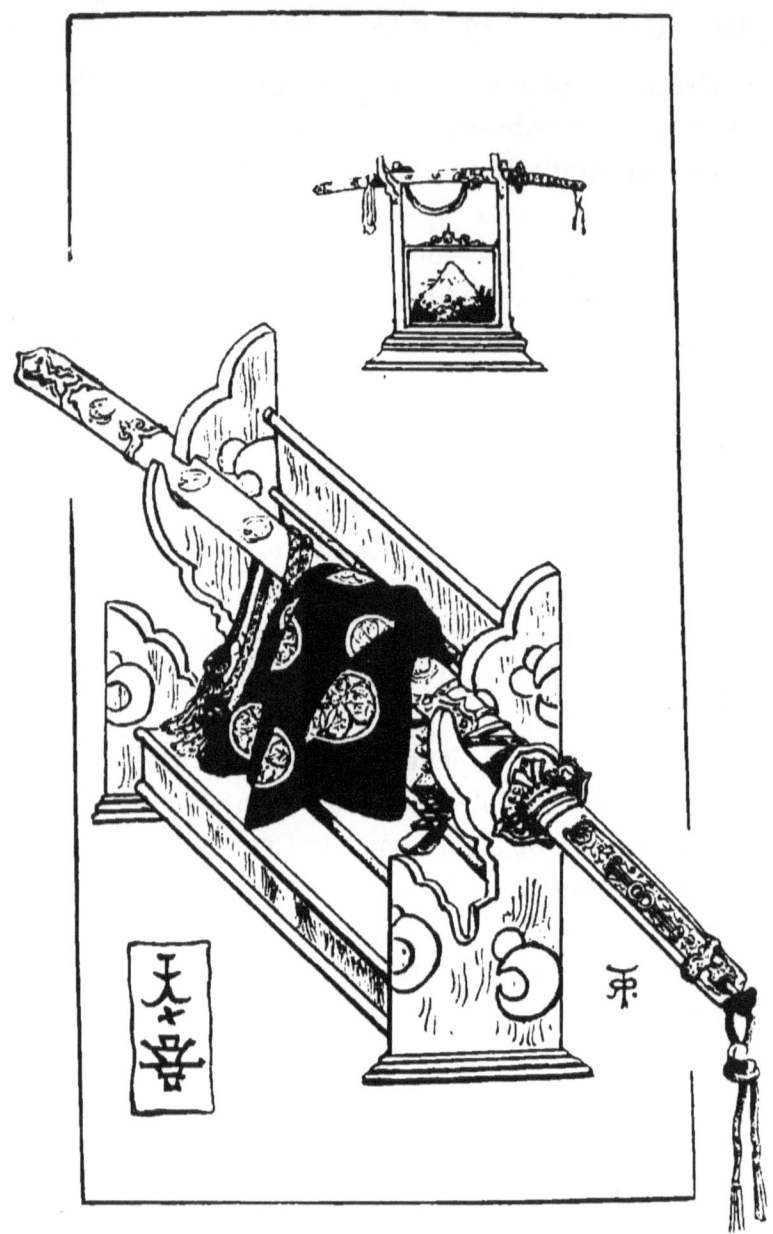

SWORD REST, JAPAN.   P. 342.

ciliated, would that pious artisan take his hammer in hand.

The blade was beaten out of steel alone—*muku-gitai,* the "pure make"—or of steel blended with iron. Great heed was taken to have good and well-smelted material. Each time, before the smith placed his bar in the bed of glowing charcoal, which an apprentice blew to white heat, he coated it with a paste of clay and straw ashes, so as not to burn the naked metal; and never touched it with the hand—hot or cold—since sweat would spoil the weld, and leave a blur on the steel. When he had beaten out his bar 8 inches long, $2\frac{1}{2}$ inches wide, and $\frac{3}{4}$ inch thick, he bent it midway, beat it out again to the same dimensions, thus folding and re-hammering it some fifteen or twenty times. As the original bar was in four flakes, Dr. Lyman, in his admirable treatise on the subject, calculates that at the fifteenth hammering there would be 131,072 layers, increased by five following bendings to 4,194,304 layers. This careful repetition gave the metal a texture like ivory or satin-wood. They had names for the different "watering" so produced, as "bean-grain," "pear-grain," "pine-bark grain," and "vein-grain." Afterwards the blade was forged down to its full length, the imperfect ends cut off, the point drawn out, and the tang fitted on, upon which came the tempering. But these last processes were very serious, and the sword-forger sate alone, and solemnly sang to himself while he gave to the weapon its final fashionings. They say that the difference be-

tween the swords of Masamune and of Muramasa,
two famous craftsmen, was due to their singing. A
Masamune blade brought victory and luck everywhere. A Muramasa sword was always leading its
owner into quarrels, though it carried him through
them well; and it would cause accidents, and cut
the fingers of friendly folks inspecting it, being never
willing to go back to its scabbard without drinking
blood. The real reason was, so runs the legend, that
Muramasa, while he sate at his work in the forge,
was ever singing a song, which had the chorus
of " *tenka tairan! tenka tairan*," which means
" trouble in the world, trouble in the world," whereas
Masamune, the gentle and lucky sword-maker,
always chanted while he worked " *tenka taihei,
taihei*," which signifies " peace be on earth—peace ! "
Japanese people of the old days firmly believed that
both the kindly words and the unkindly got somehow welded into the very spirit of the steel, so that
Masamune's blades prevented quarrels or brought to
their wielders a quick victory, while Muramasa's had
in them a lurking instinct for doing mischief—a sort
of itch to hurt and wound. All sorts of tales were
told to illustrate this. There was a splendid sword
of Muramasa, which had killed by *hara-kiri* four of
its possessors in succession.   Once, too, when the
Shogun was handling a spear-head embedded in a
helmet of one of his warriors, the point wounded his
august hand.   " See quickly," he said, " what is the
mark upon this accursed iron, for it must be Muramasa's ! "   And when they came to look at the

maker's mark, it was indeed a spear-head from the grim sword-maker's, who had chanted the thirst for blood into all his *yari* and *katana*.

Some of the very famous sword-forgers would never write their names or make any sign at all upon their productions. "It is enough to try a blade of mine," said Toshiro Moshimitsu; "it will tell you of itself who made it." Many of the inferior craftsmen engraved dragons, gods, and flowers upon their blades, but the best work does not bear such ornaments, which might hide an imperfection in the metal. All, however, except such men as Toshiro and Masamune, would cut into the tang the name and date of the sword and the owner's and maker's name. Swords had appellations, and might be christened with such titles as *Osoraku*, "the terrible," or *Hiru*, "the blood-sucker." On a long sword noted by Dr. Lyman the inscription ran " *Motte shisubeshi, Motte ikubeshi*," " Defend yourself with me—die with me." But when the blade had been forged and shaped—whether it were the straight *tsuragi* or the *tachi* and *katana* carved into the lines of " the falcon's wing," or the " cormorant's neck " —it had to be very carefully and skilfully tempered. The Japanese sword-smiths effected at one operation what European craftsmen do in two, namely, the high annealing of the edge and the low tempering of the body of the blade. They covered it with *sabi-doro*, a paste of red earth and charcoal, and then, before this hardened, they drew the paste away from a narrow streak along the edge, afterwards putting

it into the fiercest part of the fire. Very heedfully
did the smith move the precious sword up and down
in the pine-coals till he saw the proper colour come
near the tang, which would be in a few minutes.
Then it was plunged in water of a certain tempera-
ture, which thing in itself was a great secret. Katate,
the "One-handed," a renowned swordsmith, bought
the knowledge of that precious mystery dear. His
master taught him everything else except this matter
of the right heat of the tempering bath, so, watching
his opportunity, he broke into the forge one day,
and plunged his hand into the water just as the
master was dipping a reddened blade into it. The
master smote the audacious member off there and
then with the unfinished sword, but Katate knew
his last trade-secret.

The fire, which burned the bared edge violet,
left the *mune*, or body of the blade, blue or straw-
colour; and being plunged into the water, the
sudden chill turned the former very hard, but brittle,
making the latter tough, elastic, and "mild." The
edge so obtained was called *yakiba*, "baked-leaf"
—but there must not be too much breadth of it,
as it would necessarily be brittle. Then was the
cold blade carefully cleaned and rough-ground, and
at this stage the smith could know whether his
work must be wasted or not. If the smallest fault
manifested itself, the true craftsman flung the failure
aside—the false one cut a dragon or a Sanskrit letter
or two over the blemish. The grooves were now
chiselled into the sword, especially the *chi-nagashi*

or blood-channel, which in the case of spear-heads would be afterwards filled up with vermilion lacquer. A hole was drilled in the tang to receive the *mekugi*, or bamboo peg holding the handle on; and then followed the real and final grinding. This was performed by a special handicraftsman. Holding the blade horizontally wrapped in cloths, and with a small part only bare, he rubbed it up and down upon whetstones of varying grit, finishing upon a fifteenth stone of very fine grain, and afterwards polishing with stone powder and oil. It would be at this stage that the beauty and value of the sword came forth. There used to be very many Japanese gentlemen, and even to-day there are some, who could tell instantly, upon inspection, by the look of a blade in this stage, who had wrought it. Official personages existed who gave governmental certificates of blades, written on special paper and stamped. The boundary between the hard, sharp, whitish edge and the grey-blue of the back must not be harsh. It must be clouded by *nioi*, misty spots and flecks, not regular like drop-marks, but fleecy and broken apart like clouds. In good steel, where the clay covering had slightly come away, there would appear *tobi-yaki*, "flying burns," isolated specks of soft white. The visible grain would look "as though the steel were water, and it were rippling." Where the tempering had been perfect there would come little points of bright silver along the edge—called *nie*, only to be seen by the educated eye. Masamune's swords were very full of such. It must be an excellent blade if, inside and underneath, as it were, the dark body of it, there flickered the *utsuri*, the "reflection," a glimmer along the dividing line of edge and breast, faintly prismatic, and resembling the "mist round the moon." Only a consummate judge could note and estimate the *chikei*, small films of white; the *niadzuma*, or "lightning flashes," fine shining lines in the *nioi*; the *sunagashi*, resembling specks of sand in a row; and the *uchi-yoke*, or narrow forge-marks. The blade which combined these virtues was fit to sit in the girdle of a daimio, and would be worth from £200 to £300; twelve to fifteen hundred of the old *yen*.

Such a sword was often mounted very splendidly indeed; the finest artists lavishing their skill upon the scabbard, *tsuka*, the *me-nuki*, or studs upon the handle, and, above all, on the *tsuba*, or hilt, which was often enriched with lovely work in gold, silver, and bronze. The scabbard was generally of magnolia wood, and ended in a richly-adorned *kojiri*, or ferrule. It held, at its upper end, two small daggers or skewers with pretty handles called *kogai*. These were used in thick of fight to stick through the ear of a slain enemy as a sort of visiting card. With such a weapon you could cut through five sheets of copper and not notch the steel, and the edge put on it might be so fine that if you held it in a river's current a stalk of grass floating down would divide upon contact with it. Masamune's blades could sever a bar of iron, or cut a falling hair in two. Muramasa's would slice bronze armour "like a melon." The point was not much used, but Iyeyasu once, for trial, put a *katana* of Yoshimitsu's clean through the iron mortar of his physician.

Immense punctilio attached to the wearing, the carriage, and the etiquettes of these precious weapons. The higher-born you were, the more you might stick up the hilts of your two swords; but soldiers of lesser degree wore them horizontally. Dr. Lyman says correctly : " To draw a sword from its scabbard without begging leave of the others present was not thought polite ; to clash the scabbard of your sword against another was a great rudeness ; to turn the sword or the scabbard, as if about to draw, was tantamount to a challenge ; and to lay your weapon on the floor and kick the guard towards another was an intolerable insult, that generally resulted in a combat to the death."

Pfoundes says that "the rules of observances connected with the wearing of the long and short sword or the single sword were very minute, but have fallen into disuse. . . . In former days the most trivial breach of these elaborate observances was often the cause of murderous brawls and dreadful reprisals. . . . To express a wish to see a sword was not usual, unless when a blade of great value was in question ; and then a request to be shown it would be a compliment appreciated by the happy possessor. The sword would then be handed with the back towards the guest, the edge turned towards the owner, and the hilt to the left, the guest wrapping the hilt either in the little silk napkin always carried by gentlemen in their girdle-books, or in a sheet of clean paper. The weapon was drawn from the scabbard and admired inch by inch, but not to the full length, unless the owner pressed his guest to do so, and then, with much apology, the sword was entirely drawn and held away from the other persons present. After being admired it would, if apparently necessary, be carefully wiped with a special cloth, sheathed, and returned to the owner as before."

A guest, on entering a friend's house, if the host was an older man or of higher rank, would take off his longer sword and either lay it down at the entrance or hand it to the servant who admitted him, who would thereupon place it on the sword-rack in the position of honour in the apartment. If on somewhat familiar or equal terms with the host, the guest might carry the long sword into the house, but detached with its scabbard from the belt, and lay it on the floor at his right hand, where it could not be drawn. The shorter sword was retained in the girdle ; but in a prolonged visit both host and guest laid that also aside.

These high manners of the steel bred that Japanese courtliness and chivalry which have survived it. The cult of the *katana* is now for ever at an end in Dai Nippon—the samurai and lords of the land have laid aside their proudly cherished weapons, and go abroad as peacefully as the *Akindo*, the merchant. Yet there are fine swordsmen still to be found among the quietest of the Emperor's senators and lieges, and I have myself seen wonderful things done by some of them with ancient blades. Moreover, the measured speech, the deep and heedful reverence, the silent dignity, the instincts of manhood which clustered round the steel, are still characteristic of the race ; and the swords, though no longer worn, are proudly and carefully preserved in many a mansion, castle, and temple. Thucydides says that " the nation which carries iron is barbarous," and under that remark the United States, where almost everybody seems to possess and carry a revolver, would stand condemned. But Japan, by a wonderful effort of abnegation on the part of her upper classes, altogether laid aside, twenty years ago, the old and perilous habit of going abroad with a girdle full of swords and daggers. It was a noble submission to new ideas—yet to this day a Japanese gentleman raises your sword to his forehead and bows deeply before he examines it. Nor will he uncover a single inch of the shining and sacred steel without gravely obtaining your permission and that of the company present.

XXI

LIMPETS

z

PATELLA
ATHLETICA (Bean)

Patella vulgata
(Linnaeus)

P. crepidula
or Slipper Limpet

unguiformis
(Malta)

XXI

LIMPETS

IT is a trite saying that an
oyster may be crossed in love,
but few people who are not
observant naturalists would
ever attribute the softer
emotions of life to a limpet.
Nevertheless, some recent
researches tend entirely to
confirm the statement which
will be found in all good
books of natural history, that
there is no creature more
attached to its own dwelling-
place than the little vulgar
mollusc in question. At-
tached in one

sense everybody well knows that it is, who knows
a limpet when he sees it. The little sub-conical
single shell sits tightly to the surface of the wave-
washed rock ; and very great force, indeed, is needed
to remove it. But the limpet is a home-loving
creature in a very different sense from this. All
close observers of nature have long ago been
familiar with the mode in which it wanders away
from the little depression upon its rock to take a
meal of sea-weed between tide and tide, and then
returns to the self-same spot and fits itself with as
much precision into the notched hole as a lid upon a
box. Lately, however, these curious little journeys
have been specially investigated. Professor Davis
described very admirably, indeed, in *Nature*, how
he had seen marked individuals coming back from
an excursion of as much as a yard distance to
settle down into its particular scar. The limpet has
tentacles and what seem like eyes. Yet it is not by
means of these that it finds its slow way home, for
the Professor removed them from two individuals
which accomplished all the same their return trips.
It then occurred to him that the road was designated
for the limpet by the smell of its own track, and the
Professor, to determine this, carefully washed the
intervening space with sea-water, only to see the
limpet readily finding its way back. Another patient
naturalist, Mr. Lloyd Morgan, confirms these observations of Professor Davis with a series of
"limpet-statistics" which are quite decisive. Out of
twenty-five of the little molluscs which he removed

to a distance of six inches, twenty-one safely returned
to their accustomed hole within two tides. Out of
twenty-one removed to a distance of a foot, thirteen
came back within two tides and five more within
the next two; and when the interval was increased
to eighteen inches and twenty-four inches respectively, eighteen out of twenty-one turned up safely
from the former journey, and five out of thirty-six,
at the interval—immense for a limpet—of two feet.
Some of these enforced wanderers were removed
round a corner of a rock and yet knew the way
home. In one case, where a limpet had taken up a
new position, it went back to this after having been
transferred to its original hole. In another case the
limpet had to pass between two other of its fellows
who were fixed, and lifted its shell in the most
intelligent manner to get over these. And, leisurely
as the little mollusc travels, there is yet a certain
amount of energy displayed to reach its familiar
abode; for in one instance the little creature
travelled ten inches, over a somewhat curved course,
in something under twenty minutes, which, by the
limpet time-table, may be considered a record speed.
In a word, if limpets could sing, their favourite ditty
would be "Home, Sweet Home." Carrying their shell
with them, that becomes, in a sense, their portable
abode; but the place they really love is that spot upon
the rock where they have wriggled and fitted the little
serrated edge of their house into the stone so as to
exactly fit, and shut out air and water. On reaching
the well-known spot they twist and turn about to

match their shell to the hole, like a belated householder getting his latchkey to fit ; and they love
that one place beyond all other, because only there
can they sit still and tightly, and defy all enemies.

That this humble little sea-creature should display
so strong a passion for home, rivalling almost the
well-known faculty and instinct of the pigeon or the
cat, must make thoughtful people desire to know
more about it. Everybody has remarked the small
grey and green cones studding the surfaces of sea-
washed stones. Scientific dictionaries denominate it
" patella," and it goes into the catalogues as a " gasteropod mollusc of the Zygo-branch section." But
under these hard words is hidden a wonderful life,
the study of which is well calculated to convince the
least reflective of the miracles of design which exist
in Nature. The life of the limpet is about equally
divided between eating and sleeping. When the
tide is ebbing out, he softly loosens himself from the
depression which he has made in his rock, and goes
about under water grazing upon sea-weeds. His
tiny mouth—if so it can be called—is armed with a
tongue of the most extraordinary construction, like
nothing so much as a long flexible blacksmith's file.
It is called the "radula," and is very much longer
than his body. It has upon its surface one hundred
and sixty rows of teeth, twelve in each row, so that
the total number of the limpet teeth amounts to one
thousand nine hundred and twenty. This is the
grazing instrument of the common or British limpet ;
but a variety of the same family, called the *patella*

variegata, although only two inches and a half long in extended body, has a tongue more than a foot long. And there is a South American species with a shell one foot wide, which is used by natives as a basin, the tongue of this being absolutely prodigious. We pass by the many curious facts about the keyhole limpets, fissurellidæ, which have orifices in the apex of the shell, and the strange slipper limpets, or acmæa, to come back to our own common or sea-shore individual. Mention was made above of the enemies of the limpet, and he has many. Man eats him cooked, in the North of Ireland and elsewhere. Fish and sea-birds greatly relish his small person, which, but for the too-great prevalence of sand in it, is nearly as toothsome when cooked as a winkle. But by far the worst of his foes is the oyster-catcher, a bird wrongly named, for it lives almost entirely upon limpets. To catch the little mollusc you must surprise him at a moment when he has detached the indentations of his shell from the hole into which they fit; and the slightest vibration of his rock, or any sudden blow or noise, causes him instantly to screw himself down into his "scar" in a manner which makes him immovable except to the edge of a sharp knife or the stroke of a big stone. But the red-legged oyster-catcher, stepping softly with his great feet upon the half-bared rocks, knows how to catch the limpet just at the moment of innocent relaxation; and with one cunning and silent insertion of his bill wrenches the small "gasteropod" from his beloved site. If once the limpet hears the

oyster-catcher coming, he locks himself into his
chiselled hole, and nothing that the "hæmatopus"
can do will detach the tiny morsel. Safe in his
corrugated shell, he listens to the futile efforts of
the bird, as secure from danger as a sailor in an
armour-clad battery. We might almost imagine that
he laughs at his baffled foe, for why should it seem
impossible for a limpet to laugh if he can find his
way home over a yard of rugged rock, and if he
loves that home with such deep devotion, and
possesses besides in what we have called his tongue
a mechanical implement of such exquisite delicacy
and perfection that any invention of Mr. Edison or
Mr. Maxim is but rude and clumsy compared to
its matchless efficiency?

For anything we know to the contrary, the limpet
enjoys his life—feels, perceives, and even thinks.
Nay, he may and must share with the oyster the sad
privilege of being crossed in love; for the sexes are
distinct in the small beings, and they have their
love-makings and little families quite regularly
every spring. It may not seem a very lively existence to adhere to a rock at low tide and nibble
sea-weed when the water is up; but a mollusc who
in this way always "comes home to tea" cannot
but possess faculties and feelings unsuspected by us.
Has he preferences among the female limpets which
all look so similar to our eyes; is he an epicure among
the sea-grasses, knowing flavours and tastes utterly
hidden from us? Does his sloppy rock, with its
barnacles and sea-anemones and mussel-shells and

bladder-weed, afford him all the charms and variety
of an extended landscape? Has anybody any idea
by what magic of evolution that "radula" has been
furnished to him by Nature which under the micro-
scope makes the finest tool of the watchmaker
ridiculous? And the minute mollusc which suggests
these unanswerable questions is but an item in the
countless company of living things filling every corner
of land and sea and air, each of them everywhere
a thousand times more wonderful than the wisest
student knows. There is a "gasteropod," a sort of
first cousin to the limpet, which swims in the Southern
Ocean and is called the "violet sea-snail." It is
one of the ianthinidæ, and in the breeding season
this strange creature forms a raft out of a special
membrane, attaches its two hundred or three hundred eggs to this improvised lifeboat, and launches
it upon the water for them to hatch out at
leisure. If you touch it when captured in the sea-
net it exudes a violet dye much more beautiful than
the purple of the Tyrian murex. This, too, is only
one of the million marvels of the deep, and only
one of the uncounted instances of the exhaustless
resources of life. Many and many a more astonishing
fact than the home-loving habits of the limpet might
be culled from that rich region of the sea-shore
between high and low water mark.

XXII

A DELICATE ENTERTAINMENT

XXII

A DELICATE ENTERTAINMENT

THERE is a pretty and refined form of social amusement in Japan which has never been mentioned on
this side, so far as I have seen, in connection with the
domestic life of that country. It well deserves description, nevertheless, being so characteristic of the highly
cultured tastes of the Japanese, and because it opens
the gate into quite a new realm of sense-pleasure,
and might, indeed, be very well introduced among
people of education and fine sensibilities in England.
It is founded upon the Eastern love of sweet odours
—a province of rare delight, far too much neglected
among ourselves, as may be seen indeed by our lack
of words with which to define different fragrances,
and the foolish fashion which has surrendered the
beautiful world of perfume almost entirely to the
female sex. Englishmen, it is true, wear button-
holes of violets, or gardenias, or rosebuds ; and some
of them are bold enough to bedew a pocket-handker-
chief with a little frangipani or eau de Cologne ; but
the habit is regarded as rather effeminate, and even
ladies are a little blamed if they indulge in the
stronger fragrances of the fashionable perfumers.
All this is deplorable, and due, it seems to me, to a

deficient olfactory gift rather than to any reasonable prejudice ; for why should we not take delight in the infinite range and exquisite variation of those mysterious odours which, not content with scattering freely among her flowers, Nature bestows upon us in many a strange and subtle corner of the animal and vegetable world ? We have, by reason of our dulness, very few satisfactory titles in the dictionary with which to name these wonderful essences ; and the nose—that most important feature—not only boasts no classic passages of its own to compare with the literature of the eye, the ear, and the lips, or even the hair, but is scarcely ever mentioned, even in poetry. Martial can find nothing better to say of that organ in his mistress except

WALL PICTURE OR "KAKEMONO."

that it is "not too great," and all that Ariosto permits himself to observe about the same part of the

lovely countenance of one of his chief heroines is
that "it stood in the middle of her face."

They do not so disregard the nose in Japan, or
neglect the delicious kingdom of sensations of which
it is the well-provided and happy channel. Less
fortunate than we are in the variety and delicacy of
manufactured perfumes, they appreciate intensely
those which they possess, and give lovely and ap-
propriate names to distinguish one odour from the
other. For the most part, Japanese perfumes are
prepared not in the liquid form, as with us, but in
powder or solid shape, necessitating the use of incense-burners to develop the aroma of each. The
Japanese word for an incense-burner is "koro," and
upon this omnipresent article of Japanese domestic
and religious life the artists of the land have lavished
their finest skill. The most divinely graceful utensils
exist in bronze, iron, silver, gold, and pottery, entirely devoted as "kogo" in which to keep the little
tablets of incense, or as "koro," and "chojiburo" in
which to burn them. Some are quaintly fashioned
in the forms of fish, birds, or animals, and richly
gilded; but the majority are of bronze, the fragrant
smoke issuing from perforations in the lid of the
little vessel.

Imagine yourself, then—oh, gentle English guest!
seeking in vain for some new social pastime—imagine
yourself in Tokyo, receiving the distinction of "O
maneki"—the honourable invitation—to a "josshuko,"
or incense-party. I must call it a distinction, because
these entertainments are only given in the upper

circles of Japanese life, and would never be addressed
to any one who was not known as a person of quiet
ways and cultivated tastes.   On the highly orna-
mental document inviting you, or in a letter accom-
panying it, will be conveyed in graceful words the

JAPANESE LADY.

request that, if it be " honourably convenient," you
will not smoke, or drink tea, or " saki," or eat scented
sweetmeats for a day or so previous to the reception.
It will also be in good form that you should not make
any employment of pomade or oil for the hair, nor
use any ordinary perfume.   On repairing to the house

of your hostess—for a lady always presides over this most dainty amusement—it will be polite and proper to enter with much caution the apartment reserved, taking care to open and shut the paper shutters, "shoji," very quietly, in order not to disturb the tranquil air of the room. Like all Japanese rooms, that chamber will be celestially clean and sweet ; but the probability is that you are entering a "yashiki," or superior abode, where, beside the cream-white "tatami" and the silvery "shoji," the woodwork around will be of finished workmanship, and the supporting columns of natural timber, the most valuable that the mountain forests can yield. With your feet bare or in socks you have knelt down in your place within a half-circle of pleasant friends, male and female, who salute you with soft words of welcome and polished compliments. Your dress will be new, or at least unsoiled ; all upper garments being left outside that no smell of the street may enter this Paradise of perfume. Opposite to the half-circle of happy guests kneels the fair hostess, in front of her being ranged a row of ten small packets of perfume, folded and tied in precisely an identical fashion, and their contents known to her alone, either by their arrangement or some private mark. Two or more incense-burners will be near her with a metal bowl of lighted charcoal and various little implements with which to handle the incense. In "josshuko" there will be ten packets, but only four different scents, and a specimen of each of these four is placed, distinctively coloured or packed, at

the left hand of the lady of the house. Let us say
that they are the sorts called " tamatsumi," in English,
pile of jewels; "shibafune," ships of grass ; " mumei,"
the unspeakable ; and a fourth fragrance, which is
not named or experimented with. In the row of ten,
all looking identical, there will be three of No. 1,
three of No. 2, three of No. 3, and one of the mysterious compound. The guests receive ten little tickets,
bearing names corresponding to this division—three
of No. 1, three of No. 2, three of No. 3, and one
for the "kyaksama," or unknown perfume. In a
box near at hand there is a division for the tickets
of each of those present ; —and now the graceful
pastime is ready to commence.

The lady of the house burns one of the extra
parcels of No. 1, and all in turn sniff at the aroma,
the name and character of which she indicates.
Then, gently wafting aside the fragrant cloud, she
gives her guests the flavour of No. 2, and afterwards,
in due turn, that of No. 3, naming them all. But
"kyakuko" is, as I say, not burned. Now then the
delicate ordeal commences. The lady host opens
one of the ten indistinguishable parcels and places
it on the glowing scarlet ashes of the "koro." The
blue vapour issues from the perforated lid, each guest
in turn of precedence savours the smoke decorously
three times, and then, making up his or her mind,
secretly drops the ticket which is thought to agree
with that particular odour. One after the other the
guests thus vote in silent ballot, not being allowed
to give any hint as to their persuasion, but softly

conversing of other things as the incense-burner goes round. Another and another packet is selected and consumed, and again and again those present cast their votes, each dropping the tickets into his own division of the ballot-box. Somewhere or other in the course of the play the secret scent will come in, but it is remarkable how often it fails to be recognised, the eager guests expecting it before it has arrived. Moreover, in spite of the frequent use of the fan, each of the fragrances intermixes with each, and it is quite astonishing how keen the nostril needs to be to analyse and separate the fine differences of the various essences. At the close of the round, when all ten perfumes have been consumed in the "koro," a scrutiny is held of the voting, and he or she who has made the highest number of happy guesses receives a little "hobi," a prize of some pretty and useful kind.

A great collection of elaborate articles is needed to carry out this graceful entertainment in perfection. The incense-burner ought naturally to be very artistic, whether of porcelain, bronze, copper, or iron. The incense-box should be of fine lacquer, and of beautiful shape and finish. It will generally have been constructed in three divisions—the first containing the incense-cakes, the second some aloes-wood, and the third a receptacle for the incense ashes. Little plates of mica must be ready, on which to lay the pieces of incense when put over the burner. The card-box ought to be charming, and the cards are sometimes little lacquered wooden blocks, with a number on one side and on the other the picture of some tree or flower—the name of which each guest will, for the time being, assume. Every person, it will be understood, receives ten tickets, with the same picture on the back, representing unmistakably the owner.

It would take me too far to go into the varieties of incense and other fragrant materials which are manufactured by the Japanese perfumer, and to quote all the playful and fanciful names given to them. There is, for example, " kokon "—" the breath of twilight " — and there is "yama-ji-no-tsuyu "—" the dew on the mountain path." The first is compounded of aloes-wood, sandal-wood, and kakko, in certain proportions. The second has clover-blossom in it, and musk or "jako"—of which the ladies of Dai Nippon are very fond. Some of them have the custom of sewing a tiny bag of musk-dust inside a velvet fillet, and fastening it under their sleeve upon the upper arm. The ingredients of these perfumes are mixed in powder and then kneaded into consistency with white honey. There are many other forms of this delicate entertainment besides "josshuko"—such as " kogusa-ko," " keiba-ko," " kagetsu-ko," " meisho-ko," all of them having some amusing or imaginative significance. But enough has been said to show the refinement, the charm, and the entertaining character of this Japanese form of indoor pastime, which might, I think, be happily introduced into those fortunate abodes in our own land where there reigns something like

Japanese tranquillity and something like the Japanese artistic instinct which can find 'true joy in the curve of a line, in the contrast of supplementary colours, or in the subtle differences of one sweet odour from another closely resembling it.

JAPANESE BOY.

Printed by BALLANTYNE, HANSON & CO.
Edinburgh and London